P9-BJR-162

CRUSHED

The troll rose to his feet, lifting his knee from her chest. One cartilage-crusted hand was balled into a fist; he held it over her, maintaining the magical spell that pinned her to the ground.

"You're a dead woman," he said in Cantonese.

"No . . . I'm not," Night Owl gasped. She knew better than to believe his threat. Gangers didn't make speeches before killing someone. They just greased them.

"You have angered Eldest Brother by cheating him," the troll said, eyes blazing. "You sold him property, then told the original owners where to find it again."

"That wasn't me . . . who told. Someone else." It was the truth—but she didn't expect the troll to believe it.

"You agreed to the contract," the troll continued in a grim voice. "You bore the ultimate responsibility."

"I can pay . . . your boss back . . . twice what he gave me," she lied.

The troll clenched his fist tightly, causing his bony knuckles to crack. Night Owl's vision swam with stars as the magical arms that were holding her squeezed the last air from her lungs She fought to take a breath, but it was as if she were underwater. Dimly, over the pounding that filled her ears, she heard the troll's final pronouncement—and realized she'd been wrong. Sometimes real-life gangers like to make speeches, too. . . .

SHADOWRUN

TAILS YOU LOSE

Lisa Smedman

A ROC BOOK

ROC
Published by New American Library, a division of
Penguin Putnam Inc., 375 Hudson Street,
New York, New York 10014, U.S.A.
Penguin Books Ltd, 27 Wrights Lane,
London W8 5TZ, England
Penguin Books Australia Ltd, Ringwood,
Victoria, Australia
Penguin Books Canada Ltd, 10 Alcorn Avenue,
Toronto, Ontario, Canada M4V 3B2
Penguin Books (N.Z.) Ltd, 182–190 Wairau Road,
Auckland 10, New Zealand

Penguin Books Ltd, Registered Offices:
Harmondsworth, Middlesex, England

First published by Roc, an imprint of New American Library,
a division of Penguin Putnam Inc.

First Printing, February 2001
10 9 8 7 6 5 4 3 2 1

Series Editor: Donna Ippolito
Cover Art: Koveck

 REGISTERED TRADEMARK—MARCA REGISTRADA

Once again, thanks to the B.C. Science Fiction Association Writers' Workshop for their aid in critiquing this book. Special thanks to Matthew Claxton, Fran Skene and Peter Tupper for their excellent advice and suggestions and, of course, to Leanne Taylor, both for her support and for always being able to suggest just the right plot twist.

Year of the Rat

Anxious not to be a failure, those born in the year of the rat use their intelligence and imagination to suceed. Charming, honest and practical, they are alert individuals who learn from experience. Their materialism is tempered by their sentimental natures; their tendency to be opportunistic is concealed by their grace and elegance.

*   *   *

Attracted to whatever is clandestine and secretive, those born in the year of the rat live for today. Restless and sometimes quick-tempered, they are calculating folk whose actions usually have an ulterior motive. Prone to gossip and grumbling, they obsessively hoard their possessions and often allow their reach to exceed their grasp.

NORTH

CIRCA 2062

TSIMSHIAN
ATHABASKAN COUNCIL
ALGONKIAN-MANITOU COUNCIL

Edmonton

Saskatoon

Vancouver
Calgary
Regina
SALISH-SHIDHE COUNCIL
Seattle
Winnipeg
Pacific Ocean
Spokane

Portland
Salem
Helena
SIOUX NATION
Butte
Bismarck
Duluth
Fargo

TIR TAIRNGIRE
Boise
Billings
St. Paul
Minneapolis

Idaho Falls
Sheridan
Rapid City
Sioux Falls

Eureka
Reno
Salt Lake City
Cheyenne
Des Moines

Provo
Boulder
Omaha

San Francisco
Denver
Colorado Springs
Kansas City

CALIFORNIA FREE STATE
UTE NATION
Pueblo
Topeka

Bakersfield
Las Vegas
Wichita

Santa Barbara
Los Angeles
PUEBLO CORPORATE COUNCIL
Tulsa

San Diego
Santa Fe
Amarillo
Oklahoma City
Little Rock

Tijuana
Phoenix
Albuquerque

Tucson
Roswell
Ft. Worth
Dallas
Shreveport

El Paso
San Angelo

San Antonio
Austin
Houston

Pacific Ocean
Chihuahua
San Antonio
Corpus Christi

AZTLAN
Monterrey
Ciudad Victoria

La Paz
Culiacan
Durango

To Tenochtitlán

AMERICA

CIRCA 2062

Ft. Albany • • Waskaganish

QUÉBEC

Sept Iles

Gulf of St. Lawrence

Thunder Bay

Charlottetown

Fredericton

Québec

Halifax

Sault Ste. Marie

Sudbury Ottawa Montpelier Montreal Augusta

Kingston

Concord

Milwaukee

Toronto Albany **Boston**

Lansing Buffalo Hartford

Chicago Detroit

Gary Cleveland

Philadelphia Manhattan

Indianapolis

Springfield Cincinnati **D.C.** **UNITED CANADIAN AND
AMERICAN STATES (U.C.A.S.)**

East St. Louis Charleston Richmond

Louisville Roanoke Norfolk *Atlantic
Ocean*

Knoxville Durham

Nashville Raleigh

Memphis Charlotte

Columbia Wilmington

Birmingham **Atlanta** **CONFEDERATED AMERICAN STATES (C.A.S.)**

Charleston

Jackson Montgomery Savannah

Albany

Mobile Jacksonville

Baton Rouge

Orlando

Tampa West Palm Beach

*Gulf of
Mexico* Miami

Key West

Havana **CARIBBEAN
LEAGUE**

CUBA

North America

- ⊚ National Capital
- Seattle • City
- – · – · International Boundary
- ── State Boundary
  (U.S.A. circa 1990)

Kilometers
0   200   400   600

Miles
0   200   400

Fidelity

The tremor struck her left hand just as she was completing the first trigram of the I Ching. Three bronze coins with square holes at their centers clattered onto the countertop as her fingers sprang open wide and then fluttered like a moth in a flame. Cupping her left hand in her right, Alma activated the timer in her cybereye and watched the glowing red numbers that appeared in her lower right field of vision. Twenty-three seconds later, the tremor passed.

When it was over, she flexed her hand once and then ran her fingers through the series of complicated gestures that were part of her daily tai chi routine. Her hand moved smoothly, fingers flowing through the forms with absolute precision. She sped the gestures up, and her hand became a blur. Her move-by-wire system seemed to be working fine, accelerating her reactions until her fingers flowed with the speed and grace of rushing water. Sighing with relief, she lowered her hand.

The tremors had started six days ago, on February 17. She'd barely noticed at first—her hand would twitch once or twice and then return to normal. But they'd gradually increased in frequency and violence, and they now struck two or three times a day, preventing her from using her hand properly until the shaking stopped.

Worried that they might be the first signs of temporal lobe epilepsy, she'd booked a scan with PCI's physicians the day after she'd first noticed them. She'd also spoken to Gray Squirrel, asking him if the experimental cyberware she'd been fitted with six months ago might be the cause of the problem. He'd promised to run some tests.

Two days after making that promise, Gray Squirrel had been extracted from PCI. In the wake of the kidnapping, Alma had canceled her CAT scan. Getting Gray Squirrel back was much more important than testing for something that would take months to become full-blown. Even if the tremors were the onset of TLE, the corrective nanosurgery could wait for a few days. The area of brain tissue that had become dysfunctional was probably still very small. She was glad it was her left hand, and not her right, that had been affected.

Alma reached for the three coins, sliding them across the countertop so that she could see them. All three had landed with Chinese characters face-down: changing yin. Together with the two lines that had already been cast, it formed the trigram for thunder.

Just as Alma was about to begin the second trigram, her cellphone chimed softly. She picked it up and flipped open its screen.

The face that appeared on the tiny monitor was a computer-generated, cartoonish image whose gestures and expressions were slaved with the caller's. Text below the cartoon listed the caller as UNKNOWN MOBILE UNIT. Whoever was telecoming her had blocked the caller ID function.

Alma thumbed the audio-only respond button. She didn't want the caller to see her face—or her apartment. "Yes?"

The voice that came out of the speaker was male and spoke English with a linguasoft-perfect accent. "Ms. Johnson?"

Alma allowed a fraction of a second's delay before answering, despite the hope that she felt. Appearing too eager would be unprofessional, especially in front of a shadowrunner. "Yes."

"This is Tiger Cat. I've uncovered some data on the 'package' that was stolen from your firm. How soon can you transfer payment?"

Alma's heart beat a little faster at the good news. Forcing herself to remain calm, she activated her retinal clock. It was 8:07 a.m.

"Are you near a cred machine?" she asked.

"I could be."

"Wait at least five minutes after this call ends, then slot your stick and call back. I'll give you an access number to key in, and you'll get the first payment. If your data checks out, a second payment will be transferred later."

"My data's good as platinum. I guarantee it."

The cellphone's screen blanked.

It took Alma two minutes and eighteen seconds to access her corporate expense account and preauthorize the transfer of three thousand nuyen to a certified credstick. As she waited for Tiger Cat's second call, she stared out through a rain-streaked window at the city of Vancouver and sipped a glass of tyrosine-boosted soymilk. Fourteen stories below her apartment, banks of artificial grow lights inside the biodome that enclosed Stanley Park illuminated it from within, making it look like a gigantic, multifaceted light bulb. Beyond it, the twinned Lion's Gate and Dan George bridges led to the North Shore, where row upon row of overpriced condoplexes climbed the foot of a blue-green mountain that rose to meet the rain clouds.

Alma picked up a remote and adjusted the window's polarization. The view of the city was replaced by a reflection of the tiny loft apartment that was kitchen and bedroom in one. Stark white walls,

counter and furniture accentuated the room's mini-
malist look. The only images on the walls were framed
certificates of appreciation from Pacific Cybernetics,
arranged in a neat row above a table that held a pot-
ted cinnamon-scented orchid. Beside the plant was an
animated holopic of a dozen children forming a
human pyramid in front of a gigantic logo of a rising
yellow sun: the Superkids. Their tiny images knelt on
a ten-centimeter-wide square of projection plastic,
grinning up at the viewer. All wore bright blue-and-
yellow New Horizons Incorporated T-shirts, and all
were exuberant and happy—except for the boy on the
bottom left, who looked pensive and troubled: Aaron.

As the kids below steadied themselves, a girl at the
top of the pyramid sprang into the air. She landed in
a handstand and then lifted her right hand to wave
while balancing on her left. Then there was a flicker,
and the girl appeared back on top of the human pyramid as the holopic cycled back to the beginning again.

The image had been captured more than two decades ago, on Alma's eighth birthday—one month before Aaron's death. Two months after that, the project
was shut down, and the corporation that had given
birth to the Superkids was torn apart.

Alma's body was still as athletic as ever under the
black tights and red silk kimono she wore while relaxing at home, but her face had grown leaner since
childhood. Straight, shoulder-length hair cut in blunt
bangs framed Eurasian features. Her cybereyes were
natural-tint models with brown irises, and the augmentations to her hearing had been done without removing or altering her natural ears. Her softlink chipjack
was hidden at the nape of her neck. The rest of her
cyberware and bionetic augmentations lay deep under
her skin. In her line of work, it didn't pay to advertise
advantages. Surprise was too effective a weapon.

When Tiger Cat called back, she took a moment to

center herself and then greeted him with a simple hello. Then she punched the credit transfer's authorization number into her cellphone. She heard the faint *beep-beep-beep* of numbers being keyed into a cred machine. Tiger Cat thanked her with a purr in his voice.

"I managed to find out what happened to the 'package' that went missing," he said. "It's being shipped to Hong Kong by Swift Wind Cargo aboard the *Plum Blossom*. The ship is loading this morning at Vanterm 5. It's a short turnaround; she's due to sail at 4:40 this afternoon."

"Will the package be going on board with the crew?" Alma asked.

"No—as cargo. It's sealed inside a container."

Alma blinked. Sealed inside a container? That was alarming news. An ocean crossing would take a week, at least—longer if the ship was delayed by a storm. Container ships didn't have insulated holds.

"Won't the package . . ." She searched for a way to say it obliquely but couldn't find a word that would convey her worries adequately. She opted instead to be blunt. "How will the package manage to stay alive?"

She heard a faint chuckle before Tiger Cat answered. Unlikely as it was that anyone was listening in on their conversation, he stuck to the prearranged code. "The integrity of the package won't be compromised. It's being shipped inside a specialized stabilization unit—the type hospitals use when a transplant patient has to be put on ice for several days when a vat-grown organ isn't immediately available. Don't worry—the folks who have your package are making sure that it's handled properly."

Alma nodded to herself. No wonder Gray Squirrel hadn't been spotted anywhere in the three days since his extraction. He was on ice—literally. At least he was still alive.

"Where's the container now?"

"It was loaded on a truck this morning. It's probably already at the terminal."

"What about the four individuals I inquired about?" Alma asked. "Were the stills I provided from the securicams any help?"

"I recognized one of the faces: the male with the prominent teeth. He's a local runner by the name of Wharf Rat. He's heavily involved in smuggling—he's got a network of contacts along the waterfront. Grabbing your package was a bit out of character for him, but I suppose he got the job because he knows whose palms to oil at the shipping companies. Someone had to turn a blind eye when an extra piece of cargo the size of a coffin was stuffed inside the container.

"Two of the other runners were just low-grade muscle that Wharf Rat hired off the street—none of my connections even knew their names. They haven't been seen locally; it looks as though they've left town. I wasn't able to find anything at all on the fourth person."

"I didn't expect you to," Alma conceded. "Her digipic didn't give you much to go on. Where is Wharf Rat now?"

Tiger Cat's cartoon image shrugged. "Nobody knows. He's disappeared."

"What about the people who hired him?"

"I located someone who's cozy with Wharf Rat, and she says the client was a typical Mr. Johnson. Untraceable—end of story. Should I keep digging?"

Alma frowned. Part of her job was to find out which of Pacific Cybernetics' competitors had hired the shadowrunners, but for now the important thing was getting the "package" back.

"I'll let you know," she told Tiger Cat. "Do you have anything else for me?"

The cartoon shook its head. "That's it. When can I expect the second payment?"

"When the package has been recovered."

"Can I call you back tonight?"

"Tomorrow," she said firmly.

"Agreed."

Alma thumbed the cellphone's disconnect icon and was just about to close the phone when she spotted a text message scrolling across the monitor. She read only part of it—HI AL. HOW'S YOUR DAY GOING? HAVE YOU FIGURED OUT WHO I AM YET—before angrily erasing the rest.

For the past three months, some crank caller who had gotten her cellphone number had been hacking their way into the phone's daytimer memo function and leaving annoying messages. Alma had tried blocking the incoming calls, but without success—the caller must have used a different jackpoint each time. She'd even switched the cellphone's number—twice. The crank messages were especially annoying now, when she needed to keep the phone clear for Tiger Cat's calls.

Alma snapped the phone closed, set it down on the counter, and consulted her retinal clock. In seven hours and fifty-six minutes, the *Plum Blossom* would sail. Swift Wind was a large shipping firm; it would have hundreds of containers on the pier. In order to search them quickly and unobtrusively, Alma would need someone with astral capability. She'd also need technical support and a vehicle big enough to carry the stabilization unit out of the terminal, once it was located.

First and foremost on the long list of preparations, however, was the I Ching; the casting that Tiger Cat's call had interrupted was only half complete. She

picked up the coins and listened to them clink together as she shook them in her cupped hands.

The coins and a text-based copy of the *Book of
Changes* had been a gift to Alma on her twelfth birthday, from the couple who had fostered her after the
Superkid creche was broken apart. The coins dated
from the mid-19th century but were not particularly
valuable. Alma had considered them no more than
curiosities that were fun to play with, until the day
they predicted the deaths of those foster parents in a
suborbital crash, back when she was seventeen. She'd
consulted the I Ching every day since then and had
committed each of the sixty-four hexagrams to memory.

About a year ago, Alma had the coins tested by a
talismonger to see if they were magically active. He'd
confirmed that the coins were exactly what they appeared to be: ordinary coins. Even so, their prophecies
were unerringly accurate. More than once, the warn-
ings they had given her had prevented her from making a terrible mistake.

Alma held the coins over the counter, deliberately
stilling the anxious voice that insisted she immediately
rush out and find Gray Squirrel. She shook the coins
and let them fall, studied the result, and then repeated
the process twice more. Each time, two coins landed
face up and one face down: fixed yang. The trigram
for sky.

She pondered the result: sky over thunder—the
hexagram Fidelity. She could recite the overall judgment by heart: *Strength comes from outside and guides
those who are loyal from within. Although those whose
fidelity is true are blameless, fidelity alone does not
guarantee success. Those who deny what is true will
not benefit from their actions.*

It was an odd prophecy, considering the task that
lay before her today. Did it mean that her own fidelity
to her corporation would give her the strength she

needed to succeed? Or had she overlooked some truth, and was failure thus indicated?

The reference to fidelity could apply equally to herself or to Gray Squirrel—the "package" that was being shipped to Hong Kong this afternoon. She knew the researcher well enough to be certain that he was innocent of any collusion in his extraction. He was as loyal to PCI as she was. Gray Squirrel and Alma had become good friends over the years that both had been working for the corporation, and they had grown even closer after Alma had volunteered to beta-test the REM inducer.

Their lives shared many parallels. Both had been separated from their families at an early age: Alma at the age of eight when the Superkids project was shut down and she was sent halfway across the continent to live with strangers in Salish-Shidhe; Gray Squirrel at ten when his parents sent him to live with an uncle in Aztlan in a misguided attempt to toughen him up. Both had been ostracized by the other children at their schools when they refused to hide their superior prowess and intellect. Alma's cybernetics made her an oddity at the "back to basics" boarding school she was sent to—a school that didn't even have Matrix access. Gray Squirrel's keen intelligence and passion for science and math set him apart from the fitness-obsessed trainees at the paramilitary Eagle Warriors Academy that his uncle insisted he attend. Both Alma and Gray Squirrel had started their childhoods as part of a close-knit circle of siblings, and both had entered adulthood looking for something to fill the empty holes that their school years had gouged into them.

Each of them had found that something at Pacific Cybernetics. Surrounded by peers who respected their talents, each had risen swiftly through the ranks. They were part of a group of dedicated professionals who spent more time together, sharing triumphs and struggles, than most families.

For Alma, the rise to the top of PCI's counterextractions department had been a smooth one, but for Gray Squirrel, his success in the research and development division was a mixed blessing. More than once, he had confided to Alma the problems he was having at home. His wife just didn't understand the importance of his lengthy business trips to the PCI labs in the Philippines and was irritated by his round-the-clock research. He'd already compromised by always knocking off promptly at 11 p.m., no matter how engrossing the research was, and coming straight home, but still she complained.

Alma had reassured Gray Squirrel that a corporation was also a family—one that made equally valid demands on his time. And it was a family he could count on. Relationships had only two people to keep them going, and they often failed, but a corporation was sustained by hundreds or even thousands of employees. If one faltered, the others would be there to ensure its survival.

Unless, of course, the corporate family was deliberately torn apart by the UCAS judicial system and scattered to the winds—as her first one had been.

Gray Squirrel was one of the top researchers in Pacific Cybernetics' R&D lab. He was the driving force behind the REM inducer, one of PCI's most cutting-edge projects, which was certain to push the Vancouver-based company into the corporate big leagues once it was released. For that reason, Alma had been keeping an eye on him. She'd been prepared for an extraction attempt once the project's beta-testing was complete and the REM inducer was officially announced.

She hadn't expected it to come so soon. The suddenness of Gray Squirrel's extraction—and its meticulous execution—had taken her completely by surprise. Even the I Ching had not warned of it.

Perhaps today's message would become clearer as the day progressed. The first line of the hexagram had been changing yang; the second two were both changing yin. At some point in the next twenty-four hours the situation would change as yang became yin and yin became yang. A different hexagram would emerge: Meeting.

Alma hoped that this change would be for the better—that the "meeting" referred to would be the result of her successful recovery of Gray Squirrel. But as always, the I Ching was silent on the specifics. The coins could provide guidance, but it was Alma's own actions that would ultimately determine how the day would unfold.

Alma stood in front of the Heroes' Totems on Georgia Street, waiting under an umbrella for Reynolds to pick her up. From a distance, the nine totem poles appeared to be smooth cylinders of polished steel. The only features that could be made out were the regimental totems that perched at the top of each pole: wolf, bear, eagle, deer, thunderbird, killer whale, salmon, frog and beaver, all cast to resemble traditional Northwest Coast carvings. It wasn't until you got closer that the names inscribed on the poles could be seen. And it wasn't until you touched the names themselves that the digipics of the Rangers who had died were revealed.

Alma pressed a finger against one of the names on the killer whale pole and watched as the face of a young elf shimmered into view on the shiny surface like a face suddenly reflected by a mirror. Peter Charlie was a handsome man with reddish-blond hair and freckles that seemed to make a lie of his strong Native cheeks and nose. He had a cocky, confident smile that contrasted with the raindrops trickling down the surface of the pole, making it look as if tears were streaming down his cheeks. Alma felt tears begin to well in her own eyes and angrily blinked them away.

Peter had only worked seventeen months at PCI before quitting his job as a security guard to fight in the Tsimshian Border War, but they had developed a close friendship over that short time. He shared Alma's love of demanding sport, and with his whiplike reflexes and wiry muscles he was one of the few people who could keep up with her in a one-on-one game of lacrosse toss. Had Alma not been his superior at PCI, they might have become lovers. They'd come close to it, on that night before his regiment was sent north. During the two months he was on active duty they'd kept in touch via telecom; the first thing Peter had done whenever he came in from a patrol was call her.

The telecom calls had stopped abruptly in May, during the major offensive that ended the Border War. In the days that followed the battle, the newsfaxes reported the horrendous details: the Tsimshian forces, harnessing the powerful ley lines that Halley's Comet had activated, unleashed new and terrible magics upon the Salish-Shidhe forces. Most of the Rangers were killed outright by the incredibly augmented stunballs the Tsimshians hit them with—their basic motor functions shutting down as the synaptic connections in their brains were torn to shreds. Others lived but suffered severe brain damage that neither the medical mages nor the cybersurgeons could repair.

Peter was one of the unlucky ones who wasn't killed outright. The lingering effects of the stunball produced an overstimulation of a part of his brain called the reticular formation. It destroyed his ability to sleep. By the time he was med-evacuated down to Vancouver, he'd been awake for nine days. Alma had been shocked by his deterioration. Hollow-eyed, trembling, unable to feed himself or form a complete sentence, he'd lingered for two days more. Alma had held his hand and told him she loved him, and she thought she heard him slur the same words back at her but couldn't be sure. Then he died.

The badly mauled Salish-Shidhe Council had drafted a peace accord with Tsimshian in the week following the battle that came to be known as the Mind Grind. That peace had been strained to the breaking point over the past nine months, as Tsimshian forces and Ranger patrols continued to clash along the border. Many of the skirmishes ended with yet another use of the deadly stunballs, putting more brain-damaged soldiers into Salish-Shidhe critical-care wards.

Alma lifted her finger from the Heroes' Totem and watched as Peter's face faded from view. His death was what had prompted her to volunteer to have a beta-test version of the REM inducer implanted in her brain. The very day that she'd been briefed on Gray Squirrel's project, she'd insisted on becoming one of the test subjects. The testing could be brought home to PCI's Vancouver laboratories, speeding up the project. The sooner a fully tested REM inducer was ready, the fewer soldiers had to die.

In the wake of Gray Squirrel's extraction, that testing had come to a complete halt. Alma glanced up Burrard Street toward St. Paul's Hospital, with its veterans' wing. The lives of the soldiers who lay wide awake in their beds, unable to sleep despite heavy doses of magic and medication, were in the hands of one Pacific Cybernetics researcher: Gray Squirrel. It was up to Alma to bring him home.

Alma activated her binocular vision and peered out through the rain-smeared windshield of the panel van. They'd parked on the uppermost level of a parking facility that afforded an excellent view of the cargo terminal—the perfect spot to set up an observation post.

On the waterfront below, containers were stacked in long rows, one on top of the other, like gigantic building blocks. Enormous automated cranes that ran the length of the pier lifted the metal containers one by one and deposited them into the holds of waiting container ships. The low whine of heavy machinery and the distant clank of steel container on steel deck drifted in through the driver's window, which Alma had cracked open in an effort to clear the smoke from the incense Reynolds had just burned. It was cloying against the heavy smell of the oil-collection containers in the back of the van.

Alma watched for signs that the port's security force had noticed the shaman's astral incursion. Nothing looked out of the ordinary, however. A Port of Vancouver patrol vehicle cruised slowly past the *Plum Blossom*'s berth but did not turn onto the pier itself. So far, so good.

Alma switched her binocular vision off and glanced over at the elf who sat in the passenger seat beside her. When he was conscious, Reynolds was a constant flutter of nervous energy, but now he slumped loose-boned in the worn bucket seat. His body was completely motionless except for his eyes, which roved back and forth under closed lids like those of a dreaming man. He wore his prematurely gray hair Native-style, in two long braids that draped across the shoulders of his Mohawk Oil coveralls. A pigeon feather was tied into the end of each braid. Both feathers suddenly fluttered, as if in an unseen breeze. A moment later, Reynolds jerked awake as his astral body and physical body merged.

"Any results?" she asked.

The shaman bobbed his head several times in the pigeonlike nod he always used. "I think I've found him. I did a quick flythrough of every container on that pier and didn't find any astral signatures. There's only one container that could possibly have anything living inside it—and it's warded against astral intrusion. I couldn't get in."

"Which one is it?" Alma asked.

"One of the yellow ones." He pointed a slender finger. "It's second from the bottom in the row under the blue crane—five back from the end of the row where the crane's working now. There's a green container above it and a red one below. Can you see it?"

Alma increased the wipers' speed and sighted along Reynolds' forefinger. When she found it, she used her binocular vision to note the blue crane's number—C21—and to get a closer look at the container itself. She saw what she expected: "Swift Wind Cargo" stenciled on the side in red Chinese characters. The container had four others stacked above it, and its ends were wedged tight against containers to either side of it in the row.

"What side is the door on?" she asked.

Reynolds pointed with a bob of his head. "West side."

She backed off her cybereyes' magnification and used her eye's camera function to snap a digital image of the terminal, marking the position of the target container with a red crosshair. Given the crane's speed—it took an average of three point five minutes to lift and load each container onto the ship—they had approximately one hour and forty-eight minutes before their target would be lifted onto the *Plum Blossom*. The Swift Wind container was in the second-best possible position; only one level up from the ground. Clearing the door meant lifting five containers out of the stack—with luck, the *Plum Blossom*'s crew wouldn't notice that those five containers were being loaded out of sequence. Once they were out of the way—a process that should take approximately seventeen minutes and thirty seconds—Alma could open the door and haul the stabilization unit out onto the top of the adjoining container in the bottom row. From there, it was a three-meter drop to the ground— a distance that Reynolds could easily handle with a levitation spell.

The only worry was the magical ward. Whoever had extracted Gray Squirrel didn't want him to be found. The ward made her wonder if any other protective measures had been put in place.

She activated the microphone that was implanted under her skin and spoke to the team's technical support member. "Rover to Base."

A female voice whispered softly from the subdermal speaker located behind Alma's left ear. "Base here." The transmissions were encrypted, but even so, her teams were trained never to use personal identifiers on air. Riva Schell was one of PCI's best Matrix-intrusion experts. Alma had hand-picked her for this job.

"Observer has located our target. It's located under unit Charlie Two One, position two from ground, five units back from area where Charlie Two One is currently engaged. Primary color 'yukon,' secondary color 'romeo.' Access is on west side and will require five relocations. Please confirm instructions, over."

There was a moment's pause. Alma waited patiently, knowing that Schell would be accessing the automated crane's monitor cameras and visual-positioning systems.

"I see it," Schell said.

Alma instructed Schell to stand by. She did a quick radio check with Reynolds, who was wired with the standard ear speaker and mini-mike favored by delivery drivers, and then cracked the door of the van.

A gust of cold wind blew in through the partially open door, and in that same moment thunder grumbled overhead. The rain suddenly intensified, drumming on the roof of the van and covering the windows in a torrent of water.

Reynolds leaned forward in his seat and cocked his head to the side to look up at the sky with a baleful eye. "Storm crows," he said, twisting his head around to peer at them with his other eye. "We're in for another bad storm."

Alma eased the door shut and glanced out the windshield herself. Just above the parking garage, dozens of large black birds were winging their way east, racing ahead of the wind. They looked like ordinary crows to Alma.

"How do you know they're storm crows?"

"Their aura. It's dark gray with streaks of white, like lightning against a storm cloud."

"Are they going to affect your ability to cast magic?"

Reynolds shook his head but kept a cautious eye on the crows. "No. I just don't like them. Crows are bad luck."

The flock wheeled out over the harbor in a ragged formation reminiscent of a lightning bolt. As the stragglers winged their way after the rest, the pounding rain lessened. Alma cracked the door a second time.

"Reynolds!"

The shaman tore his eyes away from the sky.

Alma made a quick calculation of distances and speeds. "It should take me eight minutes to reach our target once I'm inside the gate. If you start moving at the six-minute mark, we should both arrive at the target at approximately the same time."

"Don't worry, " Reynolds said, pulling up his sleeve to display an oversized, manual-wind wristwatch. "I'll be on time."

Inwardly, Alma ground her teeth at the archaic tech. The watch was more than a century old, and she could hear that its ticking was arrhythmic. Why did shamans insist on using such obsolete equipment? Reynolds was one of the best magically active sec-guards PCI had, but if magic was going to get them out, it was technology that was going to make the job possible in the first place.

Alma stood at the side of the road, pretending to use the public telecom. The filters in her cyberears allowed her to screen out the sound of rain pattering against the yellow plastic slicker she wore—the standard, if unofficial, wet-weather gear of longshore workers on the docks. The telecom booth lay just on the other side of the overpass that led to the sprawling Vanterm cargo port. To the casual observer, she'd look like she belonged here.

She heard a large truck approaching, and the distinctive metal clatter of the container on its flatbed. With her back to the road, she listened for the sound of air brakes, and for the change in the swish of tires on wet cement that meant the truck was slowing down. At the precise moment that she knew the cab of the truck would be turning onto the overpass, causing the driver to lose sight of the back of the vehicle in his side-mounted mirrors, Alma shed her rain slicker, turned and sprinted. She hit the pavement and rolled, reaching up for the underbelly of the flatbed. Fingers and thumbs viced onto a lip of metal and locked, and in the same motion she bucked her body up, bracing her feet against another ridge. The rubber soles of the rock climber's boots she wore gripped and held. Alma pushed, making her body as rigid as the metal to which she clung.

As the truck rumbled across the overpass, the container on its flatbed rattling with each bump, Alma held on tight. The smells of oil and exhaust filled her nose. Her move-by-wire system allowed her to compensate for each bump and lurch of the truck, preventing her face from striking the underside of the flatbed. Her left hand trembled, and its grip loosened for thirty-six agonizing seconds, but the fluorinated polymer that had been braided into the vat-grown muscle tissue throughout her body gave her fingers the strength of vice grips, easily allowing her to hang on with just her right hand. Using her subdermal microphone, she instructed Schell to begin clearing a path to their target.

The truck descended the far side of the overpass, rounded a bend, and came to a stop outside a gate. She filtered out the engine's grumble so she could hear the truck driver checking in with the guard at the gate, who gave the driver directions to the spot where the container would be offloaded.

Rain was still pelting down all around the truck, making it unlikely that the secguard would do a visual inspection. Even if he did, he was unlikely to spot Alma. The insulated bodysuit, boots and fingerless gloves she wore were all a dull brown, mottled to match the mud-splattered underside of the truck. So was the tool bag that was velcroed to her chest.

Alma heard the clunk of gears being shifted. The truck lurched forward again and rolled inside the razorwire-topped chainlink fence that surrounded the terminal.

"Rover here," she subvocalized into the microphone at her throat. "I'm in."

When the truck slowed to make a turn, Alma released her fingers and feet. The ground was approximately a meter below, and she timed her muscle relaxation accordingly. When she hit the ground she was as loose-limbed as a drunk and took no damage from landing on the cement. A moment later, her move-by-wire system snapped her muscles to attention, allowing her to roll out from under the truck before its rear wheels could flatten her.

As the truck disappeared behind a wall of containers, Alma crouched in the wall's shadow and uploaded the digital image she'd shot from the parking arcade earlier. She oriented herself in relation to the cross-haired container and calculated her ETA. Then she activated her retinal clock and set its timer.

"Rover to Base. Can you see me?"

"Base here," Schell answered immediately. "That's an affirmative. You're already behind smoke."

"I'm approximately eight minutes away from our target. How's the clearing going?"

"I'm two units away from our target."

Perfect. The final two containers would take approximately seven minutes to clear. Everything was going like clockwork—just the way Alma expected it to. "Good work. Prepare to start extending the smoke."

"Will do."

Reconfiguring the programming of Crane 21 so that it loaded five containers from the middle of the stack had been relatively easy for the team's Matrix specialist, but now the tricky part was about to begin. To cover Alma's movements across the terminal, Schell had to access dozens of security cameras at once and then create a one-second delay in the data that was streaming back from them. That gave her one second in which to feed an "instant replay" loop into each of the securicams just as Alma moved into its field of view. The net effect would be to render Alma invisible—all the cameras would "see" was a blank wall of containers.

"This is Rover. I'm starting my run."

Using the aerial photo of the terminal she'd snapped

earlier as a map, Alma jogged between the walls of containers, winding her way through the maze. They rose up on either side of her like gigantic, multicolored building blocks, a checkerboard of greens, brick-reds, blues, yellows and grays. Every second one seemed to be bright yellow, emblazoned in meter-high red Chinese characters with the words Swift Wind Cargo.

When she was six minutes away from her target, she instructed Reynolds to start moving. He answered—but at that same moment lightning crackled overhead, filling her subdermal speaker with a burst of static. The thunder followed a second or two later. Alma's cyberears immediately compensated, damping the sudden burst of noise down to a level that didn't impede her hearing, but static continued to crackle in her implanted speaker each time a bolt of lightning flickered in the darkening sky. The rain drummed steadily down, soaking Alma's hair and chilling her bare face and fingertips.

At the seven-minute, thirty-nine-second mark, she rounded the corner of a row of containers and spotted the one that was their target. The crane—which arched over the stack like a gigantic, upside-down U on wheels—lowered and spread metal jaws and locked them onto the dark blue container next to the target with a loud clang. Hydraulics whining, the crane lifted the blue container into the air and carried it toward the waiting ship.

Squinting against the driving rain, Alma saw that the door of the Swift Wind container was clear. She sprinted the last few meters and leaped up into the air. Her fingers found the top of the container in the bottom row adjacent to the target, and she hauled herself up onto its roof in a fluid motion, swiveling her legs to the side so that she would land on her feet.

The container was a soft-top, its canvas roof already starting to pool with rainwater. Alma's wired reflexes immediately compensated for the uneven footing, keeping her steady and level on the trampoline-like surface. Moving with the grace of an acrobat, she bounced her way across it to the door of the yellow container that was her target. She couldn't see the magical ward that had stopped Reynolds from entering; it was probably painted on the inside of the container. She listened, letting her hearing amplification detect any noise that might be coming from inside. The only thing she heard was a soft, steady beeping—probably the stabilization unit.

The door of the container was sealed with a heavy padlock and a numbered squealstrip. The former was a simple mechanical lock that could easily be removed with bolt cutters—but the squealstrip would emit an ear-piercing wail if the metal strip was severed.

Alma pulled a finger-thin spray can of quick-hardening foam from the tool bag on her chest and sprayed a healthy wad of it around the squealstrip's built-in speaker. She counted off the thirty seconds it took to dry, using the time to pull out her bolt cutters and extend their collapsible handles. When thirty seconds were up she flicked a fingernail against the bright blue foam to test its hardness and then cut through the squealstrip. The foam worked beautifully—the only sound was a muffled squeak, and even that noise was lost in the low rumble of thunder overhead. She cut through the padlock and set it aside, and then stood and pushed back the lever that would release the door.

"Rover to Observer. I'm about to access our target. What's your ETA?"

She heard Reynolds whisper a curse before he answered. "Sorry. Took a wrong turn. ETA is ... ah ..."

She heard the rustle of his sleeve as Reynolds consulted his wristwatch.

"ETA is one minute, max."

Alma's ears easily picked up the sound of the van's engine. Behind it, she could hear another vehicle—one that had a higher pitch similar to the Ford Americars that the Port of Vancouver Security used. At the same moment, Schell's voice came over the speaker behind her ear.

"Base to Rover and Observer. You'd better move quickly or you'll have company."

Alma had intended to wait for Reynolds before opening the door, in case the container was magically guarded. With Port of Vancouver Security on its way, she didn't have that luxury. She hauled on the heavy container door, dancing lightly back on the springy canvas as it opened.

The load inside the Swift Wind container had shifted during its transport to the terminal—Alma's cyberears caught the sound of cardboard sliding on cardboard, and then a wall of boxes crashed out of the open door. The canvas top of the container on which Alma stood bowed under their weight, stretching downward as it filled with tearing cardboard and clattering cans—and then the lashings that held it gave way, whipping out of their holes.

As soon as the canvas bowed enough for her feet to find purchase on the contents of the container below, Alma sprang to one side. She flipped once in midair, bringing her feet under her as her body twisted, and landed on the container's rim. As the boxes finished tumbling into the container below her, she ran lightly along the edge toward the Swift Wind container. Dangling out of its open door, its weight supported only by a shifting pile of tin cans and broken boxes, was the stabilization unit: a gigantic plastic case colored hospital green, with monitors and condition-indicator lights flashing on its sides.

The stabilization unit teetered for a moment and then fell with a crash into the container below. Alma's heart lurched as she thought of Gray Squirrel being jostled about inside, but then logic took over. The stabilization unit was designed to be shipped from hospital to hospital. A few bumps and bangs wouldn't hurt it—or the man inside.

Tires hissed to a stop on the pavement below Alma. She glanced down and saw Reynolds peering up at her through the van's windshield. His eyes searched the open end of the Swift Wind container, and his lips moved.

Alma heard his voice in her radio: "Where's the target?"

"It fell down inside," she answered, pointing. "Get up here, where you can see it. Hurry!"

The shaman flung open the driver's door and did as instructed, scrambling up onto the roof of the van. From that vantage point, he was able to peer over the lip of the canvas-topped container and get a line of sight on the stabilization unit.

Reynolds began to chant, arms bent at his sides in a posture reminiscent of wings about to unfold. As he slowly extended his arms, fingers spread wide like feathers, the stabilization unit lifted into the air. Alma wasted no time watching it, instead shouldering the Swift Wind container's door shut to cover their tracks and then leaping lightly down to the ground to wrench open the double doors at the back of the van. As Reynolds guided the heavy stabilization unit up and out of the container and down toward the open doors, Alma gave it a shove and then slammed the doors shut.

Schell was relaying a message, but Alma's cyberears were already warning her of the same thing. The Port of Vancouver patrol car must be just around the corner—she could even pick out the voice of the driver as he radioed his superiors about the Mohawk Oil van that had strayed suspiciously off course, into the container staging area.

Alma leaped into the driver's seat and gunned the engine as soon as Reynolds was on board. "Base—do we still have a smoke screen?"

"Affirmative."

"Right." She briefly deactivated the speaker in her throat and spoke to Reynolds. "Time for an illusion— and make it quick!"

The shaman began chanting once more—a soft, cooing noise reminiscent of a pigeon settling contentedly into its nest. He closed his eyes, oblivious to the rainwater that dripped from his face and braids onto his lap. To Alma's eyes, the van did not change, but she knew what was happening. Even as the Port of Vancouver Security patrol car rounded the corner of the row of containers, the van was assuming the appearance of a mobile crane carrying one of the smaller, five-meter-long containers. When the patrol car hissed past, its driver gave them no more than a passing glance.

Alma turned the van onto the road that led back to the gate, and in a few minutes more they were outside the terminal and back on city streets. In the back of the van, the stabilization unit continued to beep.

Reynolds had slumped in his seat. After a second or two, he sat up with a jerk. When he turned toward Alma, his eyes were wide. He glanced back at the stabilization unit and bobbed his head in a ducking motion.

"Bad news," he said. "I just did an astral scan of the stabilization unit. It's Gray Squirrel, all right—but he's got no aura. It looks like he's—"

"What?" Alma veered the van over to the side of the road and jammed on the brakes. Her pulse was pounding in her ears. "What happened? Did the stabilization unit fail? Is that why the alarm's beeping?"

Reynolds shook his head. His face was very pale. "The unit's working fine. It switched automatically into critical-care life-support mode—that's what the beeping noise and flashing light are about. But even critical care couldn't—"

Alma clawed her seat belt open and clambered into the back of the vehicle. She found the stabilization unit's control panel and stabbed at it with a forefinger until the locking mechanism clicked. As she wrenched open the lid, cold air rushed out of the unit, carrying with it a hospital smell that was a mix of plastic, sterilizing scrub—and another, much more pungent odor that smelled like copper: blood.

Gray Squirrel lay on his back, cocooned in supercooled blue foam. Monitor patches dotted his chest, and intravenous tubes fed into his arms. A clear plastic breathing tube snaked down into his open mouth. His scalp had been shaved so that CAT-scan monitors could be attached; the skin was nicked in several places. His face was as white as paper, his dark eyes wide and staring.

Air was still hissing into the breathing tube, but it wasn't going far. Gray Squirrel's neck had been severed down to the spine, and the oxygen-rich mixture sighed out of this gaping wound, fluttering the ragged skin. A thick layer of frozen blood covered his chest and arms—the logical part of Alma's mind noted that his throat must have been slit just after he had been placed inside the containment unit, just before the lid had been closed. Unable to deal with the sudden trauma, the unit had gone into life-support mode, but too late: there was no life left to support.

Alma touched Gray Squirrel's cheek. His skin was as cold as glass.

"It's my fault, Squirrel," she whispered. "I should have located you sooner."

A tremor began in Alma's left hand, but she didn't bother to time its duration. There didn't seem to be much point.

Meeting

Night Owl eased her Harley Electroglide into a space between two parked cars and cut the motorcycle's engine. Rain spattered on the bike's twin exhaust pipes, hissing into steam as it hit the hot metal. She pulled off her leather gauntlets and night-vision goggles, flicked wet hair out of her eyes, and then checked her face in the bike's mirror, making sure the thick blue and black lines of the Beijing Opera mask she'd painted on her face hadn't run in the rain. Then she climbed down from the bike, admiring the winking owl that she'd had custom painted on the gas tank. She heaved the metal monster up onto its kick stand and was just about to jander into the restaurant when a soggy blanket huddled in front of the building unfolded itself.

Instantly on alert, Night Owl whipped a hand back and under her leather jacket, reaching for the Ares Predator concealed against the small of her back. It was halfway out of its holster before she realized that the grotter under the blanket was just a teenage elf, looking for spare cred.

The elf was skinny, with pointed ears that stuck out of ragged holes in his black knitted hat. His plastic pants had been made of bubble wrap and duct tape, and the sleeves of his striped shirt looked as though they'd been chewed off at the elbow. He smelled of hydro-gro weed, days-old sweat and moldy blanket, but his eyes were still scanning. He'd savvied her weapon in the second she'd flashed for it.

"Hey, heavy lady, be chill. I was just going to give your chrome a polish." He held out a dirty rag and a squirt bottle that might once have held liquid polish.

Night Owl was about to tell him to frag off when she noticed the kid's left hand. It was obviously cybered, its synthetic skin peeling back to reveal the artificial metal joints, plastic tendons, and servos that lay underneath. The middle finger was frozen in an open position, as if the kid were giving the world a permanent "frag you." The hand looked too small for the arm; the flesh around the kid's wrist was puckered like a baggy shirt that had been tucked into a tight pair of jeans.

Night Owl stepped under the dripping awning the kid had been using for shelter. "How long've you had that hand, cobber?"

The kid glanced down at his hand as if he'd forgotten it was cybered. "Since I was ten."

"It's too small for you now. How come you weren't fitted with a larger hand?"

The elf shrugged. "Couldn't afford it."

Night Owl stood for a moment in silence, watching raindrops bounce off the roofs of parked cars. The going rate for a bottom-of-the-heap, alpha-grade cyberhand was forty thousand nuyen. The kid's parents had probably scrimped up everything they had to pay for it—and the fraggers who sold it to them never bothered to mention that the kid would outgrow it in a few years' time.

"Who made the hand?"

The kid turned the hand over to show her the logo on its inner wrist. A curling tsunami wave hovered over the letters "PCI." Framing the wave in a circle were the words "Pacific Cybernetics Industries—The Wave of the Future."

Night Owl's eyes narrowed. PCI had a history of dumping its outdated cyberware in third-world countries whose customers didn't have the nuyen to launch lawsuits after the drek glitched or broke down. Some of the obsolete 'ware also showed up in local chop shops, like the one this kid's parents must have taken him to.

Night Owl reached into a pocket and handed the kid a certified credstick. The kid's eyes widened when he thumbed the stick's balance and saw the one and two zeroes on the miniature screen.

"Keep an eye on the bike, kid," Night Owl told him. "I wouldn't want one of these parked cars to back into it."

The kid opened his mouth to thank her, but Night Owl didn't stick around to hear it. She turned and shoved open the door of the restaurant.

Wazubee's was always packed at this time of night. The restaurant was a favorite hangout for the artists, citizenship activists, performance poets and other chillfolk who inhabited the area around the Drive. Humans and metas of every description jammed the tables, spending their nuyen on realkaf with a water chaser and trying to talk over the rhythImpulse that droned from the speakers overhead. The crowds and noise made Wazubee's the perfect place for a shadow meet—nobody gave a runner a second glance here.

Night Owl spotted her fixer in the back of the restaurant, sitting at a table under a gigantic chandelier made from welded cutlery. The votive candle on the table in front of him was no match for Hothead's trademark flame hair, which at the moment was blazing with a steady, propane-blue flicker. Filament-thin flames twisted out of pores in the insulated dermal plating that lined his scalp, flaring to a height of nearly five centimeters, then dampening down before flaring again. The tubes that fed propane to the system ran down the back of his neck and disappeared under his shirt collar; he wore a canteen-sized, refillable tank clipped to his belt. He'd gotten the idea from the work of 12 Midnight, a turn-of-the-century artist whose stainless-steel paintings always included propane flames. Hothead figured they looked chill and decided to turn himself into a work of art.

Night Owl worked her way to Hothead's table and slapped palms with him. He flashed her a brief smile, eyes crinkling around fire-red contact lenses. The color matched the jacket of his cellosuit, which made a crinkling noise as he shifted his weight. Despite the cheerful greeting, he seemed uneasy about Night Owl joining him. He kept glancing toward the door. She wondered if he'd been waiting for a meet with another runner.

"*Ni hao*, Hothead," Night Owl said, sliding into the chair on the opposite side of the table. "Sorry about dripping on your table. It's pretty wet out there."

"Did you see the storm this afternoon?" Hothead asked.

Night Owl shook her head. "I was sleeping."

"Street buzz says there were storm crows in the clouds. A Shinto sun shaman once told me that they gather in flocks when an evil deity is about to appear."

Night Owl laughed. "As long as it's not me he's looking for, I don't care."

The sleeve of Hothead's suit crinkled as he drained the last of his 'kaf. He set down the cup and pushed back his chair as if he was about to go.

"Got any biz?" Night Owl asked.

Hothead's eyes narrowed. "After you screwed up that last job I brokered for you? I don't think so."

Night Owl frowned. "What do you mean? The extraction went down without a glitch."

"Buzz has it that your Johnson didn't receive what he paid for."

Night Owl smiled. She'd never intended that he should. Her interest in the run had been personal, and she'd accomplished what had needed to be done. "Too bad. Sometimes things get damaged in transit."

"Damaged?" Hothead gave her a careful look. "You mean lost. Someone let something slip, and the item your Johnson paid so much cred for was snatched back by its original owners before it reached its destination."

Night Owl shrugged. "Whatever."

"The Johnson wants his nuyen back."

"I've spent it." She jerked a thumb in the direction of the door. "Check out my new wheels."

"You spent *all* of it?" Hothead shifted toward the edge of his seat, as if he was about to leave. "That's bad—but I suppose it shouldn't surprise me."

"Find me some more biz," Night Owl insisted. "Then I'll at least have the option of paying the Johnson his nuyen back."

Hothead gave her a skeptical look. They both knew runners didn't give refunds.

"I know someone who needs some extra muscle tomorrow, for a run that's going down at noon," Hothead said.

"Noon?" Night Owl laughed. "You know me, Hothead. I'm a reverse Cinderella. I come out at midnight and turn into a pumpkin at dawn."

Hothead shrugged. "The only other job I have right now needs someone who can pass as a Full Blood. You look too Euro—although with a hint of something Asian underneath. Are you part Chinese? Your accent is perfect."

"Japanese," Night Owl corrected him. "And a hundred other races. I'm a walking DNA cocktail. According to my father, I've got a little bit of everything in my genetic makeup—even Native. I probably could have claimed citizenship, if I'd wanted to."

The flames on Hothead's scalp rose a centimeter. He pulled his chair back up to the table. "Does your father have citizenship?" Behind his contact lenses, his eyes gleamed with curiosity. His commodity was information—the tidbit Night Owl had just supplied to him had captured his attention like a shiny silver coin tossed before a crow.

Night Owl leaned back in her chair. Hothead had just stepped over the line that separated fixer and runner, but she didn't care. She had his attention again. Deliberately, she tossed him another tidbit. She was feeling reckless tonight and was curious to see how smart the fixer really was. Would he be able to follow the datatrail and figure out who she was?

"My father's dead," she answered. "He suicided—hung himself with a monofilament. It took his head clean off when he jumped off the chair."

Hothead swallowed and tucked in his chin. "Why?"

"The corporation he worked for screwed him over. A project he was working on crashed and burned, and he was the one blamed for it."

Night Owl saw Hothead looking down at the table and realized that she was holding a spoon in her hands. She'd bent the stainless steel nearly double without even realizing it. Carefully, she laid it back down on the table, beside the tray that held Hothead's empty 'kaf cup and glass of water.

A waitress came up to the table and asked if they'd like to eat. Night Owl ordered a 'kaf and some fries and garlic mayo.

Hothead winked at the waitress and asked for a refill and a new spoon. "Don't make the 'kaf so strong next time," he joked. "It plays hell with my nerves."

When the waitress left, his expression became seri-

ous. The flames on his scalp dimmed to a soft red
glow, and his voice fell to a whisper.

"The Red Lotus are looking for you."

Night Owl glanced nervously around the restaurant.
Red Lotus was one of Vancouver's most notorious
street gangs, "younger brother" to a powerful triad
based in the Republic of China. They dominated the
city's heroin trade and were notorious for going over-
kill on anyone who crossed them. When the Red
Lotus struck, bullets fell like hail and blood flowed
like water.

"What do they want with me?"

"Well, since they can't get their boss's nuyen back,
I guess they'll want your blood."

Night Owl leaned forward, at the same time sliding
her left hand back along the arm of her chair, bringing
it closer to her pistol. "They don't know what I look
like," she said slowly. "Unless someone has given
them a description of me."

Hothead carefully placed his hands, palms down, on
the table. His eyes never left Night Owl's, even when
her left hand started its slide under the back of her
jacket.

"They don't need a description," he said. "They
have a vidpic of you. They got it out of Wharf Rat's
eye."

Night Owl blinked, then brought her hand back in
front of her, resting it on the table again. "Frag—I
didn't know his eye was cybered." She'd noticed that
one eye was gold instead of the runner's natural
brown, but she'd assumed it was a contact—like Hothead's dramatic red lenses.

She'd also just been told that Wharf Rat was dead.

Night Owl was suddenly sorry that she'd suspected
Hothead. He was a friend—he was sitting here talking
to her, when she was probably the last person in the
world he wanted to be seen with right now.

"Thanks, Hothead," she said. "I owe you one."

Hothead smiled. "I know. Don't worry—I'll call the debt in someday."

The waitress returned with two trays of 'kaf and water, balancing Night Owl's fries on the inside of one forearm. As she set them down on the table, Hothead glanced again at the door.

Hothead drained his coffee in several quick swallows, then rose from the table. Without a word of farewell, he left Night Owl sitting with her fries and 'kaf and weaved his way between the crowded tables to the front of the restaurant. Night Owl watched him walk out into the night and tried to decide whether to finish her meal and go or hang tight in the restaurant. Either way, the gangers might find her.

She decided to let fate choose for her. Digging her lucky SkyTrain token out of her pocket, she flipped it into the air. Heads she'd stay; tails she'd turn and run. Just as she caught it in midflight and slapped it down on the back of her right hand, however, something made her look up. The street kid she'd talked to earlier was coming in through the door. He was nervous and looking for someone: her. As soon as he saw Night Owl, he ran to the table where she sat, almost colliding with a waitress along the way.

"Hey, lady, you'd better fly. There's some heavy people looking for you."

Night Owl pushed back her chair and looked at the coin on the back of her hand. Tails. She shoved it into a pocket as she stood up. "Where? How many?"

"Outside. Two men—Chinese, by the sound of 'em. They got out of a gray ragtop and crossed the street to your bike, and were scannin' it like they knew it. Then they looked up and down the street. They asked if I saw where the person riding the bike went, and I said I'd tell them for five nuyen. They liked that. I pointed them down the street, to the New Millennium

Arcade. Stupid fraggers didn't even realize that you don't park a bike two blocks away from where you're going, especially in drekky weather like this."

"I'm impressed," Night Owl said. She was already on her feet and moving to the front door. She had every reason to believe the kid—if he had tried to snag a few more nuyen by selling her out, she'd already be dead. So would most of the other poor fraggers in the restaurant. She tossed a small-denomination credstick at the waitress, telling her to keep the change, and peered out through the restaurant's front window. The kid pointed out the car—a turbocharged Saab Dynamit convertible that looked like it could crank some serious Ks. She didn't see anyone lingering near the sports car, and none of the people who were scurrying along the Drive under umbrellas looked like the gangers the kid had described.

"Stay inside until I'm gone," Night Owl warned him. "I don't want you in my way."

The kid grinned. He'd understood what she really meant.

Night Owl pulled on her gauntlets and positioned the night-vision goggles on her forehead, ready for use. Then she pulled the door open and slid outside, moving low so the parked cars hid her. She swung up into the bike's leather seat, keyed in its ignition code, and rocked the Harley forward, taking it off its kick stand in one smooth motion. The engine's loud rumble filled the street, echoing like thunder off the buildings to either side.

Just as she was wheeling away, Night Owl caught a glimpse of a running figure in her rear view mirror. He was young, Asian and armed—and looked pissed as hell. He ran out into the street, heedless of honking traffic, and leveled the Uzi he was holding. Its barrel flared red. Bullets punched into the parked cars behind Night Owl, shattering windows and exploding tires. Pedestrians on the sidewalk dived for cover.

Night Owl wrenched the bike right and disappeared around the corner onto First Avenue. Thankfully the rain had eased up a little, although the streets were still slick. She twisted the throttle, and the Harley leaped forward, exhaust roaring. Steering with one hand, she pulled the night-vision goggles down over her eyes. The world shifted into greens and grays.

She was weaving in and out of traffic when she heard the squeal of tires behind her. The bike's rear view mirror flashed her a glimpse of the Saab, hot on her trail. The ganger in the passenger seat was leaning out of his window, trying to line her up in the Uzi's sights, but there seemed to be too many cars in the way. He ducked back inside.

She swung onto Knight Street, which offered a clear, straight run. She needed to lose those fraggers— but she wasn't going to do that in this part of the city, where the roads ran grid-straight. She needed a bolt hole, and she knew just where to find one. All she had to do was stay alive for the five minutes it would take her to reach it.

Side streets and red lights flashed by, and somehow both bike and Saab managed to miss clipping any of the cars that they rocketed past. Rain stung Night Owl's bare cheeks like ice-cold shotgun pellets, and her wet hair streamed out behind her. The water-repellent jeans she'd tucked into her Daytons fluttered like tarps in a hurricane, and her leather jacket pressed back against her chest. Wind roared in her ears.

When she reached the southernmost end of Knight Street, she deked around a barrier onto the Knight Street Bridge. It had been condemned a year ago, after the Big One hit. This end of the bridge was intact, but the opposite side was a twisted skeleton, just waiting to collapse—a bridge to the ruin that had been the suburb of Richmond. A bridge to nowhere.

Bullets *spanged* off a sagging light fixture beside the motorcycle as Night Owl flashed across the bridge. Even with her night-vision goggles, she had to rely on luck to find her way—rubble and holes flashed past so quickly that only her instinctive, last-second swerves got the Harley around them. At the last moment she spotted a gaping hole in the deck of the bridge that hadn't been there last week and deked around it in a tight swerve. Then she was below the crest of the bridge and zooming down the other side. In just a few seconds more, she'd be in the ruins.

The Saab behind her was still accelerating; the driver must have managed to avoid the hole, too. As the car shot into view in her mirrors, Night Owl took the first offramp and blasted down onto what was left of Bridgeport Road.

The road was intact for a few meters beyond the offramp, but then it became chaotic. Abandoned cars lay crumpled under the light fixtures that the earthquake had toppled on them, and long-dead electric wires snaked in tangles across the street. The road itself looked like a jigsaw puzzle that had been punched from below by a giant's fist: jagged pieces of asphalt reared up at odd angles, with weeds filling the gaps. On either side of the road were the dark shadows of ruined buildings. Some had collapsed into piles of rubble; others had tilted into the air like sinking ships when the earthquake liquefied the ground beneath their foundations. Only one in ten was still intact.

Night Owl knew every centimeter of the ruined road by heart. This was one of her favorite bolt holes. Alternately revving and braking, she skittered her way across the largest and most level slabs of asphalt, leaping the bike from one to the next as if they were stepping stones.

Behind her, she heard the twin thud of car tires hitting an obstruction, and then the screech of metal grating on concrete and an engine revving into the red. The Saab's engine stuttered into a rough idle, and then car doors slammed. For a moment, Night Owl thought she was clear. Then the Uzi roared. Bullets hissed through the night and ricocheted off debris all around her. One tore a crease across her front fender; another slammed into the seat, just behind her thigh.

Night Owl skidded around a corner into the shadow of a ruined warehouse. She looped around the back of the property and entered what remained of the building through a motorcycle-sized hole in its rear wall. Braking to a stop, she cut the engine and slid off the bike, and then picked her way to the front wall of the warehouse to peek out through a rockworm hole.

She nearly laughed at what she saw. The Saab was hung up on a twisted telecom pole several hundred meters back, rear wheels spinning in the air. It wasn't going anywhere. One ganger was standing on the broken roadway, Uzi in hand and eyes searching the night. He shouted something at the driver, but Night Owl was too far away to hear what he said. The driver shut the car down and climbed out of the vehicle. Both of them stood tense and silent, as if listening. The chase had suddenly turned into a game of cat and mouse—and neither one of the gangers knew where Night Owl was hiding. Behind her, the motorcycle made faint *tic-tic-ticking* noises as its engine slowly cooled.

Night Owl was surprised they'd followed her this far. Even the hardest-hooped gangers balked at entering the Richmond Ruins. The suburb had been leveled by a quake a year ago and left to rot ever since. Rock-

worms had made Swiss cheese of the concrete apartment blocks and office towers that still stood, making
much of the terrain so unstable that the vibrations
from someone walking along the sidewalks out front
could tumble them. Devil rats had bloated themselves
on the tens of thousands of people who had died when
the quake leveled the 'burb, and now they roamed the
ruins in swarms. But most fearsome of all were the
ghosts of the dead. There were a lot of restless, angry
spirits in Richmond—and none of them knew who it
was, exactly, that they ought to be pissed at.

Everyone agreed that the quake had been magical
in origin—the silty ground under Richmond had been
jackhammered up and down by what looked like an
earthquake of more than nine on the Richter scale,
but just across the river in Vancouver, the seismo-
graphs hadn't even twitched. Street buzz had it that a
gang of secret Feng Shui masters had miscalculated
the "straight-arrow" formed by the two-kilometer-
long suborbital runway on neighboring Sea Island and
accidentally triggered the quake. But nobody really
knew for sure—and that was the scariest part of living
in the Awakened world.

Outside on the ruined street, the Red Lotus boys
were having a shouted conversation. After a few minutes of cursing, they turned and jandered back in the
direction of the Knight Street Bridge. They seemed to
have given up the chase.

Chuckling, Night Owl walked back to her bike. She
was just swinging a leg up over the seat when someone
kicked her other foot out from under her. She went
down across the bike, and her weight overbalanced
the heavy machine. The Harley slammed onto its side
on the rubble-strewn floor, sending broken bits of concrete skittering. Night Owl twisted just in time to
avoid getting tangled in it and landed face-up. She
kicked against the floor, sending herself sliding back-

ward, at the same time twisting and reaching behind her back for her Predator.

Something heavy landed square on her chest, slamming her back onto the ground and trapping her left arm underneath her. She tried to shift the weight, but invisible arms locked around her torso, hugging her tight. A musky animal odor filled her nostrils, and she felt coarse hair pressing against her skin. Something magical was holding her, making it impossible to move. She heard a creak and felt a sharp pain under her breasts as the magical arms squeezed tighter. She couldn't tell if the sound had come from her leather jacket creaking or her ribs straining to the breaking point.

A shape suddenly appeared in her night-vision goggles: a troll twice her size, with Asian features and two spiraling horns that angled out from his temples, giving his forehead the shape of a V. His long hair was gathered in a bun at the back of his head like that of an ancient Chinese warrior and was tied with a wide band of cloth that she guessed would have been red in daylight: the hallmark of the Red Lotus. A bear's claw pierced the lobe of each ear. The troll had dropped the invisibility and silence spells he'd used to sneak up on Night Owl, and now he rose to his feet, lifting his knee from her chest. One cartilage-crusted hand was balled in a fist; he held it over her, maintaining the magical spell that pinned her to the ground.

"You're a dead woman," he said in Cantonese.

"No . . . I'm not," Night Owl gasped. She knew better than to believe his threat. Entertainment trids to the contrary, gangers didn't make speeches before killing someone. They just greased them. "You . . . want something."

She could feel her right eye twitching—an annoying quirk that cropped up whenever things got too close to the edge. She suddenly realized that there had been three gangers in the Saab—not two. The other two men had only pretended to leave. She could hear their footsteps outside even now, as they circled back toward the ruined warehouse—or maybe that was just the rain, starting up again.

"You have angered Eldest Brother by cheating him," the troll said, eyes blazing. "You sold him property, then told the original owners where to find it again."

"That . . . wasn't me . . . who told. Someone . . . else." It was the truth—she and Wharf Rat had probably been sold out by that joygirl Wharf Rat had been dossing down with this past month. Night Owl didn't expect the troll to believe it, however.

"You agreed to the contract," the troll continued in a grim voice. "You bore the ultimate responsibility."

Night Owl pretended to be listening, but all the while she was testing her strength against the invisible arms that held her. She could rock back and forth slightly, although it felt as though the weight of a grizzly were on top of her. And she could still move her fingers. If she could just hook one of them around the Predator, she might be able to roll over and pull the trigger. With luck, she might hit the troll in the leg— if she didn't shoot her own hoop off first. As she strained her hand closer to the holster in the small of her back, she stalled for time.

"I can pay . . . your boss back . . . twice what . . . he gave me," she lied. "There's twenty K on registered credsticks . . . back at—"

The troll clenched his fist tightly, causing his bony knuckles to crack. Night Owl's vision swam with stars as the magical arms that were holding her squeezed the last of the air from her lungs. She fought to take a breath, but it was as if she were underwater, with no air to breathe. Dimly, over the pounding that filled

her ears, she heard the troll's final pronouncement—
and realized she'd been wrong about the trids. Sometimes real-life gangers liked to make speeches, too.

"Your death will be a lesson that the other shadowrunners will remember."

Night Owl's world dimmed to a dull red. Static filled
her ears, and in her chest she could hear her heartbeat, so frenzied a moment ago, slow and falter. She
was dying . . .

A voice floated into what remained of her consciousness—a voice that sounded as ancient and wet
as rotted silk tearing.

That will be enough, Wu.

The invisible bands of steel that had been tightening
around Night Owl's chest were suddenly gone. Something cold dripped on her skin—rainwater leaking in
through what remained of the roof? Eyelids fluttering,
she took a ragged breath. Somehow, she forced herself
to sit up. When her eyes could focus again, she nearly
fainted.

Looming over her, nearly filling the ruined warehouse, was an enormous eastern dragon. Its head
alone was as large as a horse, and the sinuous neck
that undulated behind it was as sleek as the body of
a snake. Long, straggling whiskers hung from either
side of its mouth, and multipointed horns jutted from
above its eyebrows like broken twigs. One of its hands
rested on Night Owl's overturned Harley, its fingers
spread to reveal webbing between them. The nails on
its fingers and thumb were nearly a meter long, as
twisted and curved as peeled tree bark.

Only the upper body of the dragon was visible—the
rest was bisected by the floor of the ruined warehouse,
as if the dragon had erupted from the earth. Wu, the
ganger who had been holding Night Owl with his
magic, was just to the right of the dragon, resting on
one knee as if paying homage to the creature. His

eyes were wide and glistening and his expression enraptured, as if he were looking upon a god. Night Owl
could see the ganger clearly, even when the dragon's
body passed in front of him. The dragon was here in
astral form only, manifesting itself visually so that
Night Owl and the troll could see it—but that didn't
make it any less dangerous.

Night Owl knew without being told that she was in
serious drek now. The Red Lotus obviously served
this dragon—this worm must be the "eldest brother"
the troll had been jabbering about. The gang was also
working for the Johnson whose intermediary had
hired her—the one whose property she had deliberately trashed. It didn't take a major synaptic leap to
figure that the dragon and her Johnson were one and
the same. Dying in the troll's magical grip was nothing
compared with what she faced now. A dragon could
think of far more exquisite torments than a metahu-
man shaman ever could. Night Owl's life and soul
were balanced on a razor's edge.

She chose her words carefully. "How can I . . . serve
you, great one?" Her right eye was twitching like
crazy, and only by concentrating all of her effort on
it could she make it stop.

The dragon smiled, baring teeth that looked like
ancient bits of bone filed to needle-sharp points. *You
are a close friend of Akira Kageyama.* Although it was
speaking to her telepathically, its "words" had a
throaty gurgle.

"I've done runs for him," Night Owl admitted.

*He trusts you. He showed his appreciation, after you
extracted the dour from the Technology Institute, by
making you an honorary member of PETAB.*

Night Owl was stunned. The dragon seemed to
know even more about her biz than the other runners
she sometimes hung with. She hadn't told any of them

about the Technology Institute run—she'd done that one solo.

After hearing the skinny on that run—that she was to set free a half-dozen dour that cybernetics students at the institute were performing vivisection on—she'd told her Johnson she'd do the job for free. Dour might be little more than animals—they were magically active chimpanzees that were transformed by the Awakening—but that didn't mean they didn't suffer and feel pain. Cutting into their living bodies was the same as experimenting on children.

Two weeks after the dour were liberated, Night Owl had been summoned to a party in one of Vancouver's most expensive condoplexes. Akira Kageyama was its host, and the guests were a small but exclusive group: a half-dozen of Vancouver's elite who contributed to the coffers of People for the Ethical Treatment of the Awakened Beings. The group was a legitimate charitable organization that vehemently denied any connection with the recent rash of raids on research facilities and testing labs, but the gleams of gratitude in the eyes of the PETAB members as they shook Night Owl's hand had confirmed her hunch they were the ones who had hired her for the Technology Institute raid.

Night Owl never did tell them that her decision to waive her runner's fee had been based on a flip of the token in her pocket.

The dragon watched her patiently, its eyes as still as pools of dark liquid. Its head remained perfectly level, despite the fact that its sinuous body was gently snaking back and forth.

"You know a lot about me," Night Owl said.

Be thankful of that, the dragon said. *If you weren't so useful to me, I would have let Wu end your life.*

The shaman folded his massive arms across his chest. His grin extended to the tips of his horns.

You are alive because there is something in Kageya-ma's home that I want—something you will get for me, the dragon continued. *It is a piece of jade: a statue. You will remove it and convey it to Wu, at a location that you and he will arrange.*

Night Owl thought that one over. She had no qualms about doing a run on Kageyama, or about using his misplaced trust to steal from his home. She was a shadowrunner, and biz was biz, after all. "Kageyama's an art dealer—his place is full of expensive drek like that. How will I know which statue you want?"

The dragon gave a bubbling sigh. *The jade has engraved upon it the character fu—happiness—and is hollow. It may feel lighter than it should when you pick it up, and it may rattle. Do not be tempted to look inside. If the statue is damaged in any way, I will let Wu finish what was begun here tonight.*

"And if I deliver the statue intact, you'll call off the Red Lotus?"

The dragon gave her a wet smile. *Of course. They will trouble you no more.*

Night Owl nodded, even though she knew she was as good as dead. The shaman would flatline her as soon as she handed the statue over to him.

Realizing she had little to lose made her bold enough to speak her mind to the dragon. "Let me scan this straight: I'm supposed to show up uninvited at the condoplex of a millionaire I barely know and ask him to look the other way while I search his doss from top to bottom for a statue that even you wouldn't recognize if you saw it. You can't even tell me how big the statue is or what it looks like. Kageyama has some pretty big pieces of art in his place. What if I need a crane to haul the fragger out of there?"

The troll shaman had risen swiftly to his feet as

Night Owl spoke. His face held a mixture of anger and outrage, as if he was amazed by her impertinence. He glanced at the dragon beside him, as if expecting it to blast Night Owl with its magic. Wu's master, however, gave only a gurgling chuckle.

There is an ancient proverb in my country, the dragon said. *"If a woman is strong in a meeting, do not try to marry her." Unfortunately, you are the only "bride" available to me at this time. You are a resourceful person—I am certain you will think of some clever way to accomplish the task I have set for you. How you do it is not my concern. All that matters to me is that you deliver the jade to Wu.*

"When?" Night Owl asked.

No later than tomorrow night. I will leave you and Wu to work out the details of the transaction.

The dragon's astral form suddenly collapsed onto the floor, deflating like one of the cloth dragons that dancers carry during the Lunar New Year celebrations. When it was gone, Night Owl and the troll shaman glared at each other.

Wu spoke first. "When you have the statue, bring it to me at—"

"Delete that," Night Owl cut in. "Here's how it's going to be: I'll get your master's statue, but I'm not going to be your delivery girl. Give me a telecom number, and I'll call you when I've got the statue. I'll tell you where I've stashed it, and you can go and fetch it for your master, like a good boy."

The troll raised a gnarled fist and growled, and for a moment Night Owl thought she'd pushed him too far. Wu was smart enough to realize, however, that harming Night Owl would limit her usefulness to his master. He eventually smiled—but Night Owl knew that the source of that smile came from the shaman imagining what he'd do to her after the statue had been boosted.

She smiled back. Let Wu threaten all he liked. By the time the statue was in his hands, she'd be safely tucked away inside the most effective bolt hole of all.

"You can call me at the Triple Eight Club," Wu said, naming a popular downtown casino. "But be certain it is early in the evening. The more I spend, the less patient I become. When my patience has run out, I will come looking for you. Rest assured that, no matter how far you run, I will find you."

Wu threw his hands out in front of him in a dramatic gesture, reactivating his invisibility spell—and in the split second before it activated, Night Owl saw the round circle of plastic he held in his right hand. As the shaman vanished, so did Night Owl's smile. Her hand flashed down to the pocket of her jacket, confirming her fears. The pocket had been torn open, and her lucky SkyTrain token was gone.

The token wasn't really lucky—it was just one that happened to have been issued in 2032, the year that Night Owl was born. She'd found it on the street a couple of months ago and had used it exclusively as her heads-or-tails decision maker since then.

But the token was unlucky now. It had Night Owl's astral "scent" all over it. No matter which bolt hole she ran to, the shaman could use it to find her.

Innocence

Two figures were waiting for Alma behind the frosted glass door of Boardroom Four. She glided down the hall and palmed the maglock next to the door. The green recognition light failed to switch on, but that might have been due to the slight tremor in her hand. She wrapped her other hand around it, forcing it into a fist. Thirty-eight seconds later, the shaking stopped. She flexed the hand and wiped a trickle of sweat from her temple. The effort of trying to control the tremor had left her feeling drained. This time, when she palmed the lock, a green light blinked and the lock clicked open.

Boardroom Four was a vast expanse of red carpet dominated by a massive faux-mahogany table with ornately carved legs. Floor-to-ceiling windows faced east, giving a view over Vancouver's high-tech industrial park toward a highway choked with rush-hour traffic. Although it was well past dawn, the skies were still a dark gray. Rain beat a steady rhythm against the thick glass, making the stream of headlights on Highway One waver as if they were underwater.

At the far end of the boardroom table sat Herbert Lali, president of Pacific Cybernetics Industries. A heavyset man in his early sixties, he was dressed in a white buckskin suit that brought out his dark skin tones. He leaned forward in his chair, elbows on the table and fingers steepled together. On his left little finger was a heavy gold PCI ring, set with microprocessor crystals. A fiberoptic cable that snaked up from the table was plugged into one of three gold-plated datajacks that studded his right temple. The right side of his scalp was shaved, but on the left hung a long black braid that was streaked with gray.

In the chair to his left sat Salvador Hu, head of security for PCI and Alma's boss. Hu had close-cropped black hair and a blocky build, and he sat with the relaxed confidence of a man who could handle anything or anyone. He was wearing casual clothes: jeans, cowboy boots, and a short-sleeved dress shirt that showed off his arms, which looked natural but were heavily cybered. At least three weapons that Alma knew about—and probably several she didn't— were concealed under their precisely tone-matched skin.

Alma bowed a greeting to both men. Hu nodded, but Mr. Lali remained silent. His eyes were impassive chips of black stone. Alma had expected Mr. Lali to be as saddened by Gray Squirrel's death as she was, but she hadn't anticipated this cold, angry silence. A reprimand wasn't required—she'd already chastised herself a thousand times since yesterday for not finding the missing researcher sooner. Turning to the shadowrunner had been a mistake—his information was accurate, but the wait for it had cost Gray Squirrel his life.

Mr. Lali shifted in his seat as Alma closed the door behind her. A frown creased his high forehead, puckering the skin around his softlink ports. "Sit down," he said, indicating a chair halfway down the table.

Alma settled into the leather chair, eyes flicking back and forth between the two men. She wondered why Hu had insisted on her coming to the PCI complex this morning. She'd already encrypted a full report of yesterday's events and sent it to a secure mailbox on his telecom. She decided that Mr. Lali must have wanted to hear the report in real time and ask questions. The REM inducer was PCI's pet project, after all. Gray Squirrel had been within a week or two, at most, of running the final diagnostics on the beta-test models. With its project leader dead, the REM inducer's release could be set back several months.

Mr. Lali cleared his throat, and Alma took it as an invitation to speak. She pushed the gruesome image of Gray Squirrel from her mind and spoke in as professional a voice as she could muster.

"Mr. Lali, I must apologize for my failure. As you must have seen from my report, Gray Squirrel was killed at approximately the time that he was placed in the stabilization unit. Perhaps if I had made better use of our corporate resources, I could have reached him before—"

Hu held up a finger, and Alma immediately fell silent. She knew his favorite admonition by rote: there are no excuses, only reasons. Hu didn't want to hear excuses. That wasn't why she had been called into the office.

She waited for Hu to ask her a question, but instead it was Mr. Lali who spoke. His words surprised her.

"How are you sleeping?" He said it in a casual tone, but Alma's instincts told her the question was anything but offhand.

"Quite well, thank you," she answered. She glanced at Hu, but the head of security gave her no clues as to whether she'd answered correctly. Hu seemed to be studying her carefully, weighing each word she said. She suspected that he was using his voice-stress analyzer.

"Have you activated your REM inducer during the past week? Skipped any nights of sleep?" Mr. Lali's attitude appeared to be that of a concerned parent, but Alma could hear the edge in his voice.

"No," she answered. It had been one hundred and eighty-seven days since PCI's physicians had implanted the beta-test version of the inducer inside her brainstem. The tiny cybernetic device lay deep inside her pons, waiting for her mental command to trigger an increase in serotonin, acetycholine, and other sleep-inducing neurotransmitters. By activating it, she could cause her body to enter a highly accelerated version of its normal sleep cycle, one that would compress an entire night's sleep into fifteen minutes.

"The beta-test model is working well," she added. "I'm still following the schedule that Gray Squirrel laid out, despite his . . . extraction: for the past twelve days I've left it in passive mode. I haven't experienced any ill effects that can be directly attributed to the inducer—no insomnia, sudden loss of muscle tone, drowsiness, or any of the other glitches reported by the alpha-test subjects."

As she spoke, she suddenly felt the urge to yawn. She wasn't tired—the yawn was probably triggered by her nervousness, and by talking about the REM inducer and its side effects. She stifled it, but a moment later, she felt something that couldn't be attributed to the power of suggestion: a slight tremble that coursed through her left hand. She tightened her grip on the arm of her chair, and it stopped.

Hu leaned forward. "Where were you between the hours of ten-thirty and midnight, five evenings ago?"

It was Alma's turn to frown. "The night that Gray Squirrel was extracted?" she asked. "At my apartment, in bed. Asleep."

Mr. Lali coughed softly and touched an icon, activating the table's cyberdeck. Flush-mounted monitors illuminated in front of himself, Hu and Alma. "I'd like us to review the recordings that were captured on the night of the extraction. Hu thinks there may be something we missed.''

Alma saw Hu tense and braced herself. Watching the vidclips of Gray Squirrel's extraction hadn't been easy, even when she still believed that her friend was alive. Now that she knew he was dead, they stung even more. She was ashamed to have failed Gray Squirrel, and to have let PCI down—and now Hu was going to rub salt in that wound.

The monitor in the tabletop glowed a solid blue and then flashed a series of codes as it loaded the vidclips they were to view. A long string of numbers appeared briefly—81, 64, 49, 36, 25, 16, 9, 4, 1—and then a date/time sequence that flashed by so quickly Alma was unable to read it. Then the monitor checkerboarded into a dozen squares, each showing a freeze-framed vidclip of the PCI parking garage from a different angle. Some showed rows of parked cars, while others were aimed at exit doors. Still others showed the stairwells and ramps. One of the split-screen images had been shot by a remote-piloted drone and was currently freeze-framed at an angle that showed an empty access ramp.

Alma and Hu had been over the security cameras' recordings dozens of times already, in second-by-second, image-enhanced slow play. She didn't think another byte of information could possibly be wrung out of them.

Hu touched an icon on the monitor screen in front of him, and all of the vidclips began to play.

Alma watched a vidclip near the center of the screen—one that showed Gray Squirrel entering the garage through a secure door that led to the elevators. According to the clock superimposed on the vidclip, it was 11:05:02 p.m.—the same time, plus or minus one minute, that the overly punctual Gray Squirrel always left the building. The researcher walked to his

car—a four-door Toyota Elite—and activated its door
locks by voice command. Settling into the cushioned
leather seat, he reached for the car's control cable. He
was just about to plug it into his datajack when the
intruders appeared.

There were four of them, and they came out of
nowhere, emerging from behind a concrete pillar into
the vidclip that showed Gray Squirrel's car. How they
had gotten into the garage was a mystery that PCI
security had not yet solved.

First to appear was the man Tiger Cat had put a
name to yesterday morning. Wharf Rat was an Asian
male, recognizable by his oversized, protruding incisors and his mange of black hair. One of his eyes was
brown, the other gold. He jittered as if he was on
kamikaze or some other combat drug.

Wharf Rat was followed by two Caucasian males,
one dressed in Native buckskins and sporting what
looked like animal paws woven into the ends of his
dirty blond dreadlocks, the other a dwarf wearing an
Okanagan Ogopogos combat biker T-shirt and black
leather chaps. The dwarf carried an HK227 submachine gun, while Dreadlocks held what looked like an
oversized grenade launcher with an enormous barrel.

The faces of all three had been captured by the
securicams at a number of different angles. They'd
been wearing nylon stockings that squashed their
noses flat against their faces and distorted the rest of
their features, but it had been easy enough to program
the computers to account for the tensile strength of the
nylon and produce a true rendering of each face. Alma
had stored these digital mug shots in the headware
memory that was hardwired into her brain and could
call up profiles or full-face visuals on any of them at
will. By now, she knew their faces better than the
Superkids she'd grown up with.

The fourth person, however, was more careful—or

more professional—than the other three. Judging by the height and weight, this one was probably female, but that was about all the data they had on her. She wore a dark blue balaclava that seemed to have been padded to distort the features underneath; the composite faces that the securicam's Ident program had created were as smooth and featureless as animated cartoons. The only details the program had been able to define with any certainty included her ear shape, which was rounded, like a human's, and the fact that her eyelids had been painted with bright red makeup.

Judging by the woman's cautious movements, Alma had at first flagged her as the team's leader, but it had soon become clear from Wharf Rat's shouts and gestures that the shadowrunner was leading this group. Alma had later decided that the woman must be the team's technical-support member—a little smarter than the rest, and not willing to rely on a thin nylon mask for disguise.

Gray Squirrel was just starting to notice that something was wrong when the dwarf shouted and pointed the submachine gun at him. Gray Squirrel's eyes widened. For a moment it looked as though he was going to try to plug in the jack and drive away. Then he let the control cable fall into his lap.

Just as she had done when she first saw the vidclip, Alma let out a sigh. This time, however, it wasn't one of relief, but regret. Gray Squirrel's caution should have helped him survive.

Gray Squirrel made a show of surrendering to the intruders, but Alma could guess what had been running through his mind. Although the intruders had somehow breached the parking lot's security system, he must have known that help would be on the way soon. Alma watched him cock his head as he stepped out of his car, obviously listening for the hissing jets of a takedown drone.

Elsewhere on the monitor screen, one of the vidclips appeared to be in fast motion—cars slid past in a blur and the image wove and dodged as the drone on which the camera was mounted whipped through the parking garage. Two seconds later, the drone appeared on the vidclip that showed Gray Squirrel and his extractors, and the researcher's face broke into a nervous, anticipatory grin.

He wasn't the only one who'd been expecting the drone, however. Dreadlocks raised the launcher to his shoulder and fired, and what looked like a crumpled ball of silver cloth shot into the air. The fine metal mesh fluttered open just before striking the drone and wrapped itself completely around the drone as if magnetized. A second later the mesh crackled with tiny sparks as its electric discharge unit activated.

The vidclip that had been taken by the drone's camera was now nothing more than a blur, but the other securicam showed what was happening. Hot spots glowed on the mesh where it covered the drone's jets. Two seconds later, the drone fired its takedown weapon: hollow, feather-tipped needle darts loaded with gamma scopolamine. The darts didn't go far, however—the feathered tips were caught and held by the mesh.

The drone, looking like a pincushion and bereft of its guidance camera, crashed into one of the garage's concrete support pillars and slammed into the floor. The vidclip shot by its securicam rolled through a few dizzy gyrations and came to rest pointed up at a bright white circle that must have been one of the halogen lights in the parking garage's ceiling.

On the split screen near the center of the monitor, Gray Squirrel was shoved into the back of his car. The dwarf climbed into the driver's seat and jacked in, and the others piled inside. Wharf Rat took the front seat, and Dreadlocks sat in the back with Gray Squirrel.

The female member of the team leaned over the downed drone, taking a last look at it, and then turned and ran for the vehicle. She clambered into the back, and the door slammed.

The car squealed backward out of its parking space, changed gears, and roared up the ramp. It flashed across several of the split screens on the monitor as it squealed around corners, at times narrowly missing the few parked cars that were still in the garage so late at night. The dwarf seemed to know exactly where he was going—he took the most direct route to the garage's Rupert Street exit.

The first time Alma had seen the vidclips of the extraction, she'd expected the car to be trapped at the exit. PCI's security teams had obviously been alerted to an extraction in progress—they'd already sent a drone to deal with it. By this point, the entire garage was on lockdown. The vidclips showed steel containment doors and ballistic-composite shutters blocking every exit, and secguards moving in on foot.

The barrier across the Rupert Street exit was in place—when the dwarf saw it, he brought the car to a screeching stop, front bumper almost touching the heavy steel containment door. There was a brief pause, and then one of the rear doors opened. The woman stepped out and headed for the maglock beside the door. She leaned over it, as if keypadding in a combination.

The lock shouldn't have activated. The garage was on lockdown, which meant that the ultrasonic "key" in Gray Squirrel's vehicle would no longer trigger it. The maglock had its own power source and was not accessible via the Matrix. The only way to open it was to punch in an eight-digit manual override code—a code that was changed daily and issued only to those secguards who were on duty that day.

The woman straightened, and the containment door rumbled up into the ceiling.

Alma and Hu had both come to the same shocked conclusion the first time they'd viewed this vidclip. A serious breach of security had occurred: one of their own staff must have been involved in the extraction. An extensive grilling of the secguards on both the day and night shifts, however, had turned up no evidence to support this theory. Every one of the guards had willingly submitted to an injection of gamma scopol-amine—one of the takedown drug's side effects was that it induced the same willingness to talk as a "truth serum." Not one of the guards admitted to having compromised security by divulging the code.

On the monitor, the woman got back into Gray Squirrel's car. As the vehicle pulled away into the night, the containment wall closed. The last image cap-tured on the vidclip was a shot of a PCI secguard, running up to the maglock as the door slammed shut and frantically entering the code that would open it again.

The clock on that vidclip read 11:11:28 p.m.—it had taken the four intruders just six minutes and twenty-six seconds to carry out the extraction. The shad-owrunners might look scruffy, but they operated as smoothly as any team Alma had ever put together. She hated to admit it, but she was impressed.

The tabletop monitor reverted to a blank blue screen. Alma considered what she'd just seen for a moment before looking up but came up as blank as the screen. "I didn't see anything new."

Hu shot a level stare at her across the table. "Look again."

This time, a single vidclip was playing full-frame on the monitor: the one shot by the drone's camera, after the drone had been taken out of commission. The fine-weave mesh that had wrapped around the drone obliterated all detail, and the halogen light shining directly into the lens had overloaded the camera's aperture settings. For a brief moment, however, a fuzzy black silhouette loomed in the field of view: the securicam had captured the woman as she leaned over the drone to look at it. Then the silhouette disappeared from sight.

Alma knew this portion of the vidclip frame by frame. She'd had it enhanced, magnified and run through a visual decryption and feature-recognition program several times, hoping to add detail to the female intruder's face. Nothing had worked—the face had remained a blur. As the vidclip ended, Alma looked up at Hu, puzzled.

Hu restarted the vidclip at the point where the silhouette leaned over the drone.

"I had another look at this clip last night, and I noticed something interesting," he said. "Just as the woman pulls back out of the camera's field of view, the image becomes blurrier. At first, I assumed that the mesh cloth had shifted, but then I took a closer look."

Hu touched an icon on his monitor, and the magnification increased. The clock superimposed on the vidclip slowed, stretching a single second into a minute. Alma suddenly saw something new: the blur started in the middle of the camera's point of view and spread slowly outward like flowing water. The blurring was uneven, as if the obstruction on the lens was frothy. Alma suddenly realized what it must be.

"She spit on the drone," she whispered.

Hu nodded gravely. Beside him, Mr. Lali tensed in his seat.

"We managed to collect a sample of the dried saliva from the lens," Hu said.

Alma nodded. She could guess what was coming next: PCI security would have done DNA typing on

the saliva and would have a "fingerprint" of the fourth
intruder. If they found a likely suspect, a DNA match
would prove that person's guilt or innocence. Normally, the development would have excited Alma—it
meant they were that much closer to solving the riddle
of who had conducted the extraction. But with Hu
and Mr. Lali acting so strangely, Alma found herself
dreading what was to come.

Hu was watching her intently, unspeaking, his cy-
berarms resting in too casual a manner on the polished
tabletop. Mr. Lali's eyes were puckered with lines of
sorrow and regret, like those of a father who was reluctantly facing the prospect of disciplining his child.

Mr. Lali whispered a single word: "Why?"

Alma blinked.

Hu was more direct. "The DNA from the saliva was
an exact match with the cell samples in your personnel
file. We didn't just do the usual random sampling—
we typed all twenty-three chromosome pairs. Every
single one was a match. You were the fourth person
on that team, Alma. You extracted Gray Squirrel,
then conveniently found him again yesterday—dead."

Alma shook her head, her mind whirling. "But . . .
but that makes no sense," she said. "Why would I
want to extract Gray Squirrel?"

"Gray Squirrel was a valuable commodity," Mr.
Lali said softly. "The REM inducer has both military
and civilian applications. Whichever corporation re-
leases it will be launched into triple-A status."

"We know who paid for the extraction," Hu fired
at her. "We've traced the buyer back to Tan Tien
Incorporated."

He was staring at her, as if waiting for a reaction.
The only one she could provide was surprise. She'd
been charting probabilities for days, trying to come up
with the name of the corporation that had ordered
Gray Squirrel's extraction, and had only managed to

narrow the list of possibles down to eight. How had Hu come up with the answer?

Nervously, Alma called up the corporate files in her headware memory and scanned them for Tan Tien Inc. The company was headquartered in Beijing and was one of the more prominent corporations in the Pacific Prosperity Group. Headed up by the reclusive Sau-kok Chu, it specialized in pure research. The cyberware and bioware it developed never left the drafting computers, except as copyrighted data. The corporation made its money licensing its research to other companies that actually built the hardware.

It would be easy enough for Tan Tien to claim the REM inducer as its own, especially since PCI had yet to release any information on the hot new project it was being so secretive about. But in order for Tan Tien to profit from the extraction, Gray Squirrel would have to agree to tell it about the project—in detail.

"You've seen Gray Squirrel's psych profiles," Alma protested. "He'd never willingly work for anyone else or provide data from any of our research projects. He's inno—"

Suddenly, Alma remembered the reading the I Ching had given her that morning: Innocence, with one changing yin line that would later transform the hexagram into the one called Treading. She'd thought the I Ching had been referring to Gray Squirrel, but he wasn't the innocent person the coins had spoken of.

Alma was.

As Alma looked at Hu's cold stare and poised-for-trouble posture, however, she could see it would be difficult to convince her boss of her innocence. Mind racing, she tried to puzzle out what had happened.

"I was framed," she concluded. "Someone wanted to make it look as though I was involved in Gray Squirrel's extraction. Somehow they got a sample of my DNA sequence, replicated it, and engineered that saliva." Even as she spoke, however, she realized how ridiculous her conclusions sounded. Who would go to such lengths—and why?

"What about the manual-override combination for the maglock?" Hu asked in a soft, dangerous voice. "Where did they get that?"

"I don't know," Alma agonized. "Perhaps one of our secguards managed to lie under gamma scopolamine. Have any of them shown signs of—"

"No," Hu said grimly. "You are the only suspect—your own DNA places you at the scene. I'm surprised you managed to conceal the grace of your move-by-wire system. Until last night, I was completely fooled."

Beside him, Mr. Lali nodded.

Alma protested: "But I was—"

"Home in bed," Hu said. "Just as you presumably were last night, even though you didn 't answer my urgent-flagged calls until this morning. You were alone on the night of Gray Squirrel's extraction, I presume?"

Alma nodded mutely. Hu would know from her personnel file that she lived alone and did not have a lover. There was no one to back up her alibi.

Mr. Lali stared at Alma for a long moment before pronouncing her sentence. "You've always been a loyal employee, Ms. Wei. You've provided PCI with twelve years of commendable service, but in the light of this deliberate act of sabotage, I have no other choice but termination. You will have no further access to PCI's buildings or facilities, and the personnel and security files in your headware memory will be wiped. Hu will accompany you to your home and ensure that any PCI data you have there is erased. If you cause him any trouble, he is authorized to take whatever steps are necessary to ensure your cooperation. Do you understand?"

Alma winced. She felt like a child, unable to find the words to defend herself against a parent who had unjustly accused her. "I understand. I'll cooperate."

She noticed that her left hand was trembling again. She couldn't tell if it was anxiety or the initial stages of TLE. Asking for reparative surgery, however, was out of the question now. She'd have to find some way to prove her innocence first.

"We must bear in mind one other important matter," Mr. Lali continued. "Your REM inducer." He glanced at Hu.

Hu placed both palms flat on the table and leaned across it as he rose to his feet. The pose was one that the Justice Institute taught, designed to be intimidating. His words, however, were what frightened Alma.

"If you were thinking about trying to sell the tech, don't," he said. "PCI included an additional feature in the beta-test REM inducers: a miniature cranial bomb—one just large enough to fuse the inducer's circuitry. It's activated by a 'dead man' switch—the moment all brain activity ceases, it goes off. It's also designed to trigger if anyone other than a PCI technician attempts to surgically remove the inducer. We had to be certain the inducer wouldn't fall into the wrong hands if a test subject was killed, or extracted— or tried to sell the tech to another company."

Alma nodded, unable to speak. The REM inducer was the last thing she'd been thinking about—how could Hu accuse her of wanting to betray PCI by selling it? Pacific Cybernetics Industries was her home, its staff were her family—and now she was losing them.

"The bomb wasn't intended to injure surrounding tissue," Hu continued. "But given the inducer's placement within the brain, there's a high likelihood of serious trauma. If it goes off, the resulting damage would mean you'd never be able to sleep again. You would eventually die from the physical debilitation caused by sleep deprivation. I wouldn't wish that kind of madness on anyone."

Alma was only half listening. She wasn't angry at Hu for not telling her about the cranial bomb earlier—she understood the need for that level of security on a research project as secretive as this one. If it had been Alma who had been extracted, instead of Gray Squirrel, the bomb would have ensured the project's security. Alma would willingly have paid the price. What angered her was that Hu didn't seem to realize that.

She lifted her eyes to meet those of Mr. Lali. Her voice nearly faltered when she saw the disappointment and contempt written on his face. Until today, she'd seen nothing but a father's loving pride in those eyes. He'd often praised her as one of the best counterextraction experts in the city. She was a loyal member of the PCI family—but now she was being disowned. It stung.

Mr. Lali waved a hand, dismissing her. She rose to her feet, the move-by-wire system automatically compensating for the shakiness she felt. Hu walked around the table, took Alma's elbow lightly in one cybered hand, and steered her toward the door.

Out in the hallway, she stood meekly while Hu activated the elevator's maglock. The earlier delay she'd faced in accessing the boardroom's maglock confirmed her guess: her palm prints had already been erased from the PCI building-access database.

As they waited for the elevator that would take her down to the lab where her headware memory would be erased, Hu leaned toward Alma. His words were pitched low enough that she had to activate her cyberear's amplification system to hear them, and his lips barely moved. He obviously didn't want the building's securicams to pick up what he was saying.

"Spitting on the drone was stupid, Alma," he whispered, "and you're a smart lady—too smart to have done that. When I reported that to Lali, he wanted to terminate you immediately—and I use that word literally, since he was talking about activating the cranial bomb—but I persuaded him to give you a chance to figure out what's really going on here. He agreed to four days—you have until noon on February 28. I just hope you have the intelligence and resourcefulness to find out who our unauthorized intruder really was in so little time. If you manage to discover anything, give me a call."

Alma glanced sideways at Hu, and saw that his face was carefully neutral, his eyes firmly on the elevator doors. She was shocked that Mr. Lali had considered activating the cranial bomb before hearing her protests of innocence, feeble though they were. She was relieved that Hu still believed in her—or, at least, wanted to believe in her. He'd just given her permission to continue her duties—unofficially, and without any of the corporate resources or team support that she was used to.

Alma was on her own, for the second time in her life.

She acknowledged Hu with a nod and stepped into the elevator ahead of him. As it descended, she thought back to the hexagram she had cast that morning—Innocence—and the overall judgment the I Ching had given her: *A great mystery must unfold, or a misunderstood part of your nature must come forth before progress can be made. A proper questioning attitude and receptive frame of mind bring success. Though you do not seek the innocent yourself, the innocent seek you, because your aspirations correspond.*

The last part was the most puzzling—and the most frustrating. Alma liked to act, not to wait. She could be as patient as a stalking tiger when an assignment demanded it, but there was too much yang in her soul for her to wait passively for answers to come to her. She would follow the course of action the I Ching recommended and remain open to information from new sources, but in the meantime she would do whatever it took to discover who had framed her—and why.

Alma stood poised on one foot, arms extended to the side with palms up, left leg cocked in front of her as if she were about to take a step forward. Her head was perfectly level, chin neither too high nor too low, her face turned slightly to the left. Slowly, she leaned to the right until the weight of her entire body was balanced on the outer edge of her right foot. When she was certain the form was absolutely correct, she locked her body in that position, allowing the move-by-wire system at the base of her skull to keep her as steady as a precisely weighted balance.

All around her in the park, dozens of people stood poised on the grass, moving in slow motion as they followed the master whose image was projected on the monitor screen at one end of the field. High above them, the dome that covered Stanley Park kept out the incessant rain, and banks of grow lamps and heaters kept the park consistently warm and bright.

For Alma, tai chi—the "infinite void"—was a way of forcing herself into a waiting mode. The combination of perfectly controlled movement and enforced stillness slowed her racing thoughts, quieting the storm of questions and self-doubts that had filled her mind since her meeting with Mr. Lali and Hu that morning. She had already decided on her next course of action but had to wait for Tiger Cat's call to put her plan into motion. The tai chi helped her to endure that wait.

As the figure on the monitor screen broke its frozen stance and began to move, Alma shifted gracefully into the next form. The people around her, all moving together, reminded her of the drills and exercises that had filled the days of her youth. Only two things were missing: a uniform excellence in all of the participants, and the battery of researchers who had tested and observed the Superkids as they were put through their paces.

Alma's attention should have been focused on the center of stillness she was trying to create within herself, but she found herself distracted by a man about her age, a dozen meters ahead of her. He wore loose black pants and a black suit jacket that wrapped like a kimono. His hair was long and black, clipped back in a ponytail. A slight bulge under his left armpit suggested that a weapon was holstered there. Although his tai chi forms were perfect, he never once turned in Alma's direction. He seemed to be keeping a watchful eye on the crowd, as if looking for potential threats to the Full Blood just ahead of him—an Indian who moved with formal dignity, as if used to public scrutiny.

After years in the security industry, Alma could read the relationship between the two men in a heartbeat: politician and bodyguard. When the Full Blood turned his face, Alma recognized him as Darcy Jim, hereditary chief of the Nootka tribe.

But that wasn't what held her interest. Her eyes kept coming back to the pair not because of Darcy Jim but because of the fluid movements of his bodyguard. The younger man moved with the same smooth grace and perfect control as Alma. It was almost as if Alma were watching herself in a mirror. She found herself compromising her own form, keeping her head half turned so she could watch him.

The bodyguard's instincts were as sharp as her own. Feeling her eyes upon him, he smoothly pirouetted to face her. He made the move appear casual, as though he were merely completing a tai chi form.

As the man completed the turn, Alma felt a shudder of recognition. His features matched her own, from the hint of an epicanthic fold on his eyelids to his longer, more Caucasian nose and prominent cheekbones. His eyes were a bright blue, instead of brown, and a silver datajack puckered his left temple, but aside from those minor differences, his resemblance to Alma was close enough that he might have been her brother.

Alma didn't have any brothers—not in the conventional sense of the word. But she had once had batch mates. There had been eleven other children in the Superkids "alpha batch" of 2032. One of the boys—Aaron—had died at the age of eight when he slipped while grandstanding on the New Horizons sign, on the tenth floor of the building, but ten other Superkids had presumably grown to maturity. Alma hadn't seen any of them in twenty-two years—she'd given up looking long ago. Was it possible that the random vagaries of chance had caused one of the Superkids to at last cross her path?

After a second or two, the bodyguard's blue eyes widened in recognition. He spun and spoke a word to Darcy Jim and then walked in Alma's direction. Even though he stared at her as if seeing a ghost, a portion of his attention still remained fixed on the crowd and the man he was guarding. Alma nodded, acknowledging his professionalism.

He stopped just in front of Alma and studied her.

"It's been a long time," he said in a vcice that sounded cybernetically modulated. "Which girl are you?"

"A.L.," she answered. "Alma. Are you . . . Ahmed?"

The bodyguard smiled, revealing perfect white teeth. "Ajax," he corrected her. He cocked his head the same way Alma did as he smiled, making her remember how precisely the body language of her batch mates had matched her own. For the first time in many years, she felt the return of the homesickness that had been with her constantly in the first years that followed her separation from the other Superkids. She'd forgotten what it was like to be with someone who could instinctively read and mirror you—who knew exactly what you were thinking and feeling.

"I come to the park often, but I haven't seen you here before," Alma said.

Ajax nodded at Darcy Jim. "The tai chi was Mr. Jim's idea. He's like his father—he has a thirst for other cultures."

"Do you work for him?"

Ajax fished a card-sized square of plastic out of his pocket and handed it to Alma. When she pressed the logo on its otherwise blank surface, a monologue began to play. She thumbed it off after she heard the name of the company: Priority One Security, a local bodyguard-for-hire service that had recently been acquired by the Knight Errant corporation.

"Looks like we chose the same line of work," she observed.

He smiled again. "They predicted that, didn't they? Just like identical twins, we'd be statistically more likely to drive the same kind of vehicle, have the same taste in clothes, pursue the same careers and hobbies—even choose partners with the same name."

"Or stay single into our thirties," Alma added, nodding at his ringless left hand.

"Uh-huh," Ajax said, shifting uncomfortably. He changed the subject. "What company are you with?"

Alma suddenly regretted bringing up the topic. "Pacific Cybernetics," she answered reluctantly. "But I'm . . . on leave at the moment."

"If you ever want to jump ship, let me know. Guarding the rich and famous is pretty dull most of the time, but it pays well. There'll be an opening soon at Priority One; I've leaving the company in two weeks to teach at the Justice Institute."

Alma nodded politely. Despite the unfortunate incidents of the past few days, she was still fiercely committed to PCI. She didn't want to slink away like a runaway child and beg like an orphan for work at another corporation; she wanted to redeem herself.

"I wonder how many of the other Superkids wound up in security or police work," Ajax mused. "We 're certainly tailor-made for it."

Alma blinked, startled by the thought his comment triggered—and amazed that it had not occurred to her before. The Superkids, with their superior genetics, had bodies that had been further enhanced by cyberware. Augmented muscle tissue, move-by-wire systems and skillwires were standard, and each Superkid had been fitted with a host of other cyberware, including customized eyes and ears and a host of other cutting-edge technology—all of it delta-grade. By the time the Superkids program was shut down, they were faster, stronger and smarter than children twice their age. They were the ideal candidates for security work, which demanded a combination of intelligence, brawn, speed—and corporate loyalty.

But what if that loyalty, which had also been genetically selected for, was misplaced? If that happened, a former Superkid would also make the perfect shadowrunner. And that shadowrunner's saliva, if subjected to DNA testing, would be an exact match with Alma's, across all hundred thousand chromosomes. The shadowrunner had to have been one of the other girls in Superkids Batch A, since the boy's forty-sixth chromosome would be a Y, not an X. That left five possible suspects.

"Ajax," Alma said. "Do you know what happened

to any of the other Superkids? Are any of them in Vancouver?''

Ajax shook his head. "I don't think so, but then I'm new to the city; until recently I was working out of Priority One's Seattle office. But I'm willing to bet you're the only Superkid placed in Salish-Shidhe. They scattered us pretty thoroughly and did the same with the batches below ours; they claimed this would give us as 'normal' an upbringing as possible, that it was in our best interests to separate us from anything—or anyone—that would remind us of the program. That was pure bull, of course."

"Where did they place you?" Alma asked.

"With a family in the Confederated American States, in Florida."

"Were you able to find out where any of the other Superkids were placed?" Alma asked. Her question was both nostalgic and urgent. She wanted to know if any of her batch mates had wound up in Vancouver—on the wrong side of the law.

"I was able to track down three of us," said Ajax, still scanning the area around Darcy Jim for possible threats. "We've kept in touch on and off over the years. Aimee was fostered by a family in Japan; she works for the Zurich-Orbital Bank. Agatha wound up in one of the German states and became an officer in the Alliance military, and Ahmed is a simsense tech in Denver. Ahmed managed to trace Aella to Chicago but wasn't able to contact her. He thinks she died—either during the bug infestation or when they exploded the nuke that cleared it."

Alma listened carefully. "That leaves two girls unaccounted for: Abby and Akiko."

Ajax nodded. "Three of the boys have vanished into thin air as well. None of the Superkids I've been in touch with has any idea what happened to Acheson, Afandi, or Adam."

He sighed and added: "I still think of them, even after so many years." They stood for a moment in silence, each mirroring the other's painful memories.

On the monitor at the far end of the field, the master bowed. Music welled from the speakers at either side of the screen; the day's tai chi session was over. All around them, people broke ranks and began walking away. The Nootka chief mopped his brow with a towel and turned to see where his bodyguard had gone.

Ajax immediately turned in his direction. "Duty calls," he said over his shoulder. "But I'd like to hook up with you again. Call the number on the card."

"What time does your shift end?" Alma asked. "Could we meet later today? It's very . . . important that we talk some more, as soon as possible."

Alma could hear the strained urgency in her voice but didn't care. Ajax was her one link to the surviving Superkids—perhaps the first link in what could be a long chain of information. Someone, somewhere, had to know where the missing Superkid girls were. Alma needed to begin following that datatrail—today.

"I'm off at seven o'clock tonight," Ajax called back over his shoulder as he walked away. "Call me at five minutes after seven and we'll arrange something."

As she watched Ajax walk away with Darcy Jim, Alma felt a childish urge to run after him. She noticed that he kept glancing back at her until he was out of sight. Then her cellphone chimed.

She flipped it open and heard Tiger Cat say hello. He was using a different stock image this time—a cartoon face with oversized eyes and a Cheshire cat's ear-to-ear grin. This time, Alma activated her cellphone's vidcam, allowing him to see her. It was vital that she establish a certain level of trust before she made her proposal.

"I hear that you succeeded in recovering your package," Tiger Cat said. "'I'm pleased. I assume I can expect my second payment momentarily?"

Alma had already decided to be blunt. "There's a slight problem."

Tiger Cat's smile faded. "What do you mean?"

"I'm temporarily unable to access my corporate account."

"I thought we had a deal," Tiger Cat growled. "You owe me three thousand nuyen. What about your personal assets?"

"I don't have that much credit."

She listened to him swear softly in Cantonese and then completed her pitch. "There's only one way you're going to get your money."

"How?"

"I need an insider's look at the Vancouver shadowrun community. To get it, I'll have to pose as one of you. I want you to broker a contract for me. Find me a job that I can carry out in the next day or two, preferably one that will require minimal support from one or two other shadowrunners and that will let me do the bulk of the work. That will buy me the legitimacy I need to assemble a team of shadowrunners for a second, fictitious assignment. You can keep whatever payment the employer provides for the first assignment—even if the total is more than three thousand nuyen. Then my corporation's debt to you will be canceled."

Alma waited, wondering if Tiger Cat was going to accept her offer. Her only other option was to pose as someone who'd heard of the PCI extraction and wanted to hire the team that had carried it out. But that wasn't likely to work. As soon as the woman heard that someone from the corporate sector was looking for her, she'd vanish.

Alma needed to pose as a shadowrunner instead. The shadow community, however, was like a private party: you had to have an invitation to enter it. Tiger Cat could provide her with that invitation by hiring her for an illicit assignment. Alma would have her way in—and Tiger Cat would have a full credstick.

"I'll see what I can do for you," Tiger Cat said finally. "But I'll have to know a little bit more about your areas of expertise. That will let me know if I should be looking to find you a courier run, a structure hit, a datasteal . . . Can I assume that wetwork is out of the question?"

"You can." Alma considered a moment. "Try to find an extraction. That's the type of 'run' that I'd be best at."

"All right," Tiger Cat said. "I'll see what I can do."

Alma thumbed the cell off. Once again, a message from her crank caller scrolled across the monitor screen. This time, Alma read it in its entirety.

HEY AL, JUST A THOUGHT. MAYBE IT'S TIME YOU RETIRED. I HEAR THAT THINGS AREN'T GOING TOO WELL FOR YOU AT PACIFIC CYBERNETICS, ESPECIALLY NOW THAT THINGS HAVE STARTED GOING MISSING. OH WELL. I NEVER DID LIKE THOSE FRAGGERS MUCH, ANYWAY.

As soon as she realized that the crank caller was talking about the extraction, Alma knew who the message was from: the shadowrunner who had killed Gray Squirrel. One of the other Superkids.

Alma only realized that she was squeezing the cellphone too hard when she heard its plastic case crack. She hit the delete icon, and the message faded from the screen. She didn't need to keep it—the words were seared into her memory.

"Watch your step, you 'fragger,' " she whispered angrily. "I'm coming to get you."

* * *

Ajax lived in an apartment in Metrotown, a sprawling mall surrounded by high-rise towers that was a twentieth-century precursor to the arcology. His suite was a studio unit on the twelfth floor, just large enough to hold his futon, an elegant folding rice-paper screen, a telecom, and some Moroccan rugs and throw pillows. Alma felt entirely at home here, amid the blank white walls and big windows. Even the smell in the air seemed right. Lemon-scented wind chimes hung over a small end table that held a holopic of a blond woman with pointed ears, wearing a UCAS military uniform. As Ajax went to the kitchen unit to warm some vitamin-enriched sake, Alma watched the elf in the holopic blow the viewer a kiss. She wondered if the woman was still alive—or if Ajax, too, had lost someone he loved to war.

Alma settled in a lotus position on a plush brown rug. Ajax joined her a moment later with two cups and a porcelain sake bottle on a tray. He sank gracefully into a cross-legged position that mirrored her own, placing the tray on the carpet between them. He poured steaming sake into one of the cups and then held it out to Alma. She noticed that he filled his cup to precisely the same level before lifting it to clink against her own. A love of tidiness and order was one of the personality traits that had been genetically selected for when the alpha batch of Superkids was created.

Alma chatted with Ajax for a few minutes, filling in the blank between age eight and the current day, telling him about her foster parents, her training at the Justice Institute, and her years at PCI. They reminisced about the jokes they used to play on the technicians: swapping wrist badges and pretending to be one of the others in their batch was a favorite trick. Sometimes they even managed to fool each other. The one person at New Horizons who never fell for it, however, was the company's CEO. He never once got them mixed up; he got their names right every time, even without looking at their wrist badges.

To the research technicians and scientists at New Horizons, the CEO was Mr. Louberge, very formal in his suit and tie. But to the Superkids he was just Poppy, the man who tousled their hair and told them bedtime stories. Poppy had loved each of the Superkids individually and unconditionally, as a father should.

"It was sad that Poppy died," Alma said. "My foster parents told me it was a heart attack."

"A broken heart, you mean," Ajax said. "The stress of seeing New Horizons torn apart was what killed him."

Sake splashed out of her cup and onto Alma's fingers as her hand began to shake. She quickly set her cup down and folded her arms so that the hand was hidden under her right elbow. Thankfully the tremor was a light one that lasted only thirty-two seconds. Even though she didn't try to fight it this time, it left her with the same tired feeling she'd experienced before.

Ajax didn't seem to have noticed. He was talking about Aaron—the "oldest" of their batch by virtue of being the first to be born to a surrogate mother. "Ironic, isn't it, that he was not only the first of the batch to be born, but also the first to die."

"I never understood how he could have fallen," Alma said. "What was he doing up there on the roof, all by himself? If he was showing off, who was supposed to applaud him? And why did he fall? Remember the 'floating stepping stone' test? Aaron was always the best at that one—he was as agile as a monkey in freefall."

"You didn't know?" Ajax asked, startled. "No—

of course not. How could you? You've been out of the datastream."

"Couldn't know what?" Alma prompted.

"Aaron's fall wasn't accidental. He suicided—his death was what caused the Superkids program to be shut down."

Alma gasped. "No! Why would he kill himself?"

"We'll never know. But Ahmed found something interesting when he hacked his way into one of the Superkids project files that the UCAS confiscated. Our batch—and the batches that followed us—weren't as perfect as they were made out to be. We were flawed. When New Horizons selected for the genes that gave Batch Alpha our unique immune systems and our high tolerance for cyberware, they also inadvertently selected for mental illness. In Aaron, it manifested as a bipolar disorder: manic depression. He was severely depressed when he jumped."

"What about the rest of the batch?" Alma asked.

Ajax shrugged. "The data in the New Horizons report was inconclusive. The gene gave us a genetic predisposition toward mental illness, but Aaron seems to have been the only one who went crazy. There was some speculation among the researchers that the defect in the gene may have been balanced by a healthy counterpart, found only in the X chromosome, making you girls no more than carriers. The net effect would be that mental illness only showed up in the boys, in the same way as hemophilia or color blindness."

Alma considered this information, searching her memories for anything that would constitute a mental illness. Aside from a slight tendency toward obsessive compulsiveness that all Batch Alpha Superkids shared— the meticulousness that Alma liked to think of as professionalism—she herself was more than stable. She'd survived every knockdown that life had thrown at her and come up swinging. Despite the disruption caused

by the closure of the Superkids project and her reloca-
tion to a foster family halfway across the continent,
she'd come through her childhood without any major
depressions. She couldn't think of a single thing that
would seem to indicate the onset of mental illness.

She caught Ajax's eye. "How are *you* doing?"

Ajax smiled. "No suicidal tendencies, if that's what
you're asking. I've had a pretty happy life, on the
whole. Just . . . minor glitches, that's all." His gaze
strayed to the holopic of the elf woman as he spoke,
and then he glanced away.

"Ahmed also thinks he found out why they scattered us," he added a moment later. "He said it had
nothing to do with our well-being—we went to the
highest bidders."

"What do you mean?" Alma wasn't certain that
she'd heard him correctly.

"It's speculation on Ahmed's part, of course," Ajax
added quickly. "But when he was compiling the data
on the four of us who managed to stay in touch,
Ahmed noticed a peculiar pattern: each of us was
placed with a foster family that had links—albeit only
distant ones, in some cases—to a corporation that was
active in bionetic or cybernetic research. My own foster father was a cousin of the head of Ares Macrotech-
nology's cybernetics division; Agatha's foster mother
was the ex-wife of a prominent shareholder in Saeder-
Krupp; Ahmed's foster father's sister was . . ."

Alma had stopped listening. Ahmed's "data"
sounded like wild speculation. She found it a stretch
that the UCAS government would auction the Superkids off like so much pirated tech—if ulterior mo-
tives were behind the foster-home placements, it was
much more likely that whoever was responsible would
keep the Superkids within the UCAS.

"Everyone in the world is linked to a major corporation, if you look hard enough," Alma countered.

"And every corporation on the planet is involved with cybertech and bionetics."

Ajax took a sip of his sake. "You may be right," he said. "Ahmed's theory sounded a little far-fetched to me, too. But think of the possibilities: if someone else wanted a Superkid, having access to one of us would provide them with all of the tissue samples they needed."

"But would they bother to clone us, if we weren't perfect?" Alma asked. She found the thought that she might be "flawed" irritating. She didn't really believe it, herself. Something other than mere genetics must have caused Aaron to jump.

The possibility that the Superkids might have been cloned, however, made her pause. What if the shadow-runner who had extracted Gray Squirrel was a Super-kid clone? But then Alma realized that the full-chromosome DNA scan that Hu had done on the saliva would have picked up one crucial difference between Alma and a clone: the length of their respective telomeres.

As humans age, biological markers on DNA called telomeres shorten. The older the cell, the shorter its telomeres. When cloning was first attempted in the 1990s, researchers noticed that the telomeres of the sheep they had cloned were just as short as those of the sheep they had obtained the genetic material from. When the resulting clone was born, "Dolly" the sheep had cells that appeared to be three years old.

This problem had been solved in the decades since. Today's clones were born with full-length telomeres. And since any clone of Alma would have to have been made after the breakup of the Superkids project, the woman who resulted would be twenty-two years old, at most. Her telomeres would be appreciably longer than Alma's.

The more Alma thought about it, the more she was

convinced it had been one of her batch mates who
had infiltrated PCI and extracted Gray Squirrel. Spitting on the PCI drone was no mere gesture of defi-
ance. Given the precision the woman had shown in
carrying out the extraction, the gesture had to have
been a deliberate attempt to frame Alma. Whoever
the shadowrunner was, her motivation was personal.

Which, once again, didn't make sense. Alma and
her batch mates had been closer than siblings: they'd
loved one another. There had been the usual rivalry
and petty spats, but Alma couldn't remember a single
significant fight in all of the eight years they'd been
together. Not one.

Certainly not one that would cause someone to hold
a grudge for twenty-two years.

Alma cleared her throat. "We're not the only Superkids in Vancouver," she said, choosing her words
carefully. "There's another one of us here from the
Batch Alpha: one of the girls. She's been seen around
town by people who said she looked enough like me
to be my twin. It wouldn't be Aimee or Agatha,
would it?"

Ajax shook his head. "Aimee's in space with Zurich-
Orbital, and Agatha's on active duty with her unit.
She hasn't left the German Alliance in years."

"And Aella—how certain is Ahmed that she's
dead?"

"The address he tracked down for her in Chicago
was at ground zero. I doubt that she made it."

"Whoever this other Superkid is, I need to find
her," Alma continued. "I need to speak to her about
something. It's a . . . PCI security matter that I can't
tell you much about."

She'd almost forgotten how mentally agile and per-
ceptive another Superkid could be: Ajax immediately
scanned between the lines. The conclusion he reached,
however, was the wrong one.

"You want her to double for you while you go undercover," he guessed, his blue eyes glowing mischievously. "That's what you meant when you said you were 'on leave' from your job at PCI."

Alma decided to go with it. "That's right. I'd use Aimee or Agatha, since you're in touch with them—but it doesn't sound as if they're available right now. I thought, instead, that you could help me to track down the Superkid who's been spotted here in town. It could be Abby, or Akiko—or even Aella, if she somehow survived Chicago. Whichever one of us she is, I need to find her ASAP."

Ajax had picked up on her sense of urgency; he had already risen and was walking toward his telecom. "I'll get in touch with Ahmed for you," he said, picking up the telecom's interface cable. "He's an expert when it comes to surfing the Matrix; when I talked to him a month ago, he said he might have a lead on another one of us. If anyone can find out who your Vancouver 'twin' is, it's him."

Alma forced herself to wait patiently while Ajax slotted the telecom cable into the port in his left temple and contacted Ahmed via the Matrix. When he unplugged the jack at the end of their silent conversation, Ajax looked shaken. He sat down and poured himself another sake and then drained it.

"Ahmed's got the goods, all right," he said. "He managed to track down Akiko. It took him awhile; she changed her name to Jacqueline Boothby. She's in the Confederated American States, in a Texas prison. She's on death row."

"How long has she been there?" Alma asked.

When Ajax gave her a strange look, Alma realized that it had been an odd question. But he answered just the same: "She's been in prison for two years—throughout numerous appeals. She's due to be executed three days from now, on the twenty-seventh."

Alma nodded. Assuming that Aella really was dead, that left only one of the girls from Batch Alpha unaccounted for: Abby.

"What crime was Akiko charged with?" she asked.

"First-degree murder. She slashed the throat of a man who was convicted of raping her, six years ago. The day after he got out on parole, Akiko killed him."

Alma's heart skipped a beat as she heard how the murder was committed. Involuntarily touching a hand to her throat, she wondered if Akiko had also been framed.

"How do they know Akiko did it?" she asked. "Was she convicted on the basis of DNA finger-printing?"

Once again, Ajax scanned between the lines. "You're suggesting that it might have been another Superkid from Batch Alpha, right?" he asked. He shook his head. "But that wasn't it. Akiko killed the man in front of a bar filled with witnesses, then sat down at his table to wait until the police arrived. When they arrested her, she presented them with a signed confession she'd prepared in advance—that's what got her the first-degree charge. She's a murderer, all right."

He refilled his sake cup and sighed. "It makes me wonder about the rest of us."

Alma nodded, thinking about the shadowrunner and the gruesome way in which Gray Squirrel had been killed. When Alma finally located the Superkid who had framed her, she wondered what sort of demon she'd find.

Treading

So far, so good. Akira Kageyama had bought the excuse, and Night Owl was in. As she rode the elevator down to his underwater condoplex, she cradled the plastic packing case in her hands. She didn't want the contents to break. Not yet.

The elevator was studded with four round portholes, allowing her to look out through the stainless-steel, open-mesh tube that was the elevator shaft. The rain-splattered surface of Burrard Inlet was already high overhead, and the water was rapidly darkening from green-gray to black. Dark blurs that were either large fish or seals swept past the elevator shaft, and a clump of seaweed that had been caught on the bottom of the elevator bubbled its way to the surface. Inside the elevator, all Night Owl could hear was the steady whir of machinery and the soft hiss of circulating air. As she leaned back against the rear wall, the empty holster dug into the small of her back. She felt naked without her handgun—but "naked" was the only way you could hope to enter the dragon's den.

That's what the condoplex was—literally. Built back in the 2050s, it was designed to be one of the many residences of Dunkelzahn, the great dragon who had earned far more than his fifteen minutes of fame after being elected president of the UCAS in 2057. The worm had built the condoplex on a whim, just offshore from the expensive waterfront properties of West

Vancouver, after reading in a Chinese storybook that
dragons lived in crystal palaces under the sea. This
particular whim had cost nearly twenty million nuyen
to build, and he never did get the chance to move
into it. Just a few months after it was completed, the
Big D was flatlined. Later, it turned out that he'd
willed the Vancouver doss to one Akira Kageyama,
a "financial advisor" who'd been chummers with the
big worm.

Street buzz had it that some of the artworks in the
condoplex were priceless—and not just because they
were old. The first time Night Owl had visited this
doss, she'd nearly salivated at the thought of boosting
something from the hoard, which was rumored to con-
tain more than one magical focus. She'd been smart
enough, that time, to realize that you didn't tread on
the tail of a dragon—even one that was five years
dead. But now she was going to do just that.

Walls slid up around the elevator as it clunked to a
stop at the bottom of the shaft. The door slid open,
and Night Owl's ears popped as the pressure equal-
ized. She stepped out onto a plush carpet, between
walls of frosted glass.

Night Owl had prepared for this run by popping a
hearing amplification plug inside her right ear; she
didn't want anyone sneaking up on her when she was
boosting the statue. Through the amp, she could hear
the distant sound of water dripping. The condoplex
was plagued with leaks; Kageyama had spent hundreds
of thousands of nuyen over the past five years trying
to get rid of them, but as soon as one leak was
patched, another appeared. The sound set Night Owl's
nerves on edge. Being underwater already made her
claustrophobic enough.

All of the interior walls in the condoplex were on
rollers and could slide back and forth like the rice-
paper screens in Japanese houses. Kageyama had re-

arranged his entrance hall so that it was long and narrow, leading to double doors that had an elaborate dragon design sandblasted on them. Somehow, the dragon seemed to breathe fire: tiny sparks of red flickered out of its nostrils and spread in a fan shape through the glass, then slowly faded away. Each of its hands appeared to be holding a doorknob that had been set with an enormous pearl.

A drone rolled to a stop in front of her, just outside the elevator. It extended a telescoping pole topped with what looked like an octagonal mirror, framed in red plastic. When the "mirror" reached Night Owl's eye level, the monitor screen shimmered into life as Kageyama's image appeared on it.

The first time she'd met Kageyama, Night Owl had been struck by how ordinary he looked. She'd expected Vancouver's best-known millionaire to be as flamboyant and striking as the condoplex he'd inherited. But Kageyama had a face that would have blended into any crowd. His straight, blue-black hair was neat and short, his face was neither too round nor too narrow, his eyes a nondescript shade of green.

"*Konichiwa*, Night Owl," he said. "I like the mask you've painted on yourself tonight. The silver becomes you. Does that case hold the egg?"

Night Owl nodded and flipped open the hasps that held the packing case shut. She knew better than to hide anything inside the case; Kageyama might trust her, but he wasn't so stupid that he let large packages into his home without seeing what was inside. Setting the case carefully down on the ground, she opened its lid so that the drone's security camera could scan the contents.

The drone's cameras tilted, allowing the camera to get a better angle of the egg that was nested in a bed of spongelike foam inside the case. About the size of a football, the oval egg had a leathery surface and an iridescent sheen. Lighter patches on the surface bulged outward slightly, like weak spots in an overinflated ball. Waves of heat shimmered in the air above the egg, courtesy of a chemical heat pad Night Owl had placed underneath it.

"What kind do you think it is?" Night Owl asked. "Chimera? Firedrake? Leatherback turtle?"

She glanced up at the drone's monitor screen and saw that Kameyaga's pupils had dilated. *Got him*, she thought. She already knew what was in the case: the egg of something called a Lambton lizard, boosted from an illicit apothecary shop in Chinatown that dealt in black-market animal parts. She'd already told Kageyama where the egg had come from. What she'd failed to mention was that it was long since dead. A healthy spray coating of scent-receptor-blocking agents was masking its odor.

"It warrants a closer look," Kageyama said. "Follow the drone."

Night Owl closed the case and cradled it in her arms as she followed the drone. It led her through the double doors—which opened automatically—and into the maze of rooms and corridors that followed.

All of the walls, ceilings and floors in the condoplex were made of glass. Most of the floor was either carpeted or frosted for privacy, but there was the occasional patch of clear glass that gave a view down into the level below. Crossing them was like walking on air. Other clear patches looked down into aquariums filled with gigantic gold and white koi.

Some of the sliding panes of glass were set with geometric chunks of red or green or blue glass that glittered like multifaceted gems. Other walls were constructed from double panes of glass through which swirling currents of plankton-laden water flowed, glowing a soft blue—a living barrier against astral intrusion.

The rooms were filled with antique furniture: enormous, mirror-fronted wardrobes, velvet-upholstered chairs, and tables with elaborately carved legs with claw-and-ball feet. All of the furniture was a deep, polished red-brown or black and was made of real wood: mahogany and teak, Kageyama had told her on her previous visit. Night Owl ignored it, searching instead for anything that looked like jade.

Everywhere she looked, she saw artwork. She passed through one room that smelled thickly of oil paint; it was filled with enormous paintings so dark you could hardly see the people in them. In another room, three marble pedestals each displayed an ancient-looking, chipped clay pot, painted with figures that reminded Night Owl of the Aztechnology logo. One long hallway was lined on either side with stone carvings of multiarmed humans, posed as though they were dancing. Flecks of blue paint freckled their arms and faces. Another hallway was dominated by mannequins dressed in the armor of ancient samurai. Each area had background music, piped into concealed speakers, that was appropriate to the cultural artifacts on display.

Still other rooms held more modern pieces of art: blown-glass neon from the 20th century, atomic sculptures that could only be seen through an electron microscope, and holographic renderings of performance art that spouted fragmented sentences that were supposed to be poetry.

The first time she'd seen Kageyama's art collection, Night Owl had wondered what sort of chiphead would spend good nuyen on the stuff. Now she looked it over more carefully. Somewhere in this collection of overpriced junk was the statue she'd been sent to boost. She caught a glimpse of three jade-green shapes through the smoked glass of one wall, but the drone led her in a different direction before she could make out what they were. If she remembered correctly, the room held Chinese artwork. She put it at the top of her mental checklist of places to scan.

The drone finally led her to a room with a clear glass wall and ceiling that looked out onto the ocean. A trickle of seawater ran down the inside of the viewing wall, puddling on the floor. Just outside, brilliant halogen lights illuminated the water, lightening it to a dark forest green. Bullheads and skate swam close to the floor of the ocean, sending up clouds of sand as they scavenged for food. Bright red crabs scuttled from rock to rock, and pinkish-yellow sea anemones waved delicate tendrils in the air, sifting the ocean for scraps. In the distance, far overhead, the hull of a freighter slid silently past, a darker patch of black against the surface.

Night Owl carefully set the packing case on the only piece of furniture in the room: an enormous, leather-padded bench near the viewing wall. The drone hovered for a moment and then disappeared back through the only door leading to the room. A moment later, Kageyama entered.

He was wearing gray slacks, a white shirt and a plain black tie flecked with red. Even his shoes—which were obviously expensive, given the soft creak of new leather—were nondescript. It was the sort of outfit that would allow him to blend into any crowd—just toss a black leather jacket over it and lose the tie, and he'd even be able to hang with runners. But while Kageyama could fade into the background better than anyone else Night Owl knew, he also had the ability to turn on the charm. When he wanted to, he could conjure up a presence that made people instantly stop, listen and nod.

He was turning it on big time tonight. "Night Owl," he said, striding forward and drinking her in with his eyes. "Good to see you again. Thank you for bringing the egg to me, instead of taking it to your patron. Will that place you in any danger?" His voice was rich and his smile genuine. Just as she had the first time she met him, Night Owl found herself getting a sensual buzz off the man. Kageyama had something about him—tailored pheromones, maybe—that caused both men and women to instantly warm up to him.

"I had a little trouble from gangers on this run, but the important thing is the egg," Night Owl answered. "Do you think it might still be alive?"

"We'll see," Kageyama said. He nodded at the case. "Open it."

Keeping her face carefully neutral, Night Owl did as she was instructed. As she flipped back the lid of the case, she kept an eye on Kageyama. His nostrils flared—just for a moment—and she realized that the odor-masking spray hadn't worked. Her right eye began to twitch. Time to accelerate her plan.

"That's an Awakened reptile egg, all right," Kageyama said. "Very rare, and quite valuable in its own right. But I'm afraid it's—"

Before he could finish his sentence, Night Owl reached into the packing case and lifted the egg from it. She heard Kageyama gasp—he knew what was coming, as well as she did—and saw his eyes widen. In that same instant the fragile egg ruptured in her hands like a rotten melon. Putrid jelly squelched out onto the front of Night Owl's cheap cotton jacket and smeared her hands and arms; a squirt of it even landed on her cheek. Gagging at the smell, she dropped what remained of the egg onto the floor, where it landed with a wet *splotch*, spraying her boots.

When she'd planned this run, Night Owl figured she'd have to fake her revulsion, but now she found that no acting was required. The smell of the egg was worse than anything she could have imagined, and the liquid that covered her hands was slimy and hot.

Kageyama backed away, holding a hand in front of his mouth. He looked as though he was about to vomit.

Night Owl glanced around, as if searching for something to wipe her hands on. "I'm so sorry," she croaked. "I didn't know . . ." She swallowed back the bile that rose in her throat. "Is there a washroom . . . ?"

Kageyama pointed to the door. "Down the hall," he gulped, pinching his nostrils shut. "Turn right, then left. It's the third door on the left."

Night Owl hurried from the room. As soon as she turned the corner, she headed for the room where she'd spotted the greenish shapes. It was some distance away, but the rotten egg would give her an excuse to be away from Kageyama for some time. As she hurried through the corridors, she pulled a package of sani-wipes she'd placed in her pocket earlier and ripped open its foil seal. By the time she reached the door she was looking for, her hands and face were clean. She stuffed the egg-fouled wipes back in her jacket pocket and zipped it shut.

The door she was looking for wasn't locked. Night Owl pushed it open and walked into a room filled with Chinese artwork. Delicate yellow and pink vases, intricately carved ivories and painted silks were everywhere. The floor was set with a gold-tile mosaic of a snarling dragon, and enormous wooden statues of men and animals filled the room like a forest. Against the opposite wall stood a huge wooden bookcase, elaborately carved from polished red wood. On it were a number of smaller statues, in ceramic, bronze—and jade.

Just at eye level were three statues, each about a foot tall. Carved from pale green jade, they depicted three men: one with an enormously domed bald head who leaned on a staff; the second wearing richly decorated robes and an elaborate winged headdress; the third holding an accountant's scroll. Night Owl recognized them at once as the three gods that decorated every Chinese home, although they were usually in the form of holopics.

As she stood in the doorway, Night Owl felt a tickling on the back of her neck. She had the sudden feeling that someone was watching her. She glanced over her shoulder, worried that Kageyama might have followed her, but didn't see him. Then she listened through the amplification plug. Aside from the dripping of water into a bucket in a nearby room, everything was quiet. The feeling of being watched, however, wouldn't go away.

Night Owl's gut told her to abort the run. Kageyama was a millionaire with resources she couldn't even dream of. If he caught Night Owl trying to steal from his home, she'd be in deep drek.

Her head, however, told her to stick to the plan. The statue in the middle—Fu Shen, god of good fortune—had to be her target. It was sitting right out in the open, just begging to be boosted.

Continue . . . or abort? Night Owl thrust a hand into her jeans. She'd popped open a parking meter earlier that evening and pulled a fistful of tokens from it. The one she pulled from her pocket now had a longhouse on one side and the smiling faces of the Salish-Shidhe Council on the other. Night Owl flipped it into the air. Heads, she'd steal the statue. Tails, she'd walk out of here and take her chances with the Red Lotus and their dragon master.

The coin landed council-side up. Heads.

Night Owl strode toward the display case, picked the middle statue up—it was surprisingly heavy, for something that was supposed to be hollow—and gave it a slight shake. She didn't hear any rattle, and when she turned it over in her hands and examined it closely, she couldn't see any joins: the figure of the god had been carved from a single piece of jade. She did notice one thing, though: the character "bat" engraved on the god's back. That made her grin. The word bat, which in Cantonese was pronounced *fu*, was a homonym for "good luck." Even if it wasn't hollow, this was definitely the statue the dragon wanted her to steal.

Night Owl wondered what was inside, and for just a moment was tempted to try to break it open. Then she decided that it might be better not to know.

Now that she had what she'd come for, she had to move quickly. Stripping off her jacket, she wrapped it around the statue. Fortunately, the piece of jade was neither big nor bulky—the jacket hid it entirely. Carrying it under one arm, she ran back to the bathroom. She made it back just in time; as the door clicked shut behind her, Kageyama knocked on it and asked if she was all right.

"I'm fine!" she called out, running water into the marble sink. "It's more difficult to get the smell out than I thought. I'll be right there."

She wadded her jacket into a garbage chute in the wall and hit the disposal icon. The chute closed and filled with seawater, pumps gurgled, and the jacket was swept out of sight.

Night Owl sighed with relief. The statue was on its way. She knew where it would wind up: inside a metal mesh bag that, when it was full, would be automatically lifted by balloon up to the surface, where a garbage scow would pick it up. Night Owl knew the junker who operated the garbage scow that serviced the West Vancouver waterfront—Skimmer was a chummer of Wharf Rat's. She'd already made him promise not to collect any of the trash bags that rose from Kageyama's condoplex until she gave the go-ahead. That favor was going to cost her a couple hundred nuyen, but it was worth it. She relished the thought of Wu having to pick through Kageyama's garbage to find the statue. It would serve the fragger right for forcing her into this run.

When she'd realized that the garbage-disposal system was a hole in the condoplex's security, the discovery had seemed too good to be true. Then she realized that Kageyama's security depended not on keeping track of what left the building but on screening those who came in. Night Owl, thanks to the PETAB run, had managed to slip through the cracks.

Kageyama was waiting for her when she stepped out of the washroom and immediately noticed that she'd trashed her jacket. He seemed to have anticipated it, in fact: draped over one arm was an expensive-looking jacket cut from soft brown suede.

"Please," he said. "Allow me to lend you this."

He held it out in front of him, and Night Owl slipped her arms into the sleeves. The jacket was a perfect fit and smelled of new leather. Although it looked like something a corporate slitch would wear, it was seductively soft. Night Owl found herself leaning back into it until she and Kageyama were nearly pressed against each other. Kageyama let his hands linger on her shoulders for just a moment longer than necessary before he stepped back and bowed.

"It is a pity about the egg," he said. "Even though it turned out to be rotten, I appreciate you bringing it to me. How much was your patron going to pay for it?"

Night Owl shrugged as if cred didn't matter. She told him the first figure that popped into her head: "Three thousand nuyen."

Kageyama nodded. He slipped a hand into the pocket of his trousers and pulled out a credstick, offering it to Night Owl. "This should compensate you."

Night Owl started to reach for it and then paused. Her fingers ached to take the credstick; to Kageyama, three thousand nuyen was no more than petty cash. But her gut told her to be careful—she'd bought her way into the condoplex, albeit unwittingly, by refusing payment for liberating the dour. She wondered if Kageyama was testing her. Maybe her ticket out of here was to . . .

Kageyama pressed the credstick into her palm and used both of his hands to close hers around it. "Take it," he whispered. "If you don't want the credit yourself, you can always give it away to charity." His lips twitched into a smile.

She gave him a wary look, wondering how much he really knew about her. To everyone she rubbed shoulders with in the shadows, Night Owl was a spendthrift who frittered away her cred as soon as she earned it. If they ever found out she gave the bulk of the cred from each run to a charity that provided medical care and cybernetics to third-world children, she'd be laughed off the streets.

She found herself regretting having stolen from Kageyama. Then she mentally shook her head. Biz was biz—and the goal of this particular run was to keep herself alive. Kageyama was a fool to have trusted her—and more of a fool to have given her the nuyen. She pulled her hand away from his and shoved the credstick into her pocket.

"Thanks for the cred," she said. "I appreciate it. If I find any more eggs, you'll be the first to know."

As Kageyama walked her back to the elevator, Night Owl caught a glimpse of an elderly Asian man peering into the entry hall through one of the glass walls. He looked ancient, with a bald, age-spotted head and hands as withered as fall leaves, and he wore clothing that was at least three decades out of style. The man raised a hand and waved at her, a bemused expression on his face.

"I thought you lived alone," Night Owl said. "Who's that? Your grandfather?"

"Who?" Kageyama glanced at the wall, but the elderly man had disappeared. Then he laughed. "Ah, you mean Kelvin. He's the man who created the glass for this building. He was a master craftsman before the Awakening and became a master mage after it. I am told that he somehow managed to fuse his essence with the glass and lives on inside these walls in astral form."

Night Owl swallowed nervously. "He must be . . . interesting company." Why was Kageyama telling her this?

Kageyama's green eyes twinkled. "Not as interesting as some."

The elevator door sighed open. Night Owl stepped inside and nodded goodbye to Kageyama through the window in the door as the elevator began its ascent. Only when she'd stepped out onto the rain-lashed platform at the surface did her shoulders begin to unknot. She'd done it: the run was over and she could fade away into the night.

She still couldn't shake the feeling, however, that Kageyama had put one over on her—that he wasn't nearly as stupid as he made himself out to be.

Gradual Progress

Alma walked into the fitness center and looked around at the straining, sweating bodies, wondering which one was her "Johnson." The gym was an old-fashioned one, with equipment several decades out of date. Weights clanked against each other inside exercise machines, shadowbox booths pinged whenever a point was scored against a virtual opponent, and exer-flexers creaked as people strained against a spiderweb pattern of stretchable bands. The room smelled of machine oil, rubber and sweat.

Alma waited until the ork who was using the bench press finished his set and then asked if she could work in. The ork, a squat East Indian with a dense black mat of curly hair covering his arms and legs, grinned up at her with chipped tusks. His face was heavy with five o'clock shadow, even though it was not yet 10 a.m.

"You sure you can handle it?" he asked, wiping his face with a tattered towel. "I've got a hundred and fifty kilos on the bar."

"I'll manage," Alma said.

"Want me to spot you?"

Alma shook her head and settled back on the bench. "No thanks." She reached up and wrapped her hands around the bar, activating the release pedal with her foot. The bar gradually grew heavier in her hands as the automated system gauged the resistance in her arms and released with a sudden click.

The ork hovered next to the machine as Alma began slowly to lower and raise the bar; he stood with one hand near the override lever as if he expected her to drop the weight onto her chest at any moment. By the time she'd completed twenty reps, his hand fell away. By the time she'd done forty, his eyes were bulging. When she'd finished sixty reps, he wet his lips.

"Frag me," he whispered. "You haven't even broken a sweat. What kind of enhancements have you got?"

Alma smiled up at him as she flicked the foot lever. The bar locked in place above her, and she sat up. "Yamatetsu muscle aug," she answered. She flicked a finger against a flexed bicep. "Delta grade."

She stood and gestured at the empty bench press. "Your turn. I need to rehydrate."

A tremble started in her left hand—just a slight flutter in the fingers this time, but it lasted for fifty-eight seconds. The tremors were getting worse; with each day that went by, they seemed to be increasing in duration, and each one seemed to take something out of her, leaving a feeling of lethargy in its wake. She was glad this one hadn't struck in the middle of her set.

Balling her hand into a fist, Alma walked toward the drink dispenser and slotted the credstick that she'd pinned to her tights. She chose a tube of Electro Lite and stood by the window to drink it, watching the rain pour down on Trout Lake. More than a dozen large black birds were perched in the trees outside the fitness center. She wondered if they were storm crows.

An Asian woman with bleached-blond hair nodded at Alma as she bought a drink from the dispenser. A blue plastic rectangle—a permit for travel within the Salish-Shidhe nation—hung from an elasticized band around her left wrist, next to a bracelet-shaped cellphone. She was shorter than Alma, but just as slender, with a washboard stomach and good muscle definition in her arms and legs. She carried herself as if she expected trouble—and was prepared to meet it. Her eyes had a guarded look about them, as if she'd spent time on the streets.

The woman's eyes ranged up and down Alma's body with an almost sensual appreciation. "You're fit," she said. "And you walk smooth. I bet you're fast."

Alma nodded and continued sipping her drink. She wondered what the woman wanted. She'd walked over to the dispenser with the perfect balance and springy step of someone trained in the martial arts; Alma hoped she wasn't going to try to pick a fight. She hoped the woman would be as easy to dust off as the ork—she didn't want a stranger listening in when Mr. Johnson pitched his assignment.

Alma continued scanning the room, casually sipping her drink. If no one approached her in the next five minutes, she'd do another sixty-rep set in the hope that the Johnson would notice. It was the signal that she'd told Tiger Cat to pass along when he confirmed the time and place of the meeting.

The blond woman's eyes narrowed. "Speed and strength won't mean squat on this run, unless you can get close to your target."

Alma turned, realizing at last that *this* was the Johnson she was to meet. She gave the woman a closer scrutiny, quietly focusing her eyecamera on the woman's distinguishing characteristics. The only one visible was a tattoo above her left breast, partially hidden under her sports bra: a black wolf's head, with what looked like an Asian character superimposed in white across it.

"Do you speak Korean?" the woman asked.

Alma scanned through the menu of her headware memory. She'd loaded it with the contents of more than a dozen linguasofts that covered all of the most common languages in Vancouver: Cantonese, Mandarin, Punjabi, Hindi, Vietnamese, Tagalog, Korean, Spanish—even Salish, in case Mr. Johnson turned out to be a Full Blood.

"*Ye*," Alma answered, switching to Korean. "I speak it."

"*Choun*," the woman said. "Follow me."

They walked through the changing room toward the whirlpool. A sign hanging from a mop propped in a bucket proclaimed it to be closed for cleaning and rechlorinating—the blond woman flipped aside the mop like a turnstile and entered. When they were both inside the tiled, echoing room, she shut the door and flicked on the whirlpool's bubble jets. Alma had to activate the noise filters in her cyberear to hear the woman's voice above the gurgle of the water.

"Tiger Cat says you're an expert at extractions," the woman said.

"That's right," Alma lied smoothly. "I helped with a run on PCI awhile ago." She watched for a reaction. If the woman knew about Gray Squirrel's extraction, she might also know the name of the woman who had framed Alma, and where to find her.

The blond woman merely shrugged.

"I asked Tiger Cat for someone who could pass in high-cred circles," she said. "Our target is heavily insulated by nuyen; he's going to be a tough one to access. But you'll pass as a society slitch. If it wasn't for Tiger Cat's endorsement, I'd swear you were corporate."

"Who's the target?" Alma asked, wanting to deflect the conversation.

The blond woman cracked a smile. "Not so fast, Cybergirl. I want to make sure you can deliver first. How do you take down your targets?"

Tiger Cat had warned her to anticipate this question. Some Johnsons wanted their extractions "chem free" and insisted that non-lethal magic be used; others wouldn't care if the target was delivered minus a limb. Alma hoped that the blond woman wasn't one of the purists.

"Gamma scopolamine," she answered. "I'll use a compressed-air injector. He'll never know what hit him."

The blond woman's smile was feral. "Perfect," she said. "That should prep him for us nicely. Just make sure you deliver him before his lips start to loosen. We'll want him at his most talkative."

Alma nodded. "Where do you want me to bring him?"

"I'll give you a number to call. We'll be ready to take delivery anywhere in the Lower Mainland. Once he's in our hands, I'll give your second payment to your laundry boy."

It took Alma a moment to figure out what the woman was talking about. Then she got it: the woman thought that Tiger Cat was laundering the credit, ensuring that it was untraceable. It was a nice touch on his part; it explained why Alma wasn't insisting on a personal transfer of credit.

Now that she was actually negotiating the details of the shadowrun, Alma suddenly realized that she'd have to carry it out. She hadn't allowed herself to dwell on the ultimate outcome of her actions, but now she found herself wondering what would become of her "target." She had a hard time getting Gray Squirrel's slashed throat out of her mind.

"Who's the target?" she asked.

"He's a financial advisor. Akira Kageyama."

Alma nodded, relieved that it wasn't someone she knew. She was familiar with the name—few in Vancouver weren't, after Dunkelzahn's will was read. She also had a vague idea of what Akira Kageyama looked like—she'd seen him once on the society channel but had never met the man. Although he mixed in corporate circles, he'd never attended a PCI function.

"Any more questions?" the blond woman asked.

"Just one," Alma said. "After I've delivered Akira Kageyama and you've gotten the information you want, what happens to him?"

The blond woman gave a hard laugh that was answer enough. Whatever she had planned for Kageyama, it wasn't pleasant. She flicked a hand impatiently at Alma. "Give me your cell."

Alma checked it first and saw that the memo function was clear. Her nemesis, it seemed, had been too busy to send any more taunting messages. She handed the cellphone over and watched as the woman keyed a number into its autodial menu.

"What tag do you go by?"

Alma had considered a number of nicknames, but none of them seemed to fit her as well as the nickname this woman had just given her. " 'Cybergirl' will do," she said. "What should I call you?"

"Don't worry about that," the woman answered. "Just call the entry marked 'Johnson.' I'll be the one answering the phone."

She handed the cell back to Alma. "Tiger Cat said you could handle a rush job—that's why we're paying the big nuyen. You have until midnight tomorrow. If you don't manage to bag Kageyama before then, the deal is off. *Chakbyol insa*—goodbye."

Chuckling to herself, she strode out of the room, slapping the button that shut off the whirlpool as she left. In the sudden silence, Alma heard the faint beeping of a cellphone being dialed. Realizing that it must be the blond woman using her bracelet phone, she boosted her hearing just in time to catch a fragment of conversation: "—worry. We'll know where it is soon eno—'' Then the voice was gone, lost in the clank of exercise machines.

Alma had the feeling that, after the blond woman questioned Kageyama, he'd be disposed of—permanently. Alma didn't want to be responsible for an innocent man's death. That would put her in the same gutter as the woman who had killed Gray Squirrel. But she needed this run—it was her window into Vancouver's shadowrunner community.

She hadn't realized that she might have to break the glass to get in.

Alma threaded her way along a floating walkway that bobbed and dipped with each step she took. Built from scavenged wood and kept afloat by a collection of styrofoam blocks, beer kegs and driftwood logs, it weaved its way like a sidewalk among the hundreds of small boats that were anchored in False Creek. Home to a motley collection of squatters, these ranged from small aluminum speedboats with jury-rigged tarps covering them to fishing boats and cabin cruisers; there were even a handful of aging yachts. Most were in rough shape and rode low in the water, their hulls crusted with barnacles and tendrils of seaweed, their rusted upper decks dotted with tape-patched windows and splashes of graffiti. There were also a number of houseboats, some of them little more than log rafts with decrepit prefab shelters or even tents perched on top of them.

Rain dappled the surface of the water to either side of the floating walkway, stirring up smells of raw sewage and oil. The boards underfoot were rain-slick and slippery; Alma wondered how anyone managed to negotiate them without a move-by-wire system. Those who passed her, however, walked along the unstable, slippery surface like sailors on a rolling ship. Only when she looked down and saw that the boards underfoot were perforated with thousands of tiny holes did Alma realize that they must be wearing cleats.

The squatters who lived here were a mix of races and metatypes, with a high percentage of orks and trolls—"yomi" who had been exiled from Japan in the 2020s after the first big wave of goblinization hit. They eyed Alma suspiciously through cracked windows as she went past; strangers weren't welcome here in the False Creek Floats. More than once, the city had tried to clean out the "floaters," the council police sweeping in and arresting as many squatters as they could get their cuffs on and then towing the boats away and sinking them well offshore. But somehow the floaters always got wind of the raids in advance, and only the slowest and least seaworthy craft were caught. The rest upped anchor and fled, scattering like dandelion seeds and then rooting themselves in tiny clumps all over the city's waterfront.

Eventually, after the floaters had reduced property values along several areas of the city, the council herded them back to False Creek, where they could at least be contained. The tribal police still made periodic raids, however, forcing their patrol boats through the maze of walkways and boats whenever the council ordered a crackdown on BTL chips, illegal immigrants or prohibited weapons, all of which were as plentiful as fleas on a rat in the False Creek Floats.

Alma at last saw the boat she was looking for: a battered Surfstar Marine Seacop patrol boat with a superstructure pockmarked with rusted bullet holes. The holes must have been made by armor-piercing slugs; the metal armor on the boat looked several centimeters thick. The weapons had been removed from its firmpoints before the vessel was sold for scrap, and the current owner had replaced them with vidcams. Large patches of gray primer covered the boat's original Coast Patrol markings, visible now only as the slightly raised outline of a stylized killer whale. The boat's original spotlight and hailers were still in place, however. Hanging from one of the antennae that bristled from the upper deck of the boat were the two flags Tiger Cat had told Alma to look for: a pirate's skull and crossbones, and the red flag slashed with a line of white that meant "diver below."

Alma grimaced at the pun. According to Tiger Cat, the only "diving" this cyberpirate did was in the electronic waters of the Matrix. Tiger Cat had told her the man was one of the hottest deckers in Vancouver, but given the surroundings, Alma was starting to wonder about his credentials.

As Alma turned onto the walkway that led to the boat, its on-board cameras panned to follow her movements. At the same time, an ork stepped down onto the walkway from a raft and rolled one of the heavy blue plastic drums that filled every centimeter of its deck space onto the creaking boards. Diesel fuel sloshed from an opening on the top of the drum onto the walkway, which had sagged under the combined weight of troll and fuel drum until it was awash. The ork, who had a scarred, shaved head and eyes so small and squinting that it was difficult to tell whether he was Asian, turned and eyed Alma with a belligerent look.

"You got biz here, dirt-kisser? Or are you just down here slummin'?"

Alma stopped; the ork and his drum were blocking her way, and he clearly had no intention of moving. He stood braced as if he was ready to fight, ignoring the fast-food containers that washed gently back and forth around his hobnailed work boots.

The ork's timing had been too perfect; it was clear that he was intended as a first line of defense, to slow down unwanted visitors to the boat ahead. Alma had already spotted the comlink in his ear and the slight depression in his neck where a less-than-competent surgeon had implanted a subvocal microphone. The cameras on the patrol boat were just backup; this man was the eyes and ears—and muscle—of the computer hacker that Alma had come to see.

"I have 'biz' with Bluebeard," Alma answered, nodding at the boat behind him. "He's expecting me. Tell him Cybergirl is here." As she spoke, her left hand began to shake. As casually as she could, she shifted her posture so that it was hidden behind her back.

"Yeah? Well, you can tell him yourself—after I shift this drum." The ork leaned to the side for a better look at her concealed hand and then sneered, obviously thinking that he had intimidated her. "Now get your skoggin' little hoop outta my way."

He picked up the oil drum by its sling, balancing easily under its weight as the walkway rocked back and forth. His tiny eyes bored into Alma's, warning her that if she tried to stand her ground she'd get shoved aside.

Alma glared back at him, her move-by-wire system easily compensating for the rocking. Every security system had its protocols, and if she was going to pass herself off as a shadowrunner, she would have to jump through these people's hoops. She knew from her dealings with Tiger Cat—who had yet to interface with her except by cellphone—that shadowrunners liked to keep a safe distance between themselves and the rest of the world. Tiger Cat had warned her that Bluebeard was reclusive, shielding himself behind a wall of armor and tech. Alma had expected to be scanned, videotaped and chem-sniffed before getting on board the boat. She hadn't expected to have to run a gantlet of insults as well.

She wasn't about to back down—not with Bluebeard's cameras trained on her and the rain steadily soaking through her jacket. She suspected that the ork's belligerence was a test.

She liked tests.

Alma had already calculated the amount of give in the floating boards beneath her and the length of walkway beyond the ork. Crouching suddenly, she pistoned herself into the air. She landed—for just a split second—in a handstand with both hands on the ork's shoulders and then used her momentum to complete the handspring and land lightly on the walkway behind him, knees bent to compensate for the violent rocking her leap and landing had caused. Behind her, she heard a curse and a splash as the ork, unbalanced both by the fuel drum he was carrying and the sudden extra weight on his shoulders, toppled into the water. He came up sputtering and thrashing beside the bobbing drum, his face coated with diesel fuel.

"Fraggin' dirt-kisser!" he bellowed, scrambling with diesel-slicked hands for a grip on the bobbing walkway. "I'll push your face into a propeller for that!"

A chuckle erupted from one of the speakers on the patrol boat, and then a male voice spoke: *Leave her alone, Stoker. She's right. I am expecting her.*

A second later, Alma's cyberears picked up the faint whine of an electric motor and the muffled clunk of maglocks opening. A metal ladder near the stern unfolded itself against the patrol boat's hull.

Welcome aboard.

She climbed the ladder to the small deck at the rear of the boat. A square hatch in the rear deck opened smoothly on hydraulic lifts as she walked toward it.

Alma climbed down a ladder and found herself inside what looked like a dimly lit electronics repair shop. She had to activate her cybereyes' low-light vision to see anything; the only light came from the hatch above her, which was closing again, and from the spark-bright glow of red on/off indicator lights.

The interior of the patrol boat had been gutted, its separating walls removed to create one large space. Cheap metal shelving bolted to the walls held electronic parts of every description, and a host of tools dangled on spiral cords that hung from the ceiling. Gimballed tables tilted gently back and forth as the boat rocked. A profusion of computer equipment was spread across them, but there wasn't a single monitor screen in sight.

An enormously fat ork sat in the middle of the room on a reclining chair fitted with rollers. Fiberoptic cables were plugged into datajacks in his temples and into ports at the side of his head where his ears had once been. He was Asian, with black hair that had gone from receding to patchy, and fully cybered eyes with silver irises. A goatee straggled down across his bare belly to touch the faded sarong that was his only article of clothing. Mentally, Alma shook her head at his slovenly appearance. Tiger Cat had assured her that the fellow was one of Vancouver's top Matrix experts, but the man didn't have a speck of professionalism about him. He could at least have put on a shirt for this meeting.

Reluctantly, Alma took a step forward, wrinkling her nose in anticipation. But despite the man's size—he looked as though he only rarely moved from his chair—he didn't smell as stale as Alma had expected. The odor of linament lingered in the air, making Alma wonder if the hacker had a masseuse who kneaded the circulation back into his body while his mind was deep in the Matrix.

"That's close enough," he said.

Bluebeard was sitting with his chair turned partially away from Alma, his hands resting on a belly as massive as a Buddha's. He didn't bother to turn around while speaking to her, and his eyes seemed unfocused. Alma suspected that he was using the video cameras that were mounted around the interior of the boat to look at her.

Alma bowed in the direction of the nearest vidcam. "Thank you for agreeing to meet me in person."

He grunted and waved one hand in a jerky motion. "Tiger Cat can be very persuasive. He said seeing you would be worth my while. What kind of data are you looking for?"

"There's someone I'm interested in: a man by the name of Akira Kageyama. I need to know his movements, to find out where I can access him. My Johnson wants him extracted—by midnight tomorrow."

Bluebeard's eyebrows jerked up and then settled. "That's a tough order to fill without a starting point."

"I've got one." Alma reached into her jacket pocket and pulled out a credstick and the business card that Ajax had given her yesterday. "I have some—connections—with the security industry. They tell me that Kageyama has used Priority One Security's bodyguards in the past. Priority One will have a record of where Kageyama went on those occasions, and when."

Bluebeard's jowls quivered as he shook his head. "Priority One's been bought out by Knight Errant. If you want me to try and skate past their black ice, you'll have to triple your price."

Alma held up a zero-balance credstick whose optical chip had been wiped of all information save one vital piece, pulled from her own medical file: her DNA scan. She knew that Priority One would use the same scanning procedure that PCI did, taking a random sampling of the one hundred thousand genes in the human genome and looking for a one hundred percent match with that sample. The scan typically skipped the twenty-third chromosome pair, since the smaller Y chromosome found in men carried so little genetic information. That meant that it would miss the one

difference between Alma's genetic coding and Ajax's:
an XX instead of an XY chromosome pair.

"I have a way to bypass Priority One 's Matrix security: a back-door key to their network," she explained.
"That's why I insisted on coming here in person. This
credstick contains a DNA scan of a Priority One employee named Ajax Penzler. I'm not sure what kind
of clearances he has, but you should be able to use
his ID to get into the employee scheduling system.
Penzler himself may not have been assigned to bodyguard Kageyama, but someone else at Priority One
will have."

Bluebeard's lips twitched into a smile. Alma knew
what he was thinking: that she was about to hand him
a master key to Priority One and a possible entry
point to Knight Errant itself. What he didn't know
was that the credstick included a program that would
erase the optical chip after one upload of its data.
Priority One's security would be compromised only
until Bluebeard exited its system—which he'd need to
do in order to tell Alma what he'd found.

Bluebeard leaned over slowly, pausing to catch his
balance several times as he did so, and plucked the
credstick and business card out of her hand. Alma let
the card go reluctantly. She'd only just connected with
Ajax, and he was the closest thing she had to family
in this world. Now here she was, doing the same thing
to him that the shadowrunner who had abducted Gray
Squirrel had done to her. She couldn't even claim al-
truistic reasons: she was using Ajax to salvage her rep-
utation and her job.

The ironic thing was that, even if she was successful,
she'd never work in security again. Besides Aaron,
Aella and Akiko, who were either dead or about to
die—and Ajax, whom Alma trusted—there were eight
other Superkids out there. Three of them were women
whose genetic coding was nearly identical to Alma's.

Intellectually, she'd realized that they were possible security risks, but after losing contact with them for so many years, she'd doubted that their paths would ever cross. Even so, she was negligent not to have given Hu the full details when she'd first joined PCI. He'd run a background check as part of her job-application screening and learned that she was a Superkid. He knew that she'd been bionically augmented at an early age as part of an experimental program but had no idea that each of the Superkids in Batch Alpha was gentically identical to all of the others.

Bluebeard had already slotted both the credstick and the auto-call business card into a cyberdeck on the table in front of him. His body slumped like soft dough and his eyes fluttered shut as he accessed the Matrix. Six minutes and fourteen seconds later, his eyes opened again.

"It's your lucky day," Bluebeard said. "Akira Kageyama visits the Executive Body Enhancements cyberclinic in the Woodwards Arcology just twice a year, but he's got an appointment with them tomorrow at 10 a.m. A Priority One Security bodyguard has been assigned to escort him to and from the clinic, but the guard has instructions not to accompany Kageyama inside the clinic itself. That's your window of opportunity."

Alma frowned. "That's a serious breach of security. Standard ops is to wait outside the door of the examining room itself."

Alma heard the lens in a camera next to her zoom in and realized that Bluebeard was scrutinizing her closely. His body language told her that she'd just revealed a greater knowledge of security procedure than she should have.

"I wondered about that, too," he said. "So I dug a little deeper—that's what took me so long. The ice around the clinic's patient records was pretty thick, but I managed to melt it and sneak a peek at Kageyama's file. He's only got one cybernetic enhancement, but it's a strange one: the little finger of each hand. It's a cosmetic job; the fingers don't physically interface with his nervous system. They aren't even connected to muscle tissue. They operate independently, taking their cue from the other fingers of the hand and slaving to their movements—and they're battery-driven. Kageyama has to visit the clinic twice a year, for a tuneup and battery change."

"Do his medical records say how he lost the ends of his fingers? " Alma asked, even though she had a hunch that she already knew the answer. In the Japanese yakuza, subordinates who committed grave errors apologized to their superiors by ritually severing the last joint of the little finger. Kageyama was originally from Japan. On the surface, he was a law-abiding resident of Vancouver. Alma wondered if there were gang connections in his past—if that was why someone wanted to extract him.

Bluebeard seemed to be on the same wavelength. "If Kageyama was a yak, he was a real screw-up," he said with a chuckle. "His entire little finger's gone— on both hands. But we're not talking self-mutilation. According to the chopdoc's notes, it's a genetic defect, present from birth."

Alma mulled that one over. "Why cosmetic cybernetics?" she asked. "Why not just hardwire the fingers to his nervous system?"

"He must be Awakened," Bluebeard answered. "Your target has probably got magical capabilities. This isn't going to be an easy extraction for you."

He pulled an optical memory chip from his computer and held it out in Alma's direction. "I've downloaded some newsclips about Kageyama that you can scan later," he said. "I think you'll find them quite interesting."

Alma was only half listening as she took the chip.

She couldn't shake the hunch that Kageyama was somehow gang-linked. The woman who had hired her was Korean, not Japanese, but she'd had the arrogant confidence of someone who ran with a pack . . .

That was it.

"I need you to do one more Matrix search," Alma said. "This time, I'm looking for information on a tattoo: a black wolf's head, with an Asian character—probably Korean—superimposed in white across it. I suspect it's gang-related. I want to know which gang."

"That should be easy enough," Bluebeard said. "The NAN intercouncil police task force keeps detailed records on organized crime."

Once more, his body slumped.

While Alma was waiting, wondering how Bluebeard was going to access a secure police grid, her left hand began to tremble. Before she lost her grip on it entirely, she popped the chip Bluebeard had given her into a pocket. Whatever was wrong with her was getting worse: the tremors were still occurring only two or three times a day, but when they did, they bunched up like an earthquake and its aftershocks, leaving her feeling weak and muzzy. Before Alma could time this tremor, however, Bluebeard was back.

"The wolf-head tattoo is part of the initiation rite of a Seoulpa Ring, based out of Seattle: the Komun'go. There's a lot of data on them, but most of it is pretty fuzzy; I'll just give you the highlights.

"The gang has only a toehold in North America; its base is in Korea, and there's a shadowy puppet master there who pulls its strings. Shadowbuzz says the head honcho is some kind of sentient paranormal, although the jury's still out on whether he's a vampire or a dragon.

"There may also be a corporate connection. According to the Salish-Shidhe immigration department, a Komun'go gang member was arrested in Vancouver five months ago while using a false travel permit that listed him as an employee of the Eastern Tiger Corporation. The corp claimed the ID had been stolen, but it seems to have a special relationship with the Komun'go: its Seattle subsidiary is the only Korean-based firm that the Komun'go protection racket hasn't leaned on."

Alma digested that information. She still had access to the corporate data she'd stored in her headware memory; Hu hadn't erased anything that wasn't directly linked to PCI. Eastern Tiger, a prominent member of the Pacific Prosperity Group, concentrated on heavy manufacturing and petrochemical processing—areas of the corporate sector that were far removed from Akira Kageyama's areas of expertise: banking and investment. What did they want with Kageyama?

Alma suddenly realized that she was still thinking like a security professional, and not like a shadowrunner. Her job wasn't to puzzle out who wanted to extract Kageyama and why—it was to carry out the extraction.

Bluebeard shifted in his chair, obviously impatient for Alma to leave, but Alma wasn't finished yet.

"Just one more thing," she told him. "I need you to go back into the Executive Body Enhancements Matrix host and book me an appointment at the clinic—immediately before Kageyama's appointment, if possible. Can you do that?"

"Of course," Bluebeard snorted, as if the job she'd asked him to do was as easy as entering data into a personal daytimer. "What name do you want to use?"

"Jane Lee," she said, giving him an identity she'd used several months ago while on a routine surveillance assignment. She still had a resident's ID permit for the fictitious Jane Lee—it was one of the things Hu had overlooked when he'd made his sweep of her apartment.

Bluebeard nodded. "And what reason should I give for you visiting the clinic?"

Alma held up her left hand, which was quivering slightly. "Temporal lobe epilepsy."

Bluebeard stared at her hand as if mesmerized by it. "Very convincing," he said. "I'm sure the chopdocs will believe it."

His eyes met hers for a moment, and then he added: "Is Tiger Cat giving you a decent cut from this run?"

Alma wasn't sure why he'd asked, but she nodded.

"Good," Bluebeard said. "Because you're going to need it. That kind of cybersurgery doesn't come cheap."

"But I don't—"

"I had you on zoom when you were talking to Stoker, and your hand was shaking then," Bluebeard said. "That's twice in less than an hour. I'm no chopdoc, but I've seen TLE before—I used to have a move-by-wire system myself. I figure you've got a week or two, at most, before your entire nervous system seizes up. When you see the chopdoc tomorrow, you'd better ask about it. You're going to need surgery, and soon."

Alma felt a hot rush of anger. Who was this—this shadowrunner, of all people, to be telling her what to do? Her cyberware wasn't some off-the-rack street-grade junk. It was delta-grade, the best money could buy.

Bluebeard gave Alma the time of her appointment and the doctor she'd be seeing and then slumped back into his chair. He was still there in the flesh, but his mind had once again departed into the world of the Matrix.

Maglocks in the hatch overhead clunked open, and a crack of gray light filtered into the room. Alma realized that her meeting with Bluebeard was at an end. It was time for her to go.

Thankful that her hand had finally stopped shaking,

Alma turned and climbed the ladder that led outside. As the rain hit her shoulders, she realized how cold she was and shivered. Her move-by-wire system immediately rerouted the reflexive action, auto-stimulating her muscles until they were warm again, but the feeling that had caused the shiver stayed with her.

She tried to tell herself that Bluebeard was a shadowrunner, not a cybersurgeon. What did he know about TLE? As soon as Alma had tracked down the woman who had framed her and proved her innocence to Mr. Lali, she would get PCI's physicians to give her a thorough physical and book her in for cybersurgery.

But a horrible thought kept nagging her: what if Bluebeard was right about the TLE progressing to the seizure stage in a week or two? He said he'd had a move-by-wire system himself—and the operative word there was "had." His jerky movements and lack of mobility all added up to one thing: a TLE-damaged brain.

Alma had the sinking feeling that she didn't have much time.

Conflict

Night Owl jandered past the block-long line of people who were waiting impatiently outside the nightclub. Most of the "magers" who huddled under the sidewalk awnings to avoid the rain were in their late teens through early thirties, but there were a handful of older hopefuls as well. All were geared out in anything they thought would get them in the door: chill black leathers with chromed spikes, sequined button blanket capes, hoop skirts made from glow tubes, LoGo wear that flashed corporate logos like a billboard across their chests, and gold foil suits. Some were flexing cyberware, but most were unenhanced, their near-naked bodies hung with fake magical foci or tattooed with "mystic" sigils. They jostled for position in line, all eyes straining toward the door each time it opened with a rush of music and noise. Not many people were leaving; even at 3 a.m. the club was still revving.

The club was located in a warehouse on the city's east side that was three stories tall and covered with a dense, carefully tended growth of ivy. The club's owners didn't want anyone sneaking inside; the doors were warded and would only admit astrals who had paid the cover charge in advance.

The bouncer was a Caucasian troll whose curving, ram's-head horns brushed the top of the doorway she stood in. Her iron-gray hair was buzzed short. Both of her lower tusks were capped with gold, and the fingernails on her massive hands were also gilded. She wore jeans, cowboy boots with built-in spurs, and a long-sleeved black T-shirt with the words MAGIC BOX down each arm; the letters kept changing color and emitted a haze of fizzing sparks. A shock glove covered one blocky fist; she kept the other hand on the red-velvet door rope as she eyed the crowd.

" 'Lo, Tatyana," Night Owl greeted her. "Busy night."

Tatyana grinned and waved Night Owl in out of the rain. "Long time," she rumbled. "I nearly didn't recognize you—the makeup looks good. You workin'?"

"Not tonight." Night Owl ran hands through her wet hair, combing it back out of her eyes. "I'm just here to unwind and spend some cred."

Thunder grumbled in the heavy skies above the buildings, and the rain increased in intensity. Night Owl heard a hoarse *caw-caw* from somewhere up the street as she stepped into the shelter of the doorway— it was probably another of the fraggin' storm crows that Hothead had talked about. She glanced back over her shoulder nervously. She'd already had her fill of "evil deities" and didn't want to meet up with any more dragons.

As the rain thundered down, the crowd waiting outside the door drew back to avoid the drops that were splashing up from the sidewalk. A couple at the back of the line gave up and ran to flag a cab.

"You want in?" Tatyana asked.

"Sure do." Night Owl glanced back at those in line but didn't see any hostiles. "I'm trying to keep a low profile—the Red Lotus are gunning for me. Any of them inside?"

The troll shook her head. "The R.L.s tend to hang at the Triple Eight. But if any of them show, I'll send in word."

"Thanks."

Tatyana unhitched the velvet cord and stepped aside. Night Owl jandered in through the door, chuckling as she heard the troll close it on the protests of those in line. Tatyana wasn't the brightest trog on the planet, but she owed Night Owl one, and that meant she'd be extra-watchful tonight.

Night Owl climbed a short flight of stairs to a room that had been painted to look like the inside of an Egyptian tomb. Hieroglyphs framed the club's inner door, which had an illusion spell cast on it to make it look like a velvet curtain. The door was actually armored steel, as more than one overrevved chiphead had found out after trying to slip past the inside bouncer by running through the "curtain." Music pulsed behind it, only slightly muffled by the heavy door.

The inside bouncer was a young shaman dressed in skintight, black vinyl pants that bulged suggestively. A snakeskin was knotted around his neck like a tie, the empty-eyed head hanging loose against his bare chest. His scalp was shaved except for a forelock of ink-black hair, which he flipped back with a nervous flick of his head. He motioned Night Owl forward.

Night Owl stood quietly as the shaman lifted his hands to either side of her shoulders, palms facing her. He slowly sank to his knees, sweeping his hands down to the level of her feet. Night Owl's skin tickled, as if invisible snake tongues were flickering across her flesh, and then the feeling disappeared as the shaman stood and held out a slender hand.

"You'll have to check the handgun."

Night Owl reached behind the waterproof duster she wore and pulled the Ares Predator out of the holster at the small of her back. She made sure the safety was on and handed it to the shaman. He stuck his hand into the wall to his right, and the gun and his arm up to the elbow disappeared. His hand came out with a token. Night Owl took it from him and turned toward the curtain-door.

The shaman slid in front of her, blocking her way. "You'll also need to check the shuriken."

Night Owl grinned apologetically, but the shaman's face remained stony. The throwing star pinned to her duster was disguised to look like a starburst brooch; she'd worn it so long that she had almost forgotten it was anything more than a piece of jewelry. But the tranq hidden inside the star's hollow center and the needles concealed in the arms of the star must have screamed "weapon" under the shaman's detection spell.

"Can I check the entire coat?" she asked.

The shaman nodded, took the coat and pushed the entire thing through the "wall," returning with another token, which he held out to Night Owl.

The shaman then pulled aside the velvet curtain, revealing a credit-transfer machine that was set into the door. Night Owl slotted a credstick—a clean one that she'd transferred the creds from Kageyama onto, just in case the one he'd given her included a tracer chip—and watched as its balance dropped by one hundred nuyen. Then the door swung open, and Night Owl was engulfed in a wave of overamped music as she stepped out onto the crowded catwalk that circled the central dance floor.

The Magic Box was little more than a gutted warehouse, its walls and ceiling painted a flat black. There were no tables or chairs, just a series of squat pillars, each about shoulder-high and inlaid with pentagrams. Mages and shamans—both professional magic jockeys and amateur spell chuckers—sat or stood on top of these platforms, casting their spells out over the dance floor. Their target was the crowd below: humans and metas jammed shoulder to shoulder who swayed in

time with the Mood Muzak, a chest-rattling mix of
subsonic vibration, tribal drum and gongs.

Illusion spells filled the air over the crowd in a chaotic mix: exploding fireworks, snarling dragon's heads,
neon butterflies, and comets that streaked through the
air, reverberating chords of music in their wake. But
it was the emotional manipulation spells that the
crowd came for; they expected their feelings to be
stripped raw from the highest highs to the lowest lows.
Amid the confusion of images, an illusion of a cruci-
fied Christ rose into the air and pinwheeled in a frantic
circle, spraying the crowd below with blood. Those hit
by the drops of blood were immediately plunged into
a religious fervor and fell to their knees, weeping.
Elsewhere on the dance floor, people either laughed,
cowered in fear, flushed with a sexual rush, or leaped
up and down shouting like fans at a combat biker game
as emotion-controlling spells swept over them like
breaking waves, leaving them gasping in their wake.

Night Owl nodded to herself as the pinwheel Christ
faded. It had to be one of Miracle Worker's illusions—
it looked like the former shadowrunner was still
moonlighting, despite the church gig. Night Owl
searched the platforms at the edge of the dance floor
for her chummer, but she had no idea what illusion
Miracle Worker was cloaked in tonight. She could
have been any one of the mages below.

Giving up the guessing game, Night Owl squeezed
her way along the metal-grid catwalk, which was
jammed with first-time magers who were still too timid
to venture down into the wash of spells. She jumped
for one of the polished brass poles near the catwalk,
slid down to the floor of the club, and ventured out
into the crowd.

She wound up dancing beside an enormous sasquatch who turned in a slow-mo circle, his hairy white
arms extended like rotor blades, and a cluster of

dwarves whose holopic headbands were projecting re-
alistic images of West Coast Native masks. The arched
beak of a thunderbird mask swept like a ghostly sword
through Night Owl's waist as one of the dwarves
whipped his head to the side and then back again.
Another mask seemed to purse its wooden mouth and
howl like a wolf, while the dwarf wearing it scrambled
around the floor on all fours.

A wave of giggles swept through the crowd toward
Night Owl, and a moment later she found herself dou-
bled over and clutching her stomach as tears spilled
down her face. The sasquatch's hairy arm thumped
down across her back in magic-induced camaraderie,
and then the wave was past, leaving them both gasping
for breath. Night Owl peeled the heavy arm off her
shoulders and staggered away.

She found herself in the middle of a group of young
Full Blood elves in Vashon Island suits who were
spraying each other's expensive clothing with water
pistols filled with body paint. A splatter of fire-red
paint hit Night Owl just as an illusory beam of sunlight
lanced down from the ceiling above. Bright green
grass appeared to burst out of the floor below her
feet. Even though she was wearing boots, it felt as
though she were standing on the soft springy grass in
bare feet.

Instantly her irritation at getting splashed was gone,
replaced by a warm, happy glow that flashed through
her like sunshine. She embraced one of the elves, hugging him like a long-lost brother. The elf, a teenager
with model-perfect features, smiled back at her and
shouted something in Salish that was lost in the
throbbing music. It didn't matter that she couldn't understand him; she felt a rush of empathy for the kid.
She could also sense the petty jealousy of everyone
who looked at him like hot wax dripping on her ex-
posed back.

She gripped his face in her hands. "It's not our fault that we're perfect," she shouted back at him. "We were made in the year of the rat—the year of the lab rat!"

Then the beam of sunlight swept away. The kid wrenched his face out of her hands, his eyes shooting a wave of hot anger at Night Owl. She backed away, surprised to see that her hands had left bruises on his cheeks. In that same instant, a rush of excitement swept across the crowd. Caught up in its frenzy, the elf and his friends ran after it, whooping with glee. Suddenly alone, Night Owl realized she'd been projecting her own insecurities—filling in a stranger's blanks with her own past.

She sagged her way over to the edge of the room and sat on the floor with her back against one of the pillars. Here in the shadow between the pillar and the wall, with the catwalk a few meters over her head, she was temporarily out of the streams of magic that pulsed across the dance floor.

She found herself at eye level with one of the club's astral patrons: a spirit with grainy, concrete-colored skin and blinking eyes that looked as though they were covered in oil slicks. The spirit's scalp was hidden by a multicolored tangle of hair-thin electrical wires. It wore a suit made from a patchwork of discarded fast-food wrappers and had plastic bags wrapped around its feet. It smiled at Night Owl, then opened its mouth into a perfect rectangle, exposing twin rows of square teeth that were miniature computer-monitor screens.

Words scrolled across the incisors: SOMEONE'S LOOKING FOR YOU.

Night Owl sat up.

"Who?"

A MAN WITH STRANGE EYES.

"Why are you telling me this?"

TATYANA SENT ME TO FIND YOU.

Night Owl sprang to her feet, keeping the pillar between herself and the dance floor. She leaned out to scan the crowd but didn't see anyone she recognized as a Red Lotus ganger. That didn't mean anything, though. The shaman Wu had already proved that he could sneak up on her invisibly, and the Red Lotus were always recruiting new members from the city's illegals. That teenage girl in the shimmy skirt might be a ganger—she could have sneaked a blade into the club tucked into her ample cleavage. Or the old guy with flexible glow tubes braided into his beard who kept glancing over his shoulder like he was afraid someone was going to jump him. He was a Euro, but he might be with the Red Lotus, just the same. You never could tell who was going to put a bullet into your back . . .

Had the spirit moved? Night Owl spun around, her right eye twitching like crazy. Her left hand whipped to her empty holster in a futile search for her Predator. Then she realized what had just happened. When she'd leaned out from behind the pillar, she'd been caught in the edge of a paranoia wash.

Only when her heart slowed its beat from rapid-fire to single shot did her eye finally stop spasming. She leaned back against the pillar, catching her breath. Even without the emotion spell pumping her full of adrenaline, she realized she'd made a mistake in coming to the Magic Box. She needed to shift out of here, before the man with the strange eyes found her. Unless . . .

She looked down at the spirit, which was waiting patiently beside her. Crouching down so that it would hear her over the chest-rattling music, she shouted into its ear, "Did Tatyana let the man with the strange eyes inside?"

The spirit grinned. YES.

"Is he with the Red Lotus?"

NO. TATYANA SAID SHE'D NEVER SEEN HIM BEFORE.

Night Owl sighed with relief. Tatyana had run with the Screamin' Mimis for several years and knew every ganger in town. Maybe Strange Eyes wasn't looking to flatline Night Owl after all. The encounter with Wu and his dragon master two nights ago had left her twitchy. For all she knew, the guy was another Johnson with a nice, fat credstick in his hand.

"Where is he?"

The spirit slowly scanned the room. I DON'T SEE HIM.

Great. Night Owl would have to scope the fellow out on her own. She thanked the spirit, which dematerialized back into the concrete floor, leaving a scattering of food wrappers behind, and stood with her back against the wall, trying to keep out of the wash of spells. Her night-vision goggles were hanging from a clip on her belt. She snugged them down over her eyes and activated their binocular function. The most logical place to stand and look for someone was on the catwalks above. Night Owl slowly turned her head, scanning for anyone who matched the description the spirit had given her.

She spotted her target halfway down the catwalk on her left. She knew he had to be her man—he had the strangest eyes she'd ever seen: pure white, without a hint of iris or pupil. They had to be cybered—although why he hadn't opted for natural-tint models or even mirrored lenses was a mystery. The bulging expanse of white reminded her of a hard-boiled egg.

She studied his profile and then decreased the magnification until his entire body was within the goggles' field of view.

Strange Eyes was Eurasian—no surprise, so was half the population of Vancouver—with an elongated face and a high forehead creased deeply with frown lines. He seemed to be naturally bald—there wasn't any stubble on his scalp—and was probably in his mid-forties. He wore white dress linens, an Armanté cloak that hung as if it was lined with ballistic cloth, and soft black cotton slippers that were probably soaked through, given the heavy rain outside. He stood like a terra cotta statue of an ancient Chinese warrior, arms folded over his chest, his strange white eyes staring out over the crowd. Despite the throng of people moving back and forth across the catwalk, no one bumped into him. It was as if he projected an aura that defied anyone to so much as brush against him.

Night Owl reached into her pocket and pulled out a parking token, flipping it into the air and catching it without even looking at it. Heads, she'd meet with Strange Eyes and see what he had to say. Tails, she'd blow out of here and leave the freaky fragger behind. Still staring at her man through her goggles, she ran a fingertip across the token, reading the face of it by feel. She felt the squarish outline of a longhouse: tails. Time to fade.

Something about the mystery man held her attention, however, as she slipped the token back into her pocket. She zoomed the goggles back in for a closer look at his face. She was curious about those eyes— was he blind? It was odd that he never blinked. Not once.

Just as his face filled her field of view, he turned his head. Although she was more than a hundred meters away from him, Night Owl felt a chill run down her spine as his gaze met hers full on. Although she couldn't tell where those blank white eyes were looking, she was certain he had seen her. She felt as though her gut had suddenly filled with ice water.

An illusion flashed in the air between them, flooding the goggles with a bright blue-white light that left

Night Owl blinking. Yanking the goggles away from her eyes, she saw that one of the mages had filled the air above the dance floor with a roiling mushroom cloud. Surround-sound speakers spread a rumble across the dance floor, rattling Night Owl's chest until it was difficult to breathe. When the mushroom cloud cleared a second or two later, the man with the blank white eyes was gone from the catwalk.

Still blinking away the spots from her eyes, Night Owl hurried toward a spiral staircase in the corner of the room. The brief close-up of Strange Eyes had creeped her out; she wouldn't have done any biz with him even if the token had landed heads-up. She certainly didn't want to come face to face with the fragger here in the club, without the comfortable weight of her Ares Predator in her holster.

She climbed the stairs two at a time, deked her way past a slower group of giggle-gasping patrons, and burst into a run as soon as she hit the catwalk. The exit door was just ahead.

So was Strange Eyes. He stood just in front of the exit, one hand extended toward her, palm up, as if he expected her to take his hand. Skidding to a halt, Night Owl found herself mesmerized by his blank white eyes, which both repulsed and compelled her. She began backing slowly away but found herself unable to look at anything but those bulging white orbs. His fingers twitched—once, impatiently—and a voice whispered in her mind as he spoke: *Come with me.*

Like a sleepwalking child, Night Owl walked forward and took his hand, letting him lead her through the exit door. A distant part of her mind was screaming in protest, but the spell he'd used to influence her was too strong to resist. As they passed through the room at the top of the stairs, Night Owl wrenched her head to the side and shot a pleading look at the shaman with the snakeskin tie. The effort took everything she had; it was almost impossible to make her body do anything more than follow Strange Eyes through the room. Words seemed to creak out of her mouth, and sweat trickled down her forehead as she forced a hand into her pocket to pull out a token.

"My . . . coat."

Strange Eyes paused, obviously wanting to keep up the facade that Night Owl was going with him willingly. The shaman, oblivious to Night Owl's struggle, bowed and took the token from her trembling hand. He reached into the wall and came out with her duster.

Strange Eyes plucked the duster from her hand and draped it over his arm. He tugged on Night Owl's hand, forcing her to follow him down the stairs.

The door opened, and Strange Eyes walked her out of the club. As they passed Tatyana, the troll took one look and threw a slap at Strange Eyes with her shock glove. Without even looking at her, Strange Eyes whipped his body to the side, avoiding her blow. He barked two words at her: "Stand aside!" Tatyana shuddered, then slowly backed out onto the sidewalk. Rain soaking her broad shoulders, she stared helplessly as Night Owl was led away.

As they walked down the sidewalk, Strange Eyes patted down Night Owl's duster, checking its pockets, and then handed the coat to her and gestured that she should wear it. She pulled it on stiffly over her already soaking-wet shirt and followed him around the corner to a Mitsubishi Nightsky limousine with Seattle plates. A door in the back opened, and Strange Eyes climbed inside. Still compelled by the spell he had cast upon her, Night Owl followed.

The door closed with a weighty thud that told Night Owl the limo was armored, and she heard locks click into place. The inside of the vehicle was climate-controlled, but Night Owl shivered as she sat down on the plush suede bench seat that faced the one Strange

Eyes was sitting on. Somewhere behind a smoked glass panel that hid the rest of the limo's interior, a driver put the car into gear. The limo rolled smoothly out into traffic, away from the Magic Box.

Strange Eyes sat quietly, staring at nothing and everything. Unlike Night Owl, he was perfectly dry; only the soles of his feet left damp patches on the carpet. He'd dropped the spell he'd used to compel Night Owl to follow him; she could no longer feel the back-of-the-neck tingle of magic at work. But the fact that Strange Eyes was sitting alone with her in the cavernous limo interior, without any muscle to back him up, suggested to Night Owl that he was either very powerful or overly confident. She didn't want to gamble on the latter.

She took comfort in one fact: if his goal had been to flatline her, she'd be a corpse already. She steeled her voice and did her best to meet the blank look of those bulging white eyes. "What do you want?"

She almost expected a telepathic voice to accompany his words, like the one that had whispered in her mind when he worked his magic upon her. But it seemed his vocal cords did work independently after all.

"Information." He laid his hands gently on his knees. His fingers were long and narrow, and a band of green stone—a jade ring—was on the little finger of his left hand. "The dragon Chiao hired you to perform a task for him. I want to know what it was."

His English was fluent but slightly clipped; after a moment Night Owl placed his accent: Singapore. His question told her that he wasn't with the Red Lotus, and the fact that Tatyana hadn't recognized him meant that he probably wasn't local. The limo told her he was fronting for someone with nuyen—lots of it. She decided that Strange Eyes must be with a rival gang—one with a vested interest in whatever the Red Lotus was up to.

Spilling the skinny on a run wasn't something a smart shadowrunner did—not if she wanted to continue breathing. But if Strange Eyes was as powerful as he made himself out to be, he just might give the Red Lotus and its dragon master a run for their money. If a gang war broke out, maybe Night Owl would be temporarily overlooked; she could do a fade while both sides dusted it up. With luck, there wouldn't be any survivors left to remember her.

She didn't want to appear too eager to spill, however, so she pretended to stall for time. She dropped the dragon's name as if she'd known it all along.

"How do you know about my meet with Chiao?" she asked. "And how did you find me?"

Strange Eyes slid his long fingers into the breast pocket of his jacket and pulled out a SkyTrain token. "I had a little chat with Wu. He gave me your name."

He leaned forward and handed Night Owl the token. She glanced down at it and saw a crust of what looked like dried blood on one side. She rubbed the token against the wet fabric of her jeans, cleaning it. Whoever Strange Eyes was, he'd just paid for any information he wanted, as far as she was concerned.

"Chiao hired me to steal a jade statue."

"Who from?"

"Akira Kageyama."

Strange Eyes never blinked, but his posture suddenly stiffened. "Describe the statue."

Night Owl told him about the statue of Fu Shen that she'd boosted from Kageyama's condoplex. When she got to the part about a Chinese character being engraved on the statue's back, Strange Eyes practically vibrated with excitement.

"What did it say?"

"*Fu*," Night Owl answered. "Bat."

The frown lines in Strange Eyes' forehead deepened. He turned his head slightly, as if glancing elsewhere while he was thinking, and Night Owl could sense that he was no longer looking directly at her. She shrugged off the wet duster, laying it down on the seat next to her with the star-shaped "brooch" uppermost. She played with the SkyTrain token, keeping her left hand within a few centimeters of the shuriken. It was still pinned to the lapel, but if she could contrive a way to prick Strange Eyes with it, she might be able to take him down. All she needed to do was "drop" the SkyTrain token into the folds of the duster, and that would give her the excuse she needed to pick the coat up. The windows were all tinted inkblack, and Night Owl couldn't see any surveillance vidcams in the limo; she suspected that Strange Eyes wanted to keep this conversation private. That was to her advantage—there wouldn't be anyone looking on when she made her move . . .

The blank eyes swung back in her direction. "Did Chiao say why he wanted the statue?"

It was time to curry favor, to try to get Strange Eyes to relax. Night Owl tossed him another byte of data. "The dragon wasn't interested in the statue itself. Chiao wanted whatever was inside it. The statue was hollow."

Strange Eyes' bulging white eyes bored into her with an intensity that prickled Night Owl's skin.

"What was inside it?" he asked.

Night Owl paused, trying to decide whether to bluff. If she made up something that sounded valuable and told Strange Eyes that she'd have to lead him to it, maybe he'd keep her alive. On the other hand, maybe he'd decide that she knew too much. She let her gaze drop to the SkyTrain token in her hands and frowned at it as she turned it over and over, wishing she could let it make a heads-or-tails decision for her.

Strange Eyes read more into her glance than she'd intended. "A coin," he whispered. "Of course."

Night Owl could hear awe and greed in his voice. She looked up, met his blank stare, and nodded. "That's right," she said, embellishing as she went along. "A lucky coin."

Strange Eyes blinked.

Night Owl could see that she'd startled him—and that somehow, unwittingly, she'd blundered. She was within a millimeter of being flatlined—as soon as he found out whatever else he wanted to know, she could kiss her hoop goodbye. Strange Eyes leaned forward on the seat, his slender fingers curving into the shape of claws.

"It's the fourth Coin of Luck, isn't it?" he hissed. "Where is it now?"

Night Owl jerked back, pretending to be startled. Her left hand fell on the duster. She dropped her voice to a whisper, as if she were spooked. "I gave the statue to Chiao, but I took the coin out of it first. It's in—"

Strange Eyes had been leaning forward, straining to hear her. Still speaking, Night Owl whipped the duster across the space that separated them. The shuriken's points jammed up against the back of his hand, and should have bitten deeply into his flesh. Instead they merely bent, and the knockout drug inside the shuriken's hollow center flowed out onto Night Owl's fingers, wasted.

Strange Eyes knocked the duster aside with a sweeping motion so fast that his hand blurred. His other hand shot out and found Night Owl's throat.

"That was foolish," he hissed.

Night Owl tried to swallow, but couldn't.

"Where is the coin now?" he asked aloud. Then he added a mental command: *Tell me.*

As magic forced her lips open, Night Owl knew she

was a dead woman. His spell would prevent her from lying. Her right eye began twitching furiously. She had no choice but to speak the truth. "I don't have—"

From somewhere outside the limo came a tremendous explosion. The rear of the vehicle bucked up with a creaking of twisted metal, and Strange Eyes tumbled forward into Night Owl's lap. He sprang away from her as the rear of the car slammed back down onto the ground, and he twisted to look out a window. Even though the glass was heavily tinted, he stared at it as if he could see what was happening outside.

When he threw himself flat on the seat, Night Owl followed his lead. A second later, the side window bulged in and then shattered as something that sounded like a jackhammer hit it. A shower of tinted glass sprayed into the back of the limo, dusting them both like black snow, and then the window on the other side of the car exploded outward. With both side windows gone, the sound of a machine gun outside was suddenly very loud. The armor-piercing rounds that had taken out the windows chewed into the interior of the car, shredding the fabric in the ceiling. Other bullets punched into the sides of the limo, sounding like hammers on steel.

Peering up through a shattered window from where she lay on the seat, Night Owl could see traffic lights and street signs sliding by. The limo was still straining forward, even with its rear wheels blown out. She could hear the *thwack-thwack-thwack* of shredded rubber, the roar of exhaust through what was left of the muffler, and the shrieking of metal on cement as the limo dragged itself along the street by its front wheels.

The bullets were hitting the rear of the vehicle now, no longer chewing up the inside, and Strange Eyes' attention was totally focused out the back window, which was still intact. It was now or never.

Night Owl launched herself forward, grabbing the

window frame and hauling herself out of the vehicle. She flipped out the window, bending at the waist, and then tumbled forward and out of the car. As soon as her hands touched the pavement, she tucked into a somersault and rolled away from the limo. Cars veered around her, horns blaring, and then she jumped up onto the curb.

Her luck had changed: she'd bailed in an intersection. The limo was screeching away to her right, and whoever had been shooting at it was to her left. Night Owl sprinted toward a side street, turning her head left at the last moment to see who'd been tossing all the lead. She caught a glimpse of a familiar face: it was the ganger who'd been in the Saab.

Adrenaline pumping, Night Owl pounded down the block and around another corner. She heard the wailing of a siren close by; it sounded like the TPs were only a few blocks away. Behind her, the gunfire suddenly stopped. She heard the scream of tires on cement and an engine accelerating. It roared away in the opposite direction from where she was headed.

Night Owl ducked into the shadow of an alley and stopped to catch her breath as a Tribal Police cruiser flashed by.

It looked as though she hadn't needed to stir the pot: the Red Lotus and whatever gang Strange Eyes was from had already started mixing it up. But Night Owl didn't hold out the hope that either side would forget her any time soon. The Red Lotus had seen her coming out of the limo and would assume she'd tipped Strange Eyes off about Chiao and his interest in the "Coins of Luck"—whatever those were. They'd want their kilo of flesh as payback. Strange Eyes, meanwhile, would assume that Night Owl knew where the coin was. He wasn't about to just let her go, either.

Night Owl pulled the SkyTrain token out of her pocket and tumbled it across her fingers, trying to decide what to do next. It looked as though she'd jumped out of the crucible and into the fire. A coin flip wasn't going to do her much good now. No matter which she chose—heads or tails—she'd get burned.

Small
Accomplishments

Alma boarded the SkyTrain and sat down. The advertisements that lined the platform slid away as the elevated train pulled out of the station, electric engine cycling through its distinctive pattern of three rising whines. She stared at the cellphone in her hand, contemplating the message the rogue Superkid had left on it. Like the I Ching reading she'd cast earlier this morning, the message was disturbing. Her nemesis not only knew about Alma's difficulties at PCI but seemed also to be hinting, with the "sound sleep" crack, that she knew about the beta-test cyberware inside Alma's head.

Alma had thought that knowledge of the REM inducer had died with Gray Squirrel. Now she wondered if this woman had tortured it out of him before slitting his throat.

The message had been on her cellphone when Alma first checked it at 7 a.m. She had reread it twenty times in the hour and a half since then.

HI AL. HOPE YOU SLEPT WELL. BUT THEN, YOU AND I BOTH KNOW HOW SOUNDLY YOU CAN SLEEP, DON'T WE?

WATCH YOUR HOOP TODAY. THE RED LOTUS MAY COME GUNNING FOR YOU. AND KEEP A HEADS-UP FOR A GUY WITH WEIRD

WHITE EYES—HE'LL FRAG YOUR MIND UP FASTER THAN YOU CAN BLINK.

SO . . . HAVE YOU GUESSED WHO I AM YET?

Alma cleared the screen, finally erasing the message. She took a moment to compose her reply and then spoke into the cell. "I know that you're a Superkid from Batch Alpha. What I want to know now is what you want. Meet with me. Leave me a message where you'll be, and when, and I'll be there."

She watched as the phone translated her message into text and stored it as a memo. The next time the rogue Superkid accessed Alma's cell to leave a taunting message, she'd see it.

But that was the strange thing: this morning's message didn't have the same tone as the others. It hadn't been a taunt but a warning—albeit one that Alma didn't fully understand. She'd heard of the Red Lotus: they were one of the more notorious gangs in Vancouver. Presumably the man with "weird white eyes" was one of their members. Obviously the rogue Superkid had angered this individual and now faced some sort of retaliation. Because she was a dead ringer for Alma, the gang members were liable to take a shot at Alma if they saw her. The rogue Superkid wanted to warn her about them.

But that begged a question. Having gone to all that trouble to frame Alma and get her suspended from her job at PCI, why did the woman now want to keep her alive?

Alma pondered her options. If the rogue Superkid agreed to a meeting, there was no point in going through with Kageyama's extraction. But if the woman wouldn't agree, then infiltrating the shadowrunner community would be the only way Alma could get closer to her.

She decided to wait and see what happened in the

next hour and a half. If a reply message appeared on her cellphone before 10 a.m., she would abort the extraction. If not . . .

Over and above the disturbing message on her cellphone, this morning's I Ching reading was also cause for concern. The trigrams had been water over fire, two elements that opposed each other. Together they made up the hexagram Small Accomplishments. While the reading indicated that her day would begin well enough, it hinted at trouble to come, if balance and flexibility were not maintained: *What begins auspiciously may end up in chaos.* Hope was offered, however, by the fact that four of the lines were either changing yin or changing yang. Later, the hexagram would change into the one for Great Possession. The I Ching seemed to be indicating that if Alma could maintain a balanced and flexible course, then disaster and chaos could be averted long enough for her to gain a "great possession": Akira Kageyama, perhaps?

As the SkyTrain slid quietly along its elevated track, Alma stared out the window. It was raining; the clouds that had hung over the city for the past week like a wet gray blanket still stretched from one end of the city to the other. Watery daylight filtered through them, washing all color from the city. The graffiti on the buildings below, obscured by the rain that drizzled down the window, looked streaky and blurred, a pale shadow of its usual defiant colors.

Despite the rain, the streets below teemed with life. This branch of the SkyTrain line looped above the Downtown Eastside, where BTL dealers, pimps and gangers swam like sharks through milling schools of chipheads, prostitutes, street people and illegal immigrants. Back when Vancouver was still part of Canada, the area was known as "Canada's poorest postal code." During the forty-four years that the Salish-Shidhe Council had been responsible for it, the Downtown Eastside hadn't fared much better. Like a mold that grows back, no matter how powerful the cleaning solution, it resisted every attempt to scrub it free of crime and poverty. Hundreds of thousands of nuyen spent on social programs disappeared into the Downtown Eastside without a trace, like water into a sponge.

Rising out of the middle of this desolation, looking like a bar of gold that had been stood on end in a garbage heap, was the Woodwards Arcology. Twenty-two stories tall and four city blocks wide at its base, the self-contained city within a city was a rectangular slab of gold-tinted glass and concrete. The windows on its lower stories were thick enough to prevent even a T-bird from smashing through, and the only doors at ground level were heavily monitored emergency exits. The only two legitimate points of entry were the helicopter landing pads on the roof and the SkyTrain station tunnel that pierced the arcology's third story.

The Woodwards Arcology had been named after a department store that had once stood on the site—a building that activists had sought for decades to turn into housing for the Downtown Eastside's homeless. Like those dreams, the original store was long gone. The only thing that had been salvaged was the enormous "W" that had stood on top of the original building. Five meters high and illuminated by red neon, it had blazed like a beacon over Vancouver for more than a century. Urban legend had it that if you could climb the arcology's ice-slick glass to the rooftop and touch the W, you would become wealthy beyond your wildest dreams, but the only people who profited were the vultures who waited on the streets below to pick over the flattened corpses of those who fell to their deaths.

Alma looked up at the helicopters that buzzed around the rooftop of the arcology. In one hour and fifty-eight minutes—assuming he was on time—Buzz, the shadowrunner who was providing tactical support on this assignment, would be landing his sky cab on the roof. Assuming that she didn't abort the extraction before then, Alma would need to get Kageyama to the roof at 10:30 a.m. on the dot.

As SkyTrain slid into the station, Alma rose to her feet. Smoothing her silk Zoé skirt, she waited until the doors of the train car slid open and then walked with the other disembarking passengers toward the security checkpoint. She firmly resisted the urge to make sure that the yellow square of plastic that was Jane Lee's resident ID permit was still pinned above the breast pocket of her suit jacket. Secguards were trained to watch for nervous gestures; she'd be singled out for extra scrutiny unless she appeared relaxed and self-assured. As she passed a mirrored wall—probably a one-way window for visual surveillance—she pretended to be checking her appearance. She patted the neat bun that she'd rolled her hair into that morning and glanced down as if making sure her jacket wasn't creased. The ID card was still there.

The SkyTrain passengers funneled between twin plastic pillars tall enough that a troll passing between them would be bracketed from the horns down. Inside the pillars were scanners that could be calibrated to penetrate anything from cloth to inch-thick steel. The scan would reveal any weapons, explosives or hazardous materials, regardless of whether they were merely carried on the body or were built into cyberware.

Alma had hidden her two "weapons" in the spot that was most likely to be missed: inside the heels of her stylish, spike-heeled shoes. With luck, the secguard at the console up ahead would get sloppy and wouldn't scan her all the way to the ground. If he did spot the injectors, however, she had a story ready: they were part of a patented new shock-absorption system.

As she passed between the pillars, Alma held her breath. A moment later, she was through the checkpoint without any questions being asked. Curious, she angled across the station to a spot where she could see the monitor where the secguard sat. She saw the answer immediately: the scanner had been set so that it penetrated cloth only—it hadn't even scanned the interiors of her shoe heels. Naked blue-white figures walked across the screen, oblivious to the fact that the scanners were electronically undressing them.

By sheer luck, Alma had managed to smuggle her injector into the Woodwards Arcology completely undetected. She decided that it must be the first of the small but significant accomplishments the I Ching had predicted.

Dr. Silverman leaned an elbow on her desk as she studied the three-dimensional rendering of Alma's brain that hovered in the air above the projection pad. With a slight frown, she sent a signal along the fiberoptic cable that connected her to a cyberterminal on her desk, commanding the projected image to rotate and sectionalize. Like pieces of sliced bread falling away from the main loaf, slices of the image separated, fell to the horizontal plane and then vanished, allowing the cybersurgeon to look deeper into the brain.

"I don't see any evidence of chronically dysfunctional tissue," Silverman said. She pointed with her finger, and a glowing red dot materialized inside the left half of the image, which had been coded yellow and green and blue to differentiate between the different regions of the brain. "I would expect any tissue damage to be localized here, in the precentral gyrus, or here, in the premotor cortex, but both of those regions appear healthy.

"This is your move-by-wire system." The glowing

red dot drifted toward a boxy, black shape at the base of the brain and then followed the tendrils of black that stretched down from it. The display shifted to show a marquee of alphanumeric code and what looked like a circuit-by-circuit diagram.

"It seems to be functioning within normal limits, and all of its synaptic and neural connections are intact. I don't see any damaged tissue—nothing that would induce temporal lobe epilepsy."

Alma was reclining on the examining couch with a diagnostic probe plugged into one of the chipjacks at the nape of her neck. The news that her tremors weren't TLE was reassuring and frightening at the same time. It was a relief to know that her brain tissue wasn't deteriorating and that her central nervous system wasn't about to be thrown into a permanent state of seizure. But it was unnerving not to know what was causing the tremors—not to have any data on how severe the problem would become.

Dr. Silverman turned to face Alma. She looked young: she had the muscle tone and smooth skin of someone in her early twenties, but that was probably due to age inhibitors. A gold wedding band with Native totems confirmed her citizenship: only Full Bloods were allowed to wear jewelry or clothing that depicted a clan animal.

"Have you experienced any feelings of alienation or depersonalization?" she asked.

"No."

"What about perceptual distortions? Any difficulty in determining distance or locating the source of a sound?"

"No. My cyberears and eyes seem to be in perfect order. Why? Do you think they're the source of the tremors?"

"No." The doctor shook her head. "Those are just symptoms that can crop up if the move-by-wire system creates a secondary focus in the motor systems. Other symptoms include impotence, incontinence—"

"No," Alma added quickly. "Nothing like that."

Dr. Silverman turned back to the brain scan and centered the glowing red dot on a black shadow inside the pons region. Alma recognized the cyberware as the REM inducer. It had the same diameter and thickness as one of her I Ching coins and was surrounded by a series of induction wires that gave it the appearance of a flattened spider. There was a cylindrical bulge on one side that Alma guessed must be the miniature bomb that had been hardwired into the inducer.

"What's this device?" the doctor asked. "I don't recognize it."

Alma wove together fact and fiction. If she was going to find out what was really causing her tremors, she had to tell the doctor at least part of the truth.

"It's experimental cyberware," Alma answered. "I suffer from seasonal affective disorder. I volunteered six months ago to have a serotonin inducer put in, to see if it would alleviate my depression during the winter."

She gave the doctor a convivial grin and continued on in a prattling tone. "I'm so glad I volunteered for the study, especially with the terrible weather we've had lately. Normally, I'd be flat on my back for eight hours a day, under a bank of artificial lights."

Dr. Silverman nodded, her eyes on the scan. Alma could tell that she was adjusting something; a series of three-dimensional bar graphs materialized beside the holo of the brain and then disappeared.

"The device seems to be functioning," she said. "There's current flowing through it, and your serotonin levels are high—above normal range."

"Could it be responsible for the tremors in my hand?" Alma asked.

"It has to be—I can't see any other reason for them. Given the region of the brain where it's situated, the device may be triggering pontine geniculate occipital spikes. PGO spikes typically occur during sleep; they're the cause of the rapid eye movements that occur when we dream. They can also trigger involuntary motor activity elsewhere in the body, especially in the extremities. If you've ever watched a cat or dog while it's in REM sleep, you might have noticed a sudden twitching of its paws at the same time that rapid eye movements are occurring."

The doctor paused, lost in thought. "It's strange, though, that only your left hand is affected. Why not your right hand—or your feet? Have there been any signs of tremors in your other extremities?"

"None," Alma answered. "They're steady and strong."

"Have you experienced any hallucinations—any dreamlike visions?"

Alma shook her head.

"Who installed the cyberware?" the doctor asked. "I'd like to consult with the engineer who designed it."

"That's not possible," Alma said. "He's . . . unavailable at the moment. He had an accident and is recovering in a private clinic. That's why I came here. I've had the tremors for ten days, and I didn't want to put off seeing someone any longer."

Alma activated the clock in her cybereye. It was 9:47 a.m.—just thirteen minutes before Kageyama's appointment. Her examination by the cybersurgeon had run longer than her appointed half-hour. She needed to get out to the waiting room, to see if Kageyama had arrived yet. She tried to use her augmented hearing to listen for voices behind the closed door, but the room's soundproofing blocked all noise from the corridor and waiting room outside.

"Of course, your problem just might resolve itself, you know," the doctor added.

"What do you mean?" Alma asked.

The doctor touched an icon, and a number—50:12:05—glowed in the air beside the brain scan. It looked like the readout from a clock, except that the first number was too large. But the last part of the number was ticking away at one-second intervals, so Alma assumed it represented hours, minutes and seconds. She matched the number against her retinal clock, and did a quick calculation. The countdown would end two days from now, at noon on February 28.

Alma shuddered as she realized what that date meant. Hu hadn't been exaggerating during their hushed conversation outside the boardroom. When he'd said that Mr. Lali had decided to "terminate" Alma, but that he'd gained her some time, he'd been speaking literally. That countdown was coming from the cranial bomb that was slaved to her REM inducer. If Alma didn't find the rogue Superkid before noon on the 28th, it would explode.

Dr. Silverman had reached her own, erroneous conclusion: "It looks like your serotonin inducer is programmed to enter a new cycle in two days' time," she said. "Perhaps it's going to step down your serotonin dosage. If it does, it's possible that the tremors will stop when your serotonin levels return to normal. I'd like to run some further scans after the cycle changes. Are you able to come back on February 28, at 2 p.m.?"

"What?" Alma asked. It was difficult to tear her mind away from the realization that the bomb inside her head was counting down the hours, minutes and seconds until a portion of her brain was destroyed. How had the bomb been activated? Given Hu's comment about Alma having four days to prove herself innocent, it had to have been at some point during her meeting with him and Mr. Lali in the boardroom. Then she remembered the peculiar sequence of numbers that had flashed across the monitor screen just before the vidclips started: the numbers nine through one, squared and counted down to one, followed by a date that had flashed by too quickly for her conscious mind to register. The countdown had to have been the activator for the bomb, and the subliminal-message date had given the countdown its end point.

A wave of fear washed over Alma as it hit home that she was under a death sentence, and only with an effort was she able to shake it off. It's a test, she told herself. Just like the endless tests they put her through in the Superkids program. She would think of it as a test and nothing more.

She still had fifty hours. That would be plenty of time to find the rogue Superkid and prove to Mr. Lali that he'd been wrong about her. In the meantime, she had to deal with the here and now.

"Can you do something for me?" Alma asked. "Is it possible to slave the inducer's countdown with my retinal clock's countdown function?"

"Yes, but I've already told you when—"

"Please do it."

Dr. Silverman plugged a device into Alma's eye and made a few adjustments, and then asked Alma to trigger her retinal clock and put it into countdown mode. The numbers 50:03:01 appeared, and a second later blinked to 50:03:00 and continued counting down. Withdrawing the instrument from Alma's eye, the doctor motioned for her to bend her head forward and unplugged the diagnostic probe.

"I'll have our pharmacist make up a dopamine booster for you," she said, handing Alma a card with the date and time of the appointment she'd scheduled. "We'll see if that has any effect on the tremors. It will take about half an hour to prepare the inhaler. Will you be able to wait, or would you like it couriered to your home?"

Concentrate, Alma told herself, shutting the countdown off. She'd come here to do a job. She opened her cellphone and consulted it. The memo function held only the message she'd left for the rogue Superkid; there was no answering memo. It looked as though she was going ahead with the extraction.

"I'll wait for the inhaler," she told the doctor.

She folded up the cell. Aside from the anxiety of knowing that her time limit for finding the rogue Superkid was very real, everything was going smoothly. The prescription would give her an excuse to linger in the waiting room for thirty minutes—plenty of time for Kageyama to complete his appointment. Another small accomplishment.

Which made her nervous. According to the I Ching, a series of small accomplishments could be followed by a large disaster. All Alma could do was hope for the best—that the accomplishments that were stacking themselves like a house of cards didn't become so high that they tumbled.

Her target was sitting in the waiting room, channel surfing on a mini-telecom set that was built into the arm of an overstuffed chair. Alma recognized him only by the digipics she'd uploaded to her headware memory—without them, she'd never have been able to pick him out of a crowd. Kageyama was of average height and weight, with neatly cut black hair. He wore a conservative business suit and a brown leather jacket that looked casual at first glance but was carefully tailored.

Alma found herself staring at Kageyama's hands. Now that she knew what she was looking at, she could see the not-quite-natural bulge where his narrow hands had been widened to meet the cybered little fingers. Sensing her looking at him, Kageyama looked up. Alma smiled—it was hard not to, under the sensual frankness of those green eyes—and nodded at the telecom his hand rested on.

"Anything worth watching?" she asked.

"Not on the telecom," he answered. His eyebrow lifted slightly. "You seem familiar—have we met before?"

"I don't believe so," Alma said, extending her hand and leaning toward his chair. "Jane Lee."

Kageyama took her hand and inclined his head in a bow. The movement brought his lips close to the back of Alma's hand, and the warmth of his breath on her skin sent a shiver through her. She had the eerie feeling that they had met before, but it was probably just a result of her scanning the data on her target so thoroughly.

"Pleased to meet you, Ms. Lee. I'm—"

An automated receptionist—a two-dimensional image of a bronze robot with a gratingly polite English accent—shimmered into view on a wall-sized monitor beside them. "Mr. Kageyama, the technician can see you now. Please join Dr. Silverman in Examining Room Three."

Kageyama rose with a fluid grace that Alma would have sworn was the result of a move-by-wire system, had she not known about Kageyama's abhorrence for implanted cyberware. He bowed once more in Alma's direction. "Until later, Ms. Lee," he said with a twinkle in his eye. Then he turned down the corridor to the examining rooms.

Alma's anger at her instinctive attraction to him helped her to shake off the sensual lethargy that talking with Kageyama had left her with. She recognized her reaction for what it was: a magically induced effect. She'd experienced something similar once before, when, as a young secguard fresh out of the Justice

Institute, she'd been confronted with an intruder with magical capabilities. He'd used them to shape her emotions, giving her a warm, fuzzy glow that made her reluctant to taser him. Thankfully, she'd had backup; the PCI security guard she'd been teamed with at the time was out of the spell's range and took the man down with his first shot. Only later, as the intruder lay twitching, had Alma noticed the pistol in his hand. She'd been a trigger squeeze away from taking a bullet from her "friend."

She could see that she'd have to be equally careful with Kageyama. This time, there would be no backup.

The time was one minute past ten o'clock. According to Priority One Security's log books, Kageyama's visits to Executive Body Enhancements always ended within a minute or two, at most, of the appointed quarter-hour. Kageyama would return to the waiting room in fourteen minutes, plus or minus one.

She checked her cellphone for the third time—still no return message—and then stood and glided to the door of the clinic to stare out at the corridor, as if bored. The doors were one-way glass; the clinic's exclusive clientele demanded privacy from the moment they walked in the door. All anyone outside would be able to see was Alma's silhouette.

She spotted Kageyama's bodyguard at once. He was the human Euro with pale red hair just across the foyer, leaning next to the elevator and sipping from a paper soykaf cup. He was deliberately casual, but he stood with one thumb hitched into his belt, next to a holstered taser. His eyes tracked everyone who walked past the clinic entrance. Then they stopped, and his posture straightened slightly as he spotted Alma's silhouette. She waited a moment, glanced over her shoulder as if answering the call of a receptionist inside the clinic, and then turned away. Out of the corner of her eye she saw the bodyguard relax and resume his careful scrutiny of the corridor.

The man who had been seated next to Alma was called into an examining room by the receptionist, leaving Alma alone in the waiting room. She sat down and consulted the clock: eleven minutes and forty-nine seconds to go before Kageyama's appointment ended.

While she waited, she thought over what she had learned about the man. Or, rather, what Bluebeard had dug up and loaded onto the chip that Alma had slotted. She had to admit—albeit grudgingly—that the decker was good. He'd managed to dig up information that was decades old—data that had led Alma to some startling conclusions about the target of her extraction.

Kageyama's mother was a Japanese singer who became an overnight success in the 2010s when she changed her name to Benten and began performing songs inspired by Japanese mythology. Her hit song, "Tides of a Dragon's Heart," sold more vidclips in a single month than all of the other rock groups in the country sold in a year, combined.

In those days, the Japanese ate up anything that had even a tangential connection with dragons. Their country had seen the first-ever appearance of a great dragon in 2011, when Ryomyo announced himself by racing a bullet train near Mount Fuji, and the craze for dragons had built throughout that decade. Benten played upon her stage name: that of an ancient goddess of love, eloquence and music who had tamed a dragon and prevented him from devouring the children of a coastal village. She encouraged rumors that her songs, so unlike the limp pop ballads she had sung previously, were secretly written by a dragon. She even went so far as to claim that this muse—who, like all great dragons, had a voice that was audible only telepathically—was using her body as a vessel with which to sing.

One week later, in a much-hyped press conference, Benten tearfully announced that these claims were false. Her songs had actually been composed by her bass player, a mere human.

That was in 2020, when Benten was at the peak of her career. A few weeks later came the announcement that she was pregnant. In a complete reversal of her previous antics, the singer shunned the media spotlight and went into seclusion. Despite the fervent efforts of the Asian press, which speculated daily about who the father of her child might be, very little appeared on the newsnets about the birth itself. There were rumors of a stillbirth, unconfirmed reports that the child had been born with some sort of deformity, and, later, stories that the infant had been kidnapped from the hospital and a twenty-million-nuyen ransom demanded.

When Akira was presented to the media, those rumors were squashed. The baby was both healthy and whole. He had the normal complement of fingers on each hand in the vidpics that Bluebeard had provided—and, Bluebeard had discovered after noticing that a vidpic of the infant had been touched up, deep brown eyes.

Which didn't match up. Alma had just looked into the eyes of the adult Kageyama. They weren't cybered, and he wasn't wearing colored contact lenses. His eyes were a natural-looking green. While a baby's eyes will sometimes start blue-green and darken to brown, a brown-eyed baby grows up to become a brown-eyed adult.

Shortly after the birth, Benten had announced who the father was: the author of her songs, bass player Yoshi Kageyama. A DNA test that was leaked to the media confirmed that he had indeed fathered the child. A few months later, the couple split up, and a month after that Yoshi died of a BTL overdose.

Benten's songs lost their sparkle after Yoshi died,

and her popularity gradually waned. After several years of appearing only at retro concerts, she abandoned her career as a singer. She faded from the public eye and wasn't mentioned again by the newsnets until 2057—and then only posthumously, as a footnote—when Kageyama was named in Dunkelzahn's will as the recipient of the great dragon's Vancouver condoplex.

The other information that Bluebeard had gleaned added little that Alma hadn't already known. Kageyama was wealthy—the copyrights from his mother's early hits still brought in a substantial income. He had immigrated to the Salish-Shidhe nation in the early 2050s and had become a close friend of Vancouver's most famous part-time resident: Dunkelzahn.

Alma glanced up at the clock. Five minutes and eighteen seconds to go. When Kageyama emerged from his appointment, she would continue the conversation she'd initiated earlier and walk with him to the elevator. She had already prepared for what would come after the elevator doors closed—she'd broken off the heels on her pumps during an earlier visit to the washroom and changed into a pair of shoes she'd bought at the arcology. The injectors were concealed inside her jacket pockets. Taking down both Kageyama and his bodyguard with an injector to bare skin should be relatively easy, if she timed it right.

The seconds ticked away. Three minutes to go.

Kageyama would be emerging from the examining room any moment now. Alma stood up so that she could see out into the corridor. Was the Priority One bodyguard waiting outside the door or near the elevator?

The bodyguard was gone. In his place stood a Eurasian man wearing black pajama-style pants and a blood-red silk shirt. He stood with his back to the clinic, as if waiting for the elevator, but his head was turned to the side as if he was watching someone walk away from him down the corridor. Alma's hackles rose as she put one and one together and came up with a pairing she didn't like.

Behind her, she heard the examining-room door opened, and Kageyama thanked the technician. As his footsteps approached, she was just about to turn and greet him when the man near the elevator turned in her direction. A shock ran through Alma as she saw that the man's eyes were a solid white, without iris or pupil. She had the sudden, chilling sensation that those eyes could see her, despite the one-way glass. This had to be the man the rogue Superkid had warned her about: the one with the strange eyes.

In that same instant, Kageyama touched her elbow. Alma had to instantly counter her move-by-wire system—her hand came halfway out of her pocket, injector at the ready, before she was able to stop it.

The feeling of being stared at eased, as if the man with blank eyes had suddenly lost interest in her. He was still looking in the direction of the clinic, however, and now he started to walk toward it.

"Hello, Jane, " Kageyama said, oblivious to the approaching threat. He placed a slight emphasis on the name, as if saying it tongue-in-cheek. "I'm glad you're still here. I wanted to talk to you about—"

The man with the blank white eyes opened the door. Alma could sense that his attention was no longer on her; it seemed to be focused on Kageyama instead.

Kageyama blinked . . . and then a shudder ran through him. "No!" he shouted. With reflexes as fast as Alma's own, he leaped into the air and planted a martial-arts kick squarely on the other man's chin. The man's all-white eyes blinked shut as his head snapped backward, but a second later he came in through the door low and fast, sweeping Kageyama off his feet with a spinning kick as soon as he had cleared the doorway. Kageyama bounced back to his feet, and the two came together in a blur of punches and kicks. Kageyama aimed a kick at the other man's kneecap, but his target danced back out of range. The blank-eyed man grabbed a fistful of jacket and tried to use Kageyama's own momentum to hurl him across the room, but like a fish wriggling off a hook, Kageyama slipped out of his grasp, the jacket tearing off him as he wrenched free.

Had she not been cybernetically enhanced, Alma would have been left standing like a statue, watching the whirlwind fight. Only her boosted reflexes allowed her to react in time. The man with white eyes was ignoring her, concentrating on Kageyama. Her left hand was closest to him. Whipping it forward, she tried to jam the injector into his back.

Something threw her aim off—later, she wasn't sure if it was the blank-eyed man's lightning-fast reflexes or the fit of trembling that suddenly gripped her hand. She thrust shakily forward, missing the white-eyed man by several centimeters. The injector connected with Kageyama's side as he sprang back onto his feet, and the load of gamma scopolamine was injected with a loud hiss of compressed air.

Kageyama's muscles tensed. The man with the blank eyes chuckled and stepped forward to grab him as he staggered and fell. Cursing her bad luck—the chaos the I Ching had predicted had caught up to her at last—Alma whipped her right hand into her pocket.

As she pulled out the second injector, Alma forced herself to heed the advice of the I Ching: to center, to balance. She pretended to draw away from the man with the strange eyes, sliding her hand up and out of her pocket while hiding the injector it held with her body. At the last moment she whipped her hand forward and stung his arm with the second injector. A single word whispered in her mind—*Stop*—before his pupils dilated and his mouth clenched shut. Rigid as a statue, his arms still wrapped around Kageyama, he toppled to the floor.

Suddenly, everything was quiet. Behind Alma, the robot receptionist on the wall monitor was asking the "new client" to sign in, please.

Alma bent down to tug Kageyama free, only to start back in surprise as he suddenly wriggled out of the blank-eyed man's grip himself. Kageyama staggered to his feet, and for a moment Alma wondered if gamma scopolamine had any effect on him at all. Then she saw his dilated pupils and heard the slur in his voice.

"Thanksh, Ni-howl." He stared around groggily, as if uncertain what to do next.

His uncertainty matched Alma's own. She glanced back and forth between Kageyama and the man who lay on the floor, blank eyes bulging and muscles rigor-mortis stiff. She was strong enough to carry both of them out of the arcology, but there were several securicams on the way. She'd never make it. She had to choose one or the other—and Kageyama was at least mobile.

He seemed the logical choice. According to the message on her cell this morning, the blank-eyed man was looking for the rogue Superkid and knew what she looked like. But he didn't seem to have mistaken Alma for her when he had stared at her through the door. He'd discounted her, as if she was an innocent bystander. He didn't know the rogue Superkid *that* well, it seemed. Kageyama, on the other hand, had just thanked Alma as if she was his friend. Perhaps . . .

One of the examining-room doors was opening. Despite the soundproofing, someone must have heard something. That decided Alma. She scooped the blank-eyed man up and shoved him into a chair, and then grabbed Kageyama's arm and steered him out of the clinic, toward the elevator.

The elevator doors opened, and she shoved Kageyama inside. The three passengers already on board drew back slightly and wrinkled their noses, as if discreetly sniffing for alcohol. Alma punched the icon for the rooftop.

Kageyama might have shaken off the physical effects of the gamma scopolamine in record time, but he had succumbed to the drug's "truth serum" effect. He looked at Alma as trustingly as a puppy, but his eyes were rapidly clearing. She could see that it wouldn't be long before the drug wore off entirely. Despite the other passengers, she had to start asking some questions.

"Do you recognize me?"

The high-speed elevator surged upward, causing Kageyama to stagger slightly. "Of coursh," he answered with a sloppy grin. "You liberay . . . liberay . . . shtole the dour f'r us. And you shtole my shtashue. Wha'd'ya do that for?" He waggled a finger at her, then giggled when he noticed that his cybered little finger was moving back and forth of its own accord. He watched it, fascinated.

The elevator stopped at the eighteenth floor. Two passengers got off—but five more boarded. Just before the doors closed, Alma heard an alarm begin to peal in the corridor. She shifted position so that an enormous troll stood between her and the securicam mounted near the elevator's ceiling and then did the only thing she could think of to conceal Kageyama's face. Grabbing his head with both hands, she yanked him forward and kissed him.

He kissed her back with a skill she hadn't thought possible from someone whose lips were numbed by gamma scopolamine. A rush of sexual energy filled

her, flushing her skin. Her hands began to tremble—
both of them.

She held the kiss until the elevator reached the rooftop. As the doors opened onto a glass-enclosed walkway beside the helicopter landing pads, Kageyama at
last broke away and blinked. "That was ni—"

She hurried him out of the elevator, consulting the
clock in her cybereye. It was 10:32 a.m.—despite everything that had happened, her extraction was only
two minutes behind schedule. All she had to do now
was find the right sky cab, assuming the shadowrunner
had bothered to show up on time . . .

She spotted the yellow and black helicopter—Black
Chopper number fifty-one—and ran across the rooftop
toward it, dragging Kageyama by the hand. A door in
the side of the helicopter sprang open, and they clambered inside, both of them soaked with rain from their
brief dash across the roof.

Buzz—a dwarf with a crewcut and puckered pink
scar tissue on his face and throat where his beard
should have been—cocked his head to listen as Alma
and Kageyama settled into the back of the cab. His
eyes were fully cybered: twin fiberoptic cables were
jammed into the "pupil" of each, connecting him with
the helicopter's internal and external vidcams.

"Where to?" he growled in a voice like a strangled
pit bull's. Whatever injury the shadowrunner had suffered had nearly taken his voice as well as his beard.

"Circle over the city," Alma said. "I have a few
questions to ask our passenger before we drop him
off."

Buzz nodded. The rooftop sank away beneath them
as the helicopter rose smoothly into the air. Alma
breathed a sigh of relief. She'd pulled it off: she'd
extracted Kageyama. Now she just had to decide what
to do with him.

She was startled to hear Kageyama's voice beside

her, clear and crisp, the last slurrings of the drug gone: "I have a few questions for you as well."

Alma turned slowly and saw that his pupils were back to normal—which only served to confirm her suspicions about him. Gamma scopolamine would freeze up the muscles of an ordinary human or meta for an hour and would linger in the body for an hour more after that. Kageyama had shaken off the drug entirely in . . . she consulted her cybereye . . . just under fourteen minutes.

She hoped that the man with the blank eyes wasn't capable of the same thing.

She stared at Kageyama a moment, trying to decide if he was the sort of man who would succumb to a threat. The helicopter wouldn't touch down until she authorized Buzz to do so; Kageyama was a prisoner inside it. But even with his jacket gone and his shirt torn open and soaked with rain he seemed composed. His bright green eyes sparkled with curiosity—there wasn't a hint of fear in them. Alma suddenly realized that he knew he was being extracted—and was actually *enjoying* it.

"I'll trade you," she said. "Question for question, and answer for answer. All right?"

Kageyama nodded. "Please—you first."

"Do you know my real name?" she asked.

"Of course." He smiled, not volunteering one word more.

"What name did you call me, back at the clinic?"

"Sorry, but it's my turn to ask a question," he teased. He thought for a moment. "Who hired you to kidnap me?"

It was Alma's turn to be coy. She recalled Bluebeard's speculation about who—or what—was behind the Komun'go Seoulpa Ring. She had a fifty-fifty chance of being right.

"A dragon," she answered.

Kageyama's eyes widened. "Ah." Before he could
say anything else she fired off another question. "Who
do you think I am?"

He frowned. "Quit joking with me, Night Owl.
You've changed your clothes and hair—even disguised
the way you move—but I know your aura."

Alma froze. If Kageyama was indeed Awakened,
then he could read her aura. Was it really possible
that Kageyama knew one of the Superkids intimately
enough to confuse her aura with Alma's? And could
that one Superkid be the very woman Alma was
searching for?

Alma could hear her heart pounding in her chest.
Her breathing was suddenly very shallow.

Center, she told herself. Center and balance.

Her cyberears picked up the whine of a lens adjusting, and she noticed that the vidcam with its built-
in microphone was aimed straight at her. Buzz was
listening in. For all Alma knew, the shadowrunner
might be a friend of this Night Owl.

She glanced down at the city. "Buzz," she said to
the vidcam, "we're far enough from the arcology now.
Set us down on the closest landing pad. Pick one that's
not too busy."

"You got it."

As the helicopter sank toward the ground, Alma
realized that she was taking a chance. Once they
landed, Kageyama might just turn and run. The only
thing she could count on was his curiosity. He wanted
answers as much as she did.

The helicopter came to a feather-light landing in an
almost empty parking lot, in front of a large cement
building that looked like a college. Alma tossed a
credstick to Buzz, who caught it without even turning
in his seat. Then she cracked the helicopter's side
door.

"You want me to wait?" Buzz growled. "You still got cred remaining."

Alma shook her head. "You can go. I'll handle it from here."

She climbed out into the rain, followed by Kageyama. She led him to the shelter—a glass-walled enclosure with a black plastic roof that rattled under the heavy rain. Yanking the door shut behind them, she did a quick scan. Good—they were alone, and the waiting area's securicam was out of order. They'd have privacy.

She turned to Kageyama as Buzz's sky cab lifted in a wash of downdraft that smeared raindrops sideways across the enclosure's windows. "I'll make a deal with you," she told him. "I'm not who you think I am. My name isn't Night Owl, even though I resemble her closely. I want to find her. Tell me how to do that, and I'll tell you everything I know about who hired me to extract you, and why."

Kageyama thought about that one a long time. "Why are you looking for her?"

"She committed a crime," Alma answered. "The people she stole from mistook the two of us, just as you did, and I was blamed. I want to prove my innocence. After that . . ."

She paused. After that the rogue Superkid would be questioned at length by PCI security and then turned over to the tribal police to stand trial for the murder of Gray Squirrel. Like Akiko, she'd probably wind up on death row.

As for Alma herself, she would be forced to retire—permanently. Although her superiors at PCI knew that she was a former Superkid, she hadn't fully explained to them what this meant: that there were others out there who had the same genetic makeup as she did. She'd failed to recognize and disclose this potential security risk, and now she'd be lucky to keep a job—

in any capacity—with PCI. But at least she could prove her innocence to Mr. Lali.

"I can't tell you where Night Owl is, because I don't know," Kageyama answered. "My—friends and I—hired her via an intermediary, a fixer named Hothead. He can probably point you in the right direction."

Alma struggled to keep her expression cool and professional as Kageyama described the fixer and told her how to contact him. She was finally getting somewhere—she was within one degree of separation from her target.

"Describe Night Owl for me."

"She could be your twin," Kageyama said. "Her aura is even like yours: a large number of dark shadows around the eyes, ears and neck that must come from implanted cyberware. Her body language is entirely different, however, and she doesn't have your grace. In fact, she's quite clumsy—sometimes she winds up with egg on her face."

He winked at Alma, but when she failed to return his smile he shrugged, as if she had failed to get a joke.

Everything Kageyama had just said confirmed Alma's guess: Night Owl must be the Superkid who had framed her for Gray Squirrel's extraction. The woman not only had the same aura but also the same amount and type of cyberware as the others in Batch Alpha. The move-by-wire system that was standard on all Superkids should have made her as graceful as a cat. If Night Owl was clumsy, she was either faking it or her move-by-wire had shorted out. Or she'd had it removed. Maybe the move-by-wires that the Superkids had been fitted with were faulty . . .

Alma forced her mind back to the here and now. "Can you tell me anything else about Night Owl?"

Kageyama spread his hands and shrugged. His cybernetic little fingers were working properly again, in sync with his real fingers. "All I can tell you is that her 'crimes' aren't motivated by greed, but by compassion. She—"

Alma had heard enough. "She's a killer," she gritted. She felt her cheeks blaze as a vision of Gray Squirrel's mutilated throat swam before her eyes.

Kageyama lowered his hands. His voice dropped to a whisper. "You'd know that better than I."

The rain had soaked into the shoulders of Alma's suit jacket, chilling her skin. She started to shiver before her move-by-wire system shut the involuntary motion down. She noticed that Kageyama was also soaked. Several buttons had been torn from his shirt during the fight with the blank-eyed man, and his chest was bare, save for a small circle of blue stone that hung on a gold chain around his neck. The pendant trembled against his nearly hairless chest as he shivered.

Kageyama noticed her staring at it and touched a finger to it. "Pretty, isn't it?"

Alma realized what it was: a *pi*, a good-luck token traditionally given to Chinese children. It was just one of the traditions that had jumped cultures; half of the people in Vancouver had one, regardless of their ethnic background. Obviously the custom had become just as popular in Japan.

"You promised to tell me who hired you to kidnap me," Kageyama reminded her. "Do you keep your promises?"

Alma couldn't see any reason not to. She now had the name of the woman she was looking for and the name and description of a man who could tell her where to find Night Owl. She'd made contact with two shadowrunners—Bluebeard and Buzz—who could attest to her authenticity when she went to speak with Hothead. She'd gone through the motions of a shadowrun.

There was no point in completing the extraction now. At midnight, when she still hadn't heard from

Alma, the blond-haired Seoulpa member would assume that the extraction of Kageyama had failed and would look for someone else to do the job. As for Tiger Cat, Alma would have to stall him with a partial payment of the credit that PCI owed him. That should stop him from blowing the whistle on the fact that she wasn't really a shadowrunner. If all else failed, she could try to pick up the trail of the blank-eyed man who was looking for the rogue Superkid and track his movements in the hope that he would lead her to her target.

Alma had strayed far enough into the world of the shadowrunners in her attempt to find the woman who had framed her. She didn't want to cross the line by actually committing a crime. Kageyama was an innocent victim—just as Gray Squirrel had been. Alma owed him an explanation.

"Your extraction was ordered by a Seattle-based Seoulpa Ring: the Komun'go. They wanted to question you about something—what, I don't know, but it sounded as though they're looking for something."

Kageyama feigned dismay. "How distressing: that makes three dragons who have tried to kidnap me or steal from me."

Alma had no idea what he was talking about. "Three dragons?"

He counted them off on his fingers. "Mang, the dragon whose associates hired you to kidnap me. Chiao, who hired you—"

He paused to correct himself. "Who hired Night Owl to steal the statue from my condoplex. I recognized him at once when he came to collect his prize, although why he went to such pains to acquire a simple jade statue remains a mystery. I'm surprised he didn't just send one of the Red Lotus to steal it instead."

Alma nodded, recognizing another piece of the puzzle: the Red Lotus—the gang members who were after Night Owl, according to the message that had been left on Alma's cellphone this morning.

Kageyama continued: "The third dragon, Li, also wishes to kidnap me, it seems. That was his Number One who attacked me in the clinic."

When Alma looked blankly at him, Kageyama added, in a low voice: "The 88s, a triad whose bloody reach extends all the way back to Dragon Eyes' master in Singapore."

"What do they all want?" Alma asked.

Kageyama shivered and pulled his wet shirt across his bare chest. "I honestly don't know. They must think there's something of great value in my condoplex, since it used to be owned by a great dragon. Perhaps they don't realize that I was the one who furnished it—Dunkelzahn died before he had the chance to move in any of his treasures. Yet Li, Chiao and Mang think there's something extremely valuable inside—something worth fighting over. Whatever it might be, each one is willing to risk the dissolution of a very powerful alliance to get it for himself."

Alma's mind whirled as she tried to slot all of the pieces together. Kageyama had three dragons after him, each with an associated gang, Triad or Seoulpa Ring. One of them—the dragon Mang, who controlled the Seoulpa Ring—might also, according to Bluebeard, have ties to the Eastern Tiger Corporation, a powerful player in the Pacific Prosperity Group. Alma wondered if the PPG was the "alliance" that Kageyama had just spoken of—if the other two dragons also controlled corporations in that group. If so, the combined firepower of the dragon's gang members, the nuyen controlled by their corporate subsidiaries and the dragons' own magical capabilities would produce a security nightmare she wouldn't wish upon anyone.

There was just one thing she didn't understand. "Why are you telling me all this?"

From above came the sound of rotors overhead as a helicopter descended; both Alma and Kageyama glanced up. It was a black and yellow sky cab, but it wasn't Buzz's machine. Alma glanced at the floor and belatedly realized that the concrete underfoot had a pressure-sensitive pad that automatically flagged a cab once the shelter was occupied.

Kageyama reached into a back trouser pocket and pulled out a small leather case. Then he bowed slightly and presented her with a rectangle of plastic: a personal calling card. The blue stone around his neck swung forward on its chain and settled back against his chest as he straightened.

"Ms. Lee—or whatever your real name might be— you seem to be a very capable woman," he said. "If it wasn't for you, Li or one of the other dragons would have me in his clutches. I have decided that it takes a thief to protect one from thieves. I would like to hire you to provide me with additional security."

He gave her such a knowing look that for a moment, Alma wondered if he knew who she really was. "Thank you," she stammered, tucking the card into a jacket pocket. "But I have . . . another engagement . . . at the moment."

Kageyama paused with his hand on the door. "An engagement that I suspect is in jeopardy, unless you can clear your name—is that right?"

Alma kept her emotions in check, despite his too-accurate guess. The helicopter touched down outside the shelter, its rotors throwing a spray of rain against the glass.

Kageyama inclined his head as he opened the door. "If you change your mind, let me know." Then he strode out into the rain and climbed into the cab.

Great Possession

Night Owl rumbled down the street on her Electro-glide, watching for the address she'd looked up on the telecom. The streets in this part of the downtown core were quiet this time of night. The antique shops, retro clothing and music stores, and thaumaturgical supply shops were closed and dark, and only a handful of people scurried along the blustery sidewalks, hunkered down under umbrellas to shelter from the incessant rain.

She spotted the address halfway down the block. The shop was a tiny one with a barred window that overlooked the street and a short flight of worn stone steps leading up to its front door. A battered electric sign hung above the doorway, its light flickering behind the name of the shop: National Coin & Stamp. The sign looked as though it had been there a century, as did the shop. Someone was moving around inside; Night Owl hoped it was the man she was looking for.

She turned her bike in the direction of Waterfront Station and parked it at the back of a Metermate lot, in the shadow of a Eurovan that had two hours plus on its meter. Using a handful of the parking tokens she'd boosted, she purchased six hours' worth of time. If the Red Lotus did spot her bike, she wanted them to think she'd be away from it for some time. With luck, they'd assume she had taken the Seabus over to the North Shore.

Night Owl hurried across the parking lot, turned right at a bronze statue of an angel carrying a soldier up to heaven, and pushed her way in through the front doors of Waterfront Station. The large, echoing building was busy day and night, a meeting point for the SkyTrain, Seabus and express trains. People streamed through it in all directions: down escalators to the subway and train tracks, along the elevated walkway that led to the Seabus dock, or up escalators to the skycab stops on the roof. Still more people clustered in knots at its soykaf stands for a quick jolt of caffeine or stood and watched the eleven o'clock news on the enormous Tribal Newsnet screen that filled one wall.

Night Owl slipped into a washroom and exchanged her wet jacket and jeans for a dry pair of pants and the expensive suede jacket Kageyama had given her. She blew her wind-tangled hair dry at a hand blower and combed it until it hung straight and neat. Then she squirted cream onto the Beijing Opera mask she'd painted her face with earlier and scrubbed away the diagonal slashes of black and red and blue makeup. When her face was clean, she stared at herself in the mirror, relaxing her posture and trying to keep the smirk off her face.

"Hello, 'Alma,' " she said. "Ready for your next run?"

Outside the washroom, she cached her wet clothes inside a storage locker and then pulled out the cellphone she'd boosted earlier from the apartment. She flicked past the message that had been left for her in the daytimer, asking her to name the time and place for a meet, and past her response: MEET WITH YOU? ONLY IN YOUR DREAMS, AL. Then she scrolled down through the list of telecom and cell numbers that had been stored in the cell's memory, past the entry EGON, HOME to the one that read

EGON, NATIONAL COIN & STAMP. Highlighting it, she thumbed the dial icon.

When an automated answering function cut in, she disconnected and then called the same number again. Once again, the answer was automated: *National Coin & Stamp is now closed; please call back again. Our store hours are—*

"Frag off," she whispered back at it. "I know you're there. Pick up."

After five more tries, the cell's monitor screen illuminated. The bearded dwarf it projected gave her a harried glance before returning his attention to something out of vidcam range as he spoke. "The store is closed, and I'm in the middle of taking inventory. What's so important that it can't wait until tomorrow?"

The telecom that was capturing the dwarf's image was positioned at about waist height; it was probably sitting on a shop counter. His hands bobbed in and out of the field of view as he picked up and stacked plastic envelopes filled with brightly colored stamps.

Night Owl was holding the cell at arm's length. She tilted it so that the phone's vidcam would get a good shot of her face. "Egon?"

He looked back up. "Oh, it's you, Alma. What do you want?"

Paydata! Night Owl had suspected that this fellow Egon and Alma knew each other—Alma wouldn't have his home telecom number otherwise. Now she had to hope that they weren't such good chummers that he'd see through Night Owl's charade.

"Do you remember the appraisal you did for me, about a year ago?" she asked.

"Of course: three coins from the Qing Dynasty, fair condition, no detectable magic, worth about thirty nuyen each. I hope you're not still casting fortunes with them—handling the coins will reduce their value."

Night Owl nodded, impressed with the man's memory. He'd listed every significant piece of data on the appraisal fax she'd found in the drawer in Alma's apartment. The dwarf either had a photographic memory or cybernetic data storage. She hoped that his memory for body language wasn't quite as precise.

"I'm just a few blocks from your shop, at Waterfront Station," Night Owl told him. "Can I see you? I need some information on a rare coin."

"Now?" The dwarf shifted out of the monitor screen's field of view as he turned to look at something behind him. "It 's nearly eleven-thirty."

"Have you ever heard of the Coins of Luck?" Night Owl asked. "One of them is here, in Vancouver."

That got his attention. Egon stared directly into the cellphone's vidcam, his eyes wide. He'd heard of them, all right. He wet his lips. "Do you . . . have it?"

Night Owl had already decided not to extend her bluff that far—if the dwarf asked her to describe the coin, she wouldn't be able to. She chose her words carefully; she didn't want to slip up and start using shadow slang—not when she was posing as a corporate wageslave. "Let's just say I'm moonlighting for the person who owns it—someone who wants to remain anonymous. He's hired me to provide some additional security, but he wasn't willing to tell me much about the coin itself. I thought you could fill me in. I want to know what I'm dealing with."

"Let's talk about this in person," the dwarf said. "Come to my shop."

The monitor blanked, and Night Owl grinned. "Bytebrain," she whispered derisively. She folded the cellphone up and jandered out the doors and down the street, toward National Coin & Stamp's tiny storefront.

It took the dwarf a couple of minutes to open the front door after she knocked. Night Owl stood with her jacket tented over her head, both to fend off the rain and to screen herself from passing cars. There wasn't much traffic, but she didn't want to take any chances. Not with both the Red Lotus and Strange Eyes gunning for her.

The dwarf rolled open the inner, barred door and then opened the door of the shop itself. He stood only as tall as Night Owl's waist, but his stocky frame probably matched hers kilo for kilo. His hair was blond and trimmed short, as was his beard. Despite the fact that the shop was closed, his tie was still neatly knotted at his neck. The cuffs of his dress shirt were pinned together with cufflinks made from gold coins.

"Sorry to keep you waiting in the rain," he apologized. "I had to speak to the watcher spirit first, so it would accept your presence in the store. And thanks for the tip on the security system, by the way. It saved me a bundle of credit."

Night Owl nodded as she stepped into the shop. If the coin dealer hadn't just thanked her, she would have assumed he was warning her that the shop was magically guarded. But when she pulled off her dripping jacket and turned to drape it over one of the stools that lined the display counter, Egon didn't even flinch at the handgun holstered at the small of her back.

Night Owl looked around at the shelves and counters that filled the tiny shop as Egon closed and locked the door. Binders filled every shelf, and the counters were covered with metal drawers filled with clear plastic folders, each holding a single coin, old-fashioned "dollar" bill or stamp—mediums of exchange that had survived into the twenty-first century, only to vanish with the advent of the credstick and the Matrix. A large windup clock sat on a shelf behind the counter, its antique mechanism ticking loudly, and the shelves held dusty-looking books rather than optical chips. Everything in the shop, it seemed, was the product of a forgotten era—except for the cred slotter on the counter. Egon had one foot, at least, in the twenty-first century.

It took Night Owl a moment to spot the shop's watcher spirit, which was as insubstantial as a ghost; she could only see it out of the corner of her eye. It was gnome-sized, with a heavily wrinkled face, its eyes closed and covered by coins that clung to his eyelids as if glued there. The spirit sat crosslegged inside a glass-fronted display case, as still as death. Night Owl got the impression that it could see through the coins on its eyes, though, and was watching her every move.

Egon rolled the bars back into place across the doorway and turned to face Night Owl. He obviously trusted "Alma" enough to lock himself inside the shop with her—sometimes posing as a corporate suit had its advantages. Either that, or he was determined to keep her inside until she told him everything she knew about the coin.

Night Owl had the reverse in mind.

"Tell me about the Coins of Luck," she prompted. She pulled a stool into a spot where a tall shelf screened her from the street and sat with her back against the wall. "What are they worth, and what are they capable of?"

She'd already decided that the coin she was sup-posed to have must be magical—money alone wouldn't account for a dragon being interested in it.

Egon walked behind the display case that held the watcher spirit and stepped up onto a platform that brought him up to eye level with Night Owl. "The Coins of Luck are extremely old: they date back to the Xia Dynasty. That alone makes them worth several hundred thousand nuyen. But as you've alluded, there's another reason for their great worth: they're said to be powerful magical foci. According to legend,

each brings a different kind of luck: prosperity, longevity, fertility and happiness.''

That slotted. Happiness—*fu*—was the character the
dragon had said was on the back of the "hollow"
statue that Chiao had hired her to steal. Night Owl
had gone with her gut instinct—backed up by a coin
flip—that Egon would know about the Coins of Luck,
based on the fact that he did thaumaturgical testing
on Alma's coins. The long shot had paid off. She'd
come to the right man.

Night Owl leaned forward. "What's the legend?"

Egon's eyes gleamed. "The Coins of Luck were sup-
posedly created two thousand years ago by the *lung
wang*—the 'dragon kings' of Chinese mythology, dragons who controlled the seas, rains and winds. The
coins were given to humankind as a test, to see
whether mortals would use the bounty they conveyed
for good or for evil.

"The men and women who received the coins pros-
pered and became the rulers of their people. But as
you would expect in a story like this one, the mortals
weren't satisfied with one coin apiece. They went to
war with one another, each trying to acquire the other
three coins.''

Night Owl raised an eyebrow. "They weren't satisfied with just one kind of luck?''

"It wasn't just that. According to legend, the coins
collectively can grant special powers of divination.
They can predict the optimum moment at which to
cast a spell—but only if they are used together as a
set. The last time this was said to have happened was
in the thirteenth century. When the Mongols attacked
Japan in 1281, the Japanese emperor used the coins to
predict the precise moment at which his priests could
summon up a hurricane. Their 'divine wind' smashed
the Mongol fleet and destroyed the invading army.''

Egon shrugged. "Of course, this may all be nothing

more than legend. This was long before the Awakening, in an age when magic shouldn't have been possible."

Night Owl nodded, caught up in the story. The coin she'd been sent to boost was even more valuable than she'd imagined. No wonder the dragon had been interested in acquiring it.

"Over the next few centuries," Egon continued, "the ownership and whereabouts of the coins were unknown. It wasn't until 2057, when the dragon Dunkelzahn died and his will was read, that three of them resurfaced. The Coin of Luck that conveys longevity, called the Shou Coin, went to the great dragon Lung. The Feng Coin, which brings fertility, was willed to a woman named Sharon Chiang-Wu, wife of the CEO of Wuxing, Incorporated.

"The third of the Coins of Luck, the Lu Coin, was left to an impoverished fisherman in Hong Kong. Rumor had it that this man did some great service for Dunkelzahn, and the dragon wanted to reward his family with great wealth. Unfortunately, the reward brought only death: the fisherman Sun Yat-sun was gunned down by Yellow Lotus gangsters who were attempting to steal the Lu Coin. Its whereabouts are currently unknown.

"As for the fourth coin, the question of whether Dunkelzahn ever owned it is open to speculation. The Fu Coin wasn't mentioned in his will. But whoever owns it must be a very happy person, regardless of their circumstances."

That slotted with everything Night Owl had learned so far. Akira Kageyama certainly seemed happy enough—but then, having a net worth of several million nuyen probably helped. Whoever said that credit couldn't buy happiness had never lived from credstick to credstick.

"What do the Coins of Luck look like?" Night Owl

asked. She wondered if she'd be able to pawn one of Alma's coins off on Strange Eyes or the dragon Chiao. It wouldn't fool either of them for long, but it might buy her a little time.

Egon picked up the packages of coins and stamps that were spread out on the counter, neatly stacked them to one side, and reached into the display cabinet—his hands brushing past the watcher spirit—to pull out a leather-bound binder. He set it on the space he'd cleared and flipped open its clear plastic pages, each of which had multiple pockets holding coins.

"They look like these," he said, pointing to a half-dozen badly pitted coins. "The Coins of Luck are similar to other coins produced during the Xia Dynasty, except for the fact that they never tarnish. They also have some kind of magical protection on them that only very powerful magicians can see past."

Night Owl slid from her stool and moved closer to the counter. She leaned over the book, studying the coins and committing them to memory. Each was about five centimeters wide and had a square hole that took up a good third of the center of the coin. The designs on the front of each coin were worn almost smooth; she could barely tell that they were Chinese characters. "How can you tell one Coin of Luck from the others?" she asked.

"According to what I've read about the Coins of Luck, each has the same four characters on its face," Egon said. "It takes an initiated magician to work through the magical protection on the coin. Once through, one character—*fu, lu, shou* or *feng*—will glow in the astral."

He stroked his neatly trimmed beard with one hand as he speculated aloud. "The whereabouts of two of the coins are known: Lung lairs someplace in China, and Sharon Chiang-Wu resides in Hong Kong. Neither has expressed interest in selling their coin, despite repeated requests from dealers around the world. Which begs three questions: which of the other two Coins of Luck is here in Vancouver, who owns it, and is he or she interested in selling?" His voice dropped to a conspiratorial whisper. "I'm sure I could find a buyer."

Night Owl was trying to decide how best to politely decline the offer when a Ford American rolled to a stop on the street outside the store. The headlights went out, and the driver—an Asian man—stepped out into the rain.

The watcher spirit leaned forward to look, its head shimmering as it passed through the glass front of the display case. "He's here," it said in a voice that sounded like coins jingling together.

Egon peered out at the darkened street, speaking to Night Owl over his shoulder. "Ah, good. I hope you don't mind, Alma, but I invited a friend to join—"

Before he could finish the sentence, Night Owl had drawn her gun. She'd recovered her Ares Predator from the Magic Box, with Tatyana's help, and now its perforated silencer was pointed directly at Egon's head.

She understood, now, why it had taken the dwarf so long to let her into the shop. He'd been on the telecom to this fragger.

She flicked off the safety of her gun. At the click, Egon swallowed nervously.

The man outside climbed the stairs and knocked on the shop's front door. From where he stood, he wouldn't be able to see Night Owl.

"Who is he?" Night Owl gritted.

Egon started to lift his hands from the counter but thought better of it. He glanced ruefully at the watcher spirit, which was ignoring Night Owl, its gaze fixed on the door like an expectant dog. "Alma—relax. His name is Lei Kung. He's made a study of the Coins of Luck. He . . . knows quite a lot about them."

"Who's he run with?"

Egon's eyebrows rose. "How did you know he was a shadowrunner?"

Night Owl glared, angry at herself for slipping into street slang. "Who does he work with?" she corrected herself.

"Kung is strictly independent. Perhaps I should have warned you that he was a shadowrunner, but I assure you he's not a criminal. He deals in information only. I've used him myself, to crosscheck the legitimacy of some of the items my shop deals in—and the credentials of those who are selling them."

Night Owl didn't like the sound of that last part. Keeping her gun hidden, she leaned out from behind the display case and took a good look at the man through the glass in the door. He was about thirty or forty, with a mustache that was no more than a tuft of whiskers at either side of his mouth, and thick, shoulder-length black hair that was streaked with wide orange stripes. He wore a clear plastic rain jacket over tight black jeans and a long-sleeved black T-shirt woven with gold threads that gleamed under the streetlights. The jeans disappeared into high lace-up boots.

Night Owl pulled back into the shadow of the shelf as the fellow knocked on the door a second time and waved at Egon. "I don't recognize him."

"You wouldn't," Egon said. "He's from Hong Kong. He only came to Vancouver a couple of months ago. I assure you that, even though he's a shadowrunner, he's not dangerous."

Still holding the gun on Egon, Night Owl pulled the SkyTrain token from her pocket and flipped it into the air. Heads, she'd talk to this Lei Kung. Tails, she'd tell Egon to send his friend packing.

She caught the token and slapped it down on the back of her left hand, which she'd turned slightly while still holding the gun. Heads.

She reholstered her pistol. "All right. Let him in."

Egon hurried to the door and opened it. The man who had been waiting outside entered the shop, flicking rain from his fingers.

Egon grabbed his hand. "Please, Kung! You'll get water on the merchandise."

"*Dui bu qi,*" Kung answered, shedding his raincoat. He switched to linguasoft-perfect English. "Excuse me. It's raining, in case you hadn't noticed."

Egon took the coat and folded it so the dry side was uppermost before draping it over a stool, where it dripped onto the carpet. Kung, meanwhile, turned to Night Owl and inclined his head in a slight bow. "Greetings, Ms. Wei—or should I say 'Ms. Johnson'? It is so nice to meet you in person."

Night Owl suddenly realized that Kung knew Alma—and not just because Egon had mentioned Alma's name to the shadowrunner on the telecom. This shadowrunner and Alma had a professional relationship, and judging by his use of the word Johnson, she'd *hired* him.

Night Owl could think of only one reason why a high-ranking corporate security officer from PCI would hire a shadowrunner: to learn more about the extraction. That meant that Kung would have been sniffing around in Night Owl's back yard. A delicious thrill went through her at the thought of standing right in front of him, hidden behind the perfect mask: the face of the woman who had hired him. It tickled, right down to the tips of her toes.

"Egon tells me that you're a shadowrunner, Mr. Lei," she said, pumping the corpspeak to the max. "What name do you go by, when you 'run the shadows'?"

Kung tipped his head slightly, as if amused. "Tiger Cat."

"Egon tells me you know a lot about the Coins of Luck."

"He says that one of the coins is in Vancouver."

"That's right," Night Owl said. "I was hired to provide security for it."

Egon had been standing beside Tiger Cat and Night Owl, his head tilted back, glancing from one to the other as they spoke. Now his eyes settled on Night Owl. He cleared his throat and then spoke: "Lei Kung asked me to contact him if anyone ever approached my shop with an offer to sell one of the Coins of Luck."

"I never said that my . . . that my employer wanted to sell it," Night Owl said.

"Good." Tiger Cat glanced sternly down at Egon. "I would not want you to have any part in that transaction, my friend."

The dwarf's eyebrows puckered. "Why not? The commission would be a king's ransom—enough to retire on."

"To retire, yes. But death is not the retirement you have in mind." Tiger Cat sighed. "I might as well warn you both, even though . . ." he paused for a moment to glare at Night Owl. "Even though one of you doesn't deserve a warning, after the fix I was left in."

Night Owl glared back at him but held her tongue. This was getting interesting.

Tiger Cat raised his right hand, fingers pinched together as if they were gripping something small. "Five years ago, I held one of the Coins of Luck in my hand. I was there when Sun Yat-sun was killed. I thought I was a very fortunate man to escape with both my life and the Second Coin of Luck. I tried to sell it, even though Sun Yat-sun had told me it was unlucky to spend or sell the coin—that it must be given away instead.

"When a buyer and price were arranged, we set a

time and place to meet. But the people who met me were members of the same Triad that killed Sun Yat-sun. I was nearly killed—the only thing that saved me was that I 'gave' the coin away. When one of the Triad members put a gun to my head, I threw the coin at him and said, 'Take it—it's yours!' Then I ran. Somehow, I lived."

"Sounds like luck was on your side," Night Owl said, fingering the SkyTrain token in her pocket. Listening to what Tiger Cat had to say had been the right choice—she could tell he was about to spill a lot more.

Egon stared up at him, wide-eyed. "Unbelievable," he whispered, looking so enraptured that Night Owl thought he was about to cry. "You actually held the Lu Coin in your hand."

"For too short a time—it gave no wealth. Not to me, anyway. But that's another story, one I will tell in a moment.

"First I hope to warn you, Egon. Selling the Coin of Luck—even taking a commission—is unwise. And to you, Ms. Wei, I recommend that you not be tempted to aid in the sale of the coin in any way, or you may wind up like the watcher spirit here, with coins covering your eyes."

As if on cue, the spirit leaned out through the front of the display case a second time. It tilted its head as if listening and then swung its head around until its coin-covered eyes were on the front door. "Someone's coming," its voice tinkled.

"Who?" Egon asked. His hands snapped shut the binder of coins on the counter. "What do they want?"

A car hissed past on the wet street outside and slowed before reaching the end of the block.

"Someone . . . who wants to find . . ." The watcher spirit turned until its coin-covered eyes were fixed on Night Owl. "Her."

Leaning forward to look out the window, Night Owl

saw a Toyota Elite pull into a parking spot on the opposite side of the street, halfway up the block. A blond-haired Asian woman climbed out of the car, peering at something that she held cupped in her hand. She turned slowly while keeping her eyes on it, as if consulting a compass. Her eyes ranged up and down the street and then locked on the coin and stamp shop.

"Who is she?" Night Owl asked.

Tiger Cat's lips were pressed together in a thin line. His eyes darted to Night Owl. "I transferred back her credit, but it looks like she's still angry. I think it's best if you—"

"You told that woman I was here?" Night Owl growled. She didn't like the look of this. "Why?"

"No, I—"

The woman was jogging toward the shop now. As she ran, she raised her free hand and made a karate-chop motion. In that same instant, something that looked like a detached, glowing hand crashed through the front window. A metal case just above Night Owl's head dented as the wedge of magical energy hit it. The top of the case ruptured explosively, and a spray of stamps rained down on Night Owl like colorful snowflakes.

Egon croaked and disappeared behind his counter. Tiger Cat flattened himself on the floor. Night Owl had already ducked back behind a shelf; the Ares Predator was in her left hand, safety off. Her right eye began twitching. Who the frag was after her now? The woman outside looked like a ganger, but she wasn't Red Lotus. Maybe she was part of Strange Eyes' crew.

"Time to slide," Night Owl hissed, more to herself than anyone else.

Tiger Cat was scuttling across the floor, keeping low. Egon lifted a hand above the counter and began casting a spell, one that caused the empty space where window glass had been to shimmer with magical lines of force. His face was as pale as his beard as he peered up at the results of his spell through the glass of the display case.

Scooping up her jacket, Night Owl dodged around the end of the counter and ran for the back of the shop—only to find a blank wall of shelves and filing cabinets. She skidded to a stop but then spotted a bathroom with a window just large enough to wriggle out of.

From the front of the shop came a noise like an ax hitting a chainlink fence as the woman outside the shop launched another magical attack. Night Owl glanced back and saw that the magical barrier the dwarf had thrown into place across the front of the shop was holding—but for how long?

"Alma! Where are you going?" Egon shouted back at her. "Stay in the shop—I've cast a barrier spell."

Night Owl wasn't about to stick around and find out if the magical barrier would hold. Balancing precariously on the bathroom's wobbly toilet, she yanked the window open and slithered out through it.

She landed in an alley. Jacket still clenched in one hand, she ran in the direction of Waterfront Station, feet splashing through puddles of rainwater. If she could just get to her motorcycle, maybe she could lose the blond-haired slitch the way she'd ditched the Red Lotus. She'd blast out to Richmond and—

As if she'd known where Night Owl was headed, the woman appeared in the alley ahead. Frag! Blondie might have guessed that Night Owl would bolt out a back exit—but how had the woman known which end of the alley she'd head for?

Night Owl flashed for her Predator, but even as it cleared the holster the woman's hand karate-chopped down. The gun was slammed out of Night Owl's hand; the blow felt as if a sledgehammer had struck it.

Somewhere in the distance, a police siren began to howl. Night Owl had no idea whether Egon had summoned it to the shop with a 911 call or whether the TPs were headed in another direction. Even if they were headed this way, Blondie would have plenty of time to do whatever it was she had in mind. At least she hadn't attacked Night Owl—yet. That was a good sign.

"It's midnight," the woman said. "Why didn't you call, Cybergirl? We were waiting for your explanation."

For a moment, Night Owl wondered what the frag the woman was talking about. Then it hit her: Blondie thought she was talking to Alma. Night Owl glanced down at the cellphone that was clipped to her belt. "I couldn't call," she stalled. "My cell was . . ."

The cell had twisted on its belt clip until it was bottom-side up. She noticed something then, on the bottom of the phone: a piece of what looked like kleentac. She knew what she'd find under it: a homing-signal transmitter. Blondie, it seemed, had been keeping tabs on Alma: that had been a global-positioning tracker in her hand when she got out of the car. Night Owl wondered what the frag Alma had done to warrant this kind of attention.

"My master wasn't very happy about Kageyama," Blondie said.

Night Owl did a double take. Maybe it *was* her the woman was gunning for after all. "Your master?" she stammered, her right eye twitching furiously. "You mean Chiao?"

The blond woman laughed. "Good guess, but wrong dragon," she said. "It's Mang I work for. And now that I've told you that, you know what they say: a little knowledge is a dangerous thing. As are you."

Night Owl was holding herself poised, like a sprinter

in starting blocks. Even as the woman's hand began to twitch, she threw herself to the side. Magical energy blossomed from the woman's hand, and a glowing hand streaked past Night Owl with a rush of air. Night Owl landed prone, catching herself on her hands a centimeter before her face touched the cement. She'd done the impossible: dodged a magical spell. But even as she twisted her body violently to the side, trying to roll into the shelter of a parked car, she knew she wouldn't be able to duck the second attack.

That was when she heard a crackling sound and saw a blue-white streak of what looked like lightning lance out of the alley toward the blond woman. As it hit her, she grunted as if gut-punched and folded onto the sidewalk. Realizing that something had taken the woman down before she could crank off a second magical attack, Night Owl turned her roll into a tuck and sprang to her feet.

The blond woman lay on the sidewalk, groaning, barely conscious. Night Owl knew what had taken her down from the smell that lingered in the air: ozone and burnt hair. She'd been blasted with a bolt of magical energy.

Tiger Cat stepped out from behind a trash bin and bowed. "Well done," he said. "Very convincing. Very . . . cunning. I wondered who your Johnson worked for. Now I know."

Thunder rumbled overhead, and the rain intensified. Tiger Cat stepped nimbly under an awning and glanced up at the sky with a wary look. Night Owl collected her Predator from where she'd dropped it and shoved the gun in its holster. She nearly drew it again when something dark launched itself from a nearby lightpost. Then she realized it was only a large black crow.

"Storm crow," Tiger Cat muttered. "They're said to bring bad weather—and bad luck. There's an ancient Chinese saying: 'Where storm crows perch, dragons will soon lair.' "

Night Owl glanced at Blondie, who was still twitching on the sidewalk and glaring as she struggled to lift her head. "Bad luck for some, maybe."

Night Owl wanted to ask Tiger Cat who Blondie was, but that would tip him to the fact that she was only posing as Alma. Instead, she bent down and quickly patted down the woman's pockets. The ganger didn't carry a weapon; despite her reliance on the tracking device, she obviously preferred magic over technology when it came to bagging her prey. The only thing Night Owl found on her was a Salish-Shidhe visitor's visa—probably fake. She also saw a wolf's head tattoo on the woman's upper chest, which told her much more: the woman was Komun'go. Which was just drekkin' lovely. That made three gangs after her now, thanks to whatever the frag Alma had been messing with.

The sirens were drawing closer. Tiger Cat stepped out into the rain and leaned over the downed woman. "The police will be here soon, Ms. Johnson. If you're smart, you'll keep your mouth shut about us."

Night Owl tensed as a car rounded the corner and pulled up to the sidewalk but then saw that it was only Tiger Cat's Ford Americar. Egon was at the wheel, his eyes barely visible over the dash.

Tiger Cat ran around to the driver's door and clambered inside, Egon scooting over into the passenger seat. Night Owl paused just long enough to give Blondie a swift kick in the ribs and then hopped into the back seat of the car. She opened a window, peeled the kleen-tac from the cellphone and tossed the micro-transmitter out the window. With luck, it would stick to the wheel of a passing car and keep Blondie guessing about where they had gone.

As the car pulled away, Blondie struggled into a sitting position. She was trying to rise to her feet as the police cars came into view. Then Tiger Cat turned the corner, and Night Owl lost sight of her.

The shadowrunner looked in the rear-view mirror, catching Night Owl's eye. "Akira Kageyama has one of the Coins of Luck, doesn't he? That's why that woman's master wanted to extract him."

Night Owl started to shake her head, then paused. Tiger Cat was spewing data all over the place tonight. Maybe some of it could help her out of this mess. She decided to play along with the other runner. For now.

"What if Kageyama does have it?" she asked.

Tiger Cat nodded and then sighed. "I'll finish my story now—that will give you the answer."

Egon, sitting next to him, turned eagerly in his seat.

"I told you about the attack on the fisherman in Hong Kong," said Tiger Cat. "The men who killed Sun Yat-sun tried to make it look like a Yellow Lotus hit, but it was done by the yakuza. Someone set up the fake coin buy and let me 'escape' from the 'Triad.' The whole thing was planned to let me live. By telling the story of my escape, I'd make it look like someone else has the Lu Coin."

Egon leaned forward. "Who *does* have it?"

Tiger Cat's lips twitched into a smile. "A decker by the name of Snow Tiger asked that same question. It was easy for her to learn that the Yellow Lotus wasn't really behind the attack—too easy. Snow Tiger peeled back that layer of data and came up with three different answers—again, too easily. Three dragons: Mang, Li and Chiao.

"Snow Tiger wanted to find out more—why would someone leave data that suggested that one of the dragons had the coin? She found the answer when she traced each dragon to a different corporation. Mang was rumored to be the CEO of Eastern Tiger Corporation of Korea, Chiao is a major shareholder of Tan Tien Incorporated in the Republic of China, and Li sits on the board of directors of Red Wheel Engineering of Singapore. All three companies are members of the Pacific Prosperity Group."

Night Owl mentally slotted the pieces together as he spoke. Blondie was working for the dragon Mang and the Red Lotus were tied to Chiao. That meant that Strange Eyes had to be the local muscle for the dragon Li.

Tiger Cat continued, oblivious to Night Owl's slow nod. "Each dragon thinks that one of the other two has the Lu Coin. Now each believes that, unless he gets a coin too, he will be the only dragon without one. As a result, Pacific Prosperity Group isn't as congenial anymore, or as prosperous. Snow Tiger asked herself: who would profit from that?"

He glanced into the rear-view mirror again. Night Owl shrugged, but the dwarf let out a slow whistle. "If the Pacific Prosperity Group is weakened, Japan is the big winner. If there's another dragon behind all this, it has to be Ryomyo."

"Exactly," Tiger Cat said. "All Ryomyo needs to do is drop a hint to the other dragons that the coin is in Vancouver, and they'll assume that Kageyama has it. Dunkelzahn was known to have three of the coins, so why not all four? If he gave Kageyama a million-nuyen condoplex, then why not the coin, too?"

Night Owl met his gaze in the mirror and asked, "What's the skinny, Tiger Cat? Why are you telling me this?"

"I think you know where the coin is—or that you will soon find it. When you do, don't try to sell it. This is out of your league—you should leave shadowruns to professionals."

"But if she—" Egon spluttered.

"Bring the coin to me instead," Tiger Cat said firmly.

"Why the frag should I do that?" Night Owl asked. "What's in it for me?"

"Your life, Ms. Wei. After you visited Bluebeard, he tried a little experiment using the DNA calling card you left him and found that your access to PCI was denied. This intrigued him, so he dug deeper. He found out about your impending termination and learned something he thinks may be very valuable for you to know."

Night Owl was only half listening. She didn't give a flying frag if Alma got fired from her job; PCI was as morally bankrupt a corporation as they come. Alma would do well to find some honest shadow work instead.

Night Owl didn't want whatever Kung was offering; she'd insist on a cred payout instead, if the coin ever came into her hands. And since that credit wouldn't be transferred to her, technically she wouldn't be "selling" the coin. She'd be in the clear, as far as any bad luck was concerned.

"Well?" Kung asked. "Do we have an agreement?"

"Maybe—but it would have to be for credit, not information."

Kung shrugged. "You're making a big mistake."

"Maybe," Night Owl answered. "Maybe not." She fished in her pocket and pulled out her lucky token. Heads, she'd give the coin to Kung if she found it and demand he transfer mega nuyen to her favorite charity in return; tails, she'd bail here and now and tell him to frag off.

Heads.

What the hell—it might be fun. If she played her cards right, maybe she could squeeze some cred out of Tiger Cat before giving him the coin. A *lot* of cred.

Enough to make the job of the doctors who volunteered with Cybercare for Kids a frag of a lot easier.

Night Owl inclined her head toward Tiger Cat. "Count me in. If I find the Fu Coin, it's yours."

Observing

Alma woke up slowly, stretching the stiffness out of her muscles. She checked the time on her cybereye—8:12 a.m. exactly—and then activated the clock's countdown function a second later, even though she knew what the reading would be: 27:47:59. She refused to succumb to the gloom that came with the knowledge that time was running out and focused instead on the progress she'd made. Today, at 11 a.m., she would meet with the fixer Hothead. Assuming he gave her the information she needed, it was only a matter of time—hopefully not too much time—before she caught up to the rogue Superkid and proved her innocence.

She rolled over and saw that a red light was winking on her cellphone, indicating that there was something in its daytimer that required her attention. Instantly alert, she swept the phone up and flipped it open in one smooth motion. Keying the memo function, she braced herself for what she knew she would find there: a message from the shadowrunner Night Owl.

This time, the message was neither a taunt nor a warning but an acceptance of her invitation.

I'LL MEET WITH YOU, AL, ON ONE CONDITION. THERE'S SOMETHING I WANT—SOMETHING THAT COULD MAKE A LOT OF KIDS' LIVES HAPPIER.

IT LOOKS LIKE WE BOTH RUB SHOULDERS

WITH AKIRA KAGEYAMA. SMALL WORLD, ISN'T IT?

AKIRA'S GOT A PIECE OF JADE WITH A CHINESE COIN INSIDE IT. THE JADE HAS THE CHINESE SYMBOL FOR HAPPINESS ON IT. DO WHAT YOU WANT WITH THE JADE; I JUST WANT THE COIN. IF YOU MANAGE TO BOOST IT, TAKE THE COIN TO THE GOLDEN PROSPERITY BANK AT THE CORNER OF BROADWAY AND NANAIMO, AND PUT IT IN A SAFETY DEPOSIT BOX—NOT ONE WITH A COMBINATION LOCK, BUT ONE WITH A KEY.

Having reached the end of the message, Alma stared at her cellphone, elation and doubt warring inside her. The rogue Superkid had agreed to a meeting—but what she was asking for in return might not be possible. This coin that Night Owl wanted was obviously something of value—probably a rare coin that was part of Kageyama's collection of antiquities. In order to obtain it, Alma would either have to purchase the coin—an unlikely prospect, given her account balance—persuade Kageyama to lend it to her, or "boost" it, as Night Owl had suggested.

But all three options boiled down to the same problem: once Night Owl had what she wanted, there was little reason for her to follow through on her promise of a meeting. No, the better course of action was to go to the meeting she'd already set up with Hothead, in the hope that he would provide her with the data she'd need to run Night Owl to ground.

Alma rode the escalator down to the street level of Broadway Station, bracing herself for the panhandlers and dealers she knew she'd find there. She'd only visited this part of town a few times in all of the years she'd lived in Vancouver. She didn't like it much. Commercial Drive might be touted by some as the cultural highwater of Vancouver, with its trendy shops, ethnic restaurants, real-coffee cafes and theatrical venues, but it was also a hotbed of criminal activity. Its bright murals and exotic window displays made it more cheerful than the concrete grime of the Downtown Eastside, but the number of BTL and drug deals going down on the colorful sidewalks was the same. The number of illicit dealings between shadowrunners—known in street slang as "shadow biz"—was said to be just as high.

As Alma wound her way past the panhandlers and the petty thieves who hissed at her to buy their counterfeit SkyTrain tokens, she saw a grim reminder of what a life in the shadows could lead to, just outside the glass windows that fronted the station. Lying on the sidewalk in the rain was a young elf who had just died of a BTL overdose, judging by the way the police were pulling back his black knitted hat to inspect the chipjack in his temple. Alma zoomed her cybereye in for a closer look and saw that the chip he'd overdosed on was still slotted in the jack. The kid must have only recently come into some credit, judging by his ragged appearance. His pants were made from bubble wrap, and his cyberhand looked as though it had been ready for the scrap heap years ago. He'd probably gotten the credit by breaking into someone's car or home. Alma shook her head in disgust and turned away.

She made her way through the crowds of commuters to the Kaf Kounter, ordered a cappuccino, and checked the clock in her cybereye. It was 11 a.m., precisely the time Hothead had agreed to meet with her. The "fixer," as he was known in shadow slang, had been easy to track down. Bluebeard had recognized the name at once and for a small fee had agreed to get in touch with him on "Cybergirl's" behalf. So far, it seemed, the contacts Alma had made by going through the motions of a shadowrun extraction were paying off. Now she just had to hope that Hothead actually showed up.

The minutes dragged by, and the rain continued to fall outside the station. At the five-minute mark, Alma began to get restless. At the ten-minute mark, a violent trembling in her left hand caused her to drop her cappuccino. She ordered another and held it in her right hand. At the fifteen-minute mark, a dealer tried to sell her BTL chips. She gave him a surly look and told him to "frag off." At the twenty-minute mark, the station's secguards paused to eye her suspiciously as they made their pass through the station. Alma smiled to herself, pleased with the reaction. She'd deliberately dressed down for this meeting, in slashed leather pants and a faded urban brawl fleece jacket. She'd restyled and bleached her hair so Hothead—who as Night Owl's fixer would be in regular, constant contact with her—wouldn't spot the resemblance between the two women. Alma didn't want him tipping the shadowrunner off that her "twin" was looking for her. Not when she was so close . . .

Hothead finally appeared at twenty-three minutes after eleven. Alma recognized him at once by the flickering blue flames on his scalp as he scanned the people who stood at the coffee bar. She'd never in her life seen a more ridiculous-looking implant, but she managed to keep her expression neutral. She drained her cappuccino and set the cup upside down on its saucer: the signal they'd agreed upon. The fixer winked an eye that was either cybernetic or covered with a bright yellow contact lens and pointed at one of the tiny shops that lined this level of the station: a Beautiful Horns aesthetics parlor. Alma nodded and followed him.

Hothead ambled into the salon and tossed a credstick at a red-headed human who was blow-drying the polish she'd just applied to a troll's curving horns.

"Hoi, Meg," he smiled at her. "I'll need the shop for a few. You just about done?"

"Just finishing up, Hothead, then it's all yours."

Hothead sat down in the shop's second chair—a troll-sized seat that caused his feet to dangle above the floor like a child's. He rocked it gently back and forth as he waited for the redhead to finish with her customer. Alma squeezed in past the aesthetician and leaned against a back counter covered with scrollwork tools, tubes of paint, sheets of gold and silver foil, and a multitude of designer-label horn polishes and split fillers.

After a minute or two of fussing with the dryer, the redhead ushered the troll out and left the shop herself. Hothead got up from his seat to hang a "closed" sign on the door and pulled down the window blind.

"The pirate says you're looking to make a patch with another runner," he said.

"You scan that right," Alma said, slipping into the street slang that she'd studied. "She goes by the handle Night Owl. I'm assembling a team for a run, and I want her on it. I understand that you're her fixer. I'd like you to set up a meet between us—I want to suss her out."

Flickers of red crept into the flames that jetted from Hothead's scalp. His yellow-irised eyes took on a knowing look. "If you want to know Night Owl's capabilities, I can give you the rundown. If you want more, I can give you that, too . . . for a fee."

"What do you mean?"

"When you do a run with a stranger, it's good to know the skinny on them: that's always been my policy. Night Owl appeared out of nowhere three months ago. I didn't think much of it at first—runners do fades all the time from one city to another and take care not to leave a datatrail behind. But I started wondering about Night Owl the day I picked up her so-called 'night-vision goggles' and saw that they were nothing more than ordinary rain goggles with clear glass lenses. So I asked myself why a runner would want to hide the fact that she's got cyberware. A few nights ago, Night Owl accidentally let slip a byte of data about herself. I did some digging. The results were . . . very interesting. But they'll cost you. My price is sixteen hundred nuyen. Firm."

Alma couldn't believe her luck. Was Hothead offering her information on who Night Owl really was? Did he know that she was a Superkid? If his data was legitimate, Alma could finally solve the riddle that had been plaguing her and might be able to clear her name, return to PCI—and save her own life.

She could only just afford the price he had named: her savings account had just under seventeen hundred nuyen in it. Hothead's information might prove to be worthless—but Alma couldn't afford to take that chance.

"Sold," she said. Then she paused, as a paranoid thought struck her. Had Hothead *known* how much she had in her savings account? Had he seen through her disguise and realized that she wasn't really a shadowrunner? If he had, it didn't seem as though he cared. Shadowrunners were notorious for backstabbing each other. He'd just proved the old adage: there is no honor among thieves.

Hothead lifted a credstick reader from the counter of the shop, slotted into it a blank credstick he'd pulled from his suit pocket, and handed the reader to Alma. A minute later, the transfer was complete. Alma pulled the credstick out of the reader and held it up so the fixer could see the balance readout on its side.

"Let's hear what you have to say."

Hothead sat forward in his chair. "The data Night Owl let slip was about her father. He suicided in a rather unique—and overly thorough—manner, by hanging himself with a monofilament wire around his neck. Death was as instantaneous as if he'd guillotined himself."

Alma nodded, mentally putting the pieces together. The rogue Shadowrunner must have been talking about Night Owl's foster father.

"According to the Boston police reports, the body was found by a girl—Night Owl, although this obviously wasn't the name she was using at the time."

Hothead paused; it was clear he was going to stretch his story out for all it was worth. Alma didn't care—it gave her time to digest what she was hearing. Whichever one of the Superkids Night Owl was, she'd obviously been placed with a foster family in Boston, the same city that the Superkids were reared in. Given what Ajax had said earlier about the deliberate scattering of the Superkids, Night Owl had probably been the only one placed so close to home.

"What was the girl's name?" Alma asked.

Hothead's flames danced above his head. "We'll come to that in a moment," he said. "It's not as interesting as what comes next."

Alma was inclined to disagree, but she held her tongue.

Hothead pulled a slim yellow cigarette out of the breast pocket of his suit and held it above his head until it ignited. Taking a long draw, he let out a cloud of clove-scented smoke.

"Night Owl was part of a genetic experimentation program called the Superkids," he continued. "Its aim was to produce a 'super race' of humans whose bodies were genetically tailored to accept cybernetics. Seven 'batches' of children were created with varying degrees of success. Several of the children spontaneously aborted due to deformities that were accidentally introduced during the gene splicing, and others were 'terminated' when they 'failed to meet performance standards.' In other words, they were flatlined as infants or toddlers when it turned out they weren't quite perfect."

"No!" Alma gasped. She shook her head, refusing to believe it. Poppy would never permit such a thing. Nobody from Batch Alpha had ever been "terminated." A dozen children had been born, and a dozen children were raised to maturity in the New Horizons creche.

Alma suddenly realized that Hothead had paused in his narrative to stare at her. She quickly amended her comment. "That's horrible—that they killed children, I mean."

"Yeah—too bad, so sad." He flicked ash from his cigarette onto the floor. "But that's the corporate mentality for you. Today's flawed product is tomorrow's ashes."

He took another draw on his cigarette and continued. "The Superkids project was run by a UCAS-registered corporation known as New Horizons. The company doesn't exist anymore. In 2040, after one of the Superkids committed suicide, child protection workers launched an investigation of the project. The breeding program was shut down through a court order, and the existing Superkids were apprehended. Things get a little fuzzy after that—there are a lot of records missing, presumed deleted. But a police report from that year fills in one of the blanks.

"The 'father' that Night Owl mentioned—the one who suicided—wasn't her father in the conventional sense. His name was Michel Louberge, and he was the CEO of New Horizons Incorporated. According to the police reports, he suicided in his office; Night Owl was the first Superkid to stumble across the body."

Alma sagged back in her chair. She suddenly felt queasy, as if her stomach were filled with cold sludge.

All of these years, she'd believed what her foster parents had told her: that Poppy had died of a heart attack. She just couldn't bring herself to believe that he would commit suicide. He'd always seemed such a happy, loving man. An image jumped unbidden into her mind: the only true father she'd ever known lying dead at the foot of his desk, his severed neck pumping out a wash of dark red blood across the carpet, the dull thud of his severed head as the door of his office hit it when it opened. The head rolling away like a ball . . .

Alma's left hand began to shudder violently. When Hothead stared at it, Alma was glad; it meant that he wouldn't see the tears she was fighting so hard to hide. "Sorry," she said, clearing her throat, which felt like it was filled with cotton. "I've got TLE. It hits me at the damnedest times."

"That bites," Hothead agreed. "You'd better get a chopdoc to fix you before you seize up."

"I plan on it," Alma agreed. She was relieved to have steered the conversation onto less emotionally explosive ground. "That's why I'm putting together this run. Cybersurgery is expensive."

When her hand had finally stopped shaking—this attack lasted two minutes and seven seconds—Alma handed the credstick to Hothead, repeating the question she'd asked earlier. "What was the girl's name?"

Hothead's fingers closed on the end of the credstick. "She didn't have one," he said. "To the 'mengeldocs' of New Horizons, she was a letter designation: Batch Alpha, Child AB. Her nickname was Abby."

Alma let out a slow breath she hadn't realized she was holding. Now she knew: her guess had been correct. It was Abby who was going under the name Night Owl—who had framed her. She let the credstick go and watched as Hothead tucked it into a pocket. "What surname did Abby's foster parents give her?"

"She was adopted by a couple in Boston: Brad and Erin Meade."

"What happened to her after that?"

Hothead waved his cigarette in a dismissive gesture. "The story gets less interesting from that point on. Abby Meade went on to college, got a degree in recreation training, and was contracted by the UCAS military to provide fitness training to Navy SEALs. She was on leave in Frisco when the big one hit and was presumed dead after the hotel she was staying in pancaked. And there the datatrail ends."

He took another puff of clove-scented smoke. "Short and sweet, I think she took advantage of the quake to fake her death and do a fade. What she did between 2051 and three months ago, when she started running the Vancouver shadows, is anyone's guess."

He leaned back casually in the oversized chair, a glint in his eye. "So, Ms. Johnson, does that satisfy your curiosity about Night Owl?"

Alma nodded, not bothering to acknowledge the fact that he'd seen through her attempt to pose as a shadowrunner. Only one thing still mattered. "I want to meet with her."

Hothead's flames flickered as he tipped his head, his eyes assessing her. "If a tissue sample is what you want, I'm sure I can fix it for you."

It took Alma a moment to realize what he was alluding to. Then she got it: Hothead thought she was representing a corporation that was interested in cloning the Superkids. She shook her head. "I just want to talk with her."

It was a lie. In order to prove her innocence, Alma would have to deliver Abby into Hu's hands.

"All right," Hothead said. "I haven't seen Night Owl around much these past few nights, but she usually hangs on the Drive. If you want to find her, try a restaurant called Wazubee's. She usually janders in there around midnight. Just one thing, though: you tell her that I set her up, and you're as good as dead. You got that, Ms. Wei?"

Alma blinked, startled by his use of her surname. She wondered how much more information Hothead had been able to uncover about her—and who he was selling it to. She wondered if blackmail attempts would soon follow. If they did, she could kiss her career in the security field goodbye. But right now, clearing her name at PCI and getting the corporation to halt the countdown on the bomb inside her head were much more pressing issues.

Slowly, she nodded her head. "I got it," she said.

Alma spent the hour that followed her meeting with Hothead mulling over the shocking news of how Poppy had actually died. She drifted back up the escalator to the SkyTrain platform and boarded the first train that came along. She rode it back and forth across the city, staring out at the rain. The gray skies overhead and trickle of nature's tears down the windows matched her mood.

Only when the PCI building slid into view for the third time did she realize that she was riding the train she normally took to work. She stared longingly at the sprawling complex, thoughts of death filling her mind like a dark, heavy cloud. How she wished that she could turn back the clock to the day before Gray Squirrel's extraction. If only she could have seen the extraction coming and prevented it, he might still be alive . . .

She stopped herself. That sort of thinking was counterproductive. She needed to focus on the here and now, not on what might have been. She pulled her cellphone out of its belt clip and stared at it, debating the merits of calling Hu to report what she'd found out so far. The head of PCI security had cast a vote of confidence in Alma, that day outside the boardroom when he told her to call him as soon as she uncovered the truth behind Gray Squirrel's extraction. She'd come close to telecoming him several times since then but had always stopped herself. Telling Hu that the extraction had been carried out by another Superkid wasn't enough—not even now that she knew that Superkid's name. An accusation and name alone didn't constitute "proof"—she needed concrete evidence. Hu had drummed into her a sense of professionalism, a thirst for thoroughness. Nothing short of bringing Abby down to PCI in restraint strips would do.

Tonight at midnight, gods willing, Alma would do just that. She'd stake out the restaurant from across the street, follow Abby until she found a place to waylay her, and administer a dose of gamma scopolamine. She had to assume that Hothead would tip Abby off. But Alma had confidence in the training she'd received from the Justice Institute and the skills she'd honed over twelve years of security work. Even if Abby was looking for Alma, she wouldn't see her.

Alma replayed what the fixer had told her about Poppy's death, running it over and over in her mind until she convinced herself that it was really possible. Poppy hadn't died of a heart attack. He'd killed himself. Just like Aaron.

No—not just like Aaron. The Superkid had jumped off the top of the New Horizons building, and Poppy had slit his throat with a monofilament wire.

Once again, Alma paused to correct herself. No: not slit his throat. Poppy had sliced his head clean off . . .

Alma caught herself, recognizing that she'd subconsciously mixed together in her mind the way Poppy had died with the way in which Gray Squirrel had been murdered. The realization nagged at her a moment longer, and then she saw a second parallel:

Akiko, who was on death row in a Texas prison, had also killed her victim by slashing his throat. It had to have been more than mere coincidence: studies of identical twins who were separated at birth and reared independently of each other kept turning up lengthy strings of correspondences. Twins—nature's clones—married partners with the same names, chose the same professions, had the same hobbies and even bought identical pets and gave them the same names. The Superkids had been reared as a tightly knit unit for the first eight years of their lives. It made perfect sense that, when it came to murder, they'd have the same modus operandi.

That wasn't all of it, though. Not all of the Superkids had become murderers. Ajax and those Superkids he was in touch with had gone on to become honest citizens—not just law-abiding, but in some cases law-enforcing. Something environmental must have steered Abby and Akiko down the wrong path. Probably something that happened to them during the years they were fostered . . .

Or during their final days in the New Horizons creche. What was it that Hothead had said? Abby was the *first* Superkid to find Poppy's body. If she was the first, it begged the question: who was the second?

Pulling out her cellphone, Alma punched in a number. Three calls later, she had tracked down the Texas prison in which Akiko was incarcerated and was speaking to the warden. Somewhat reluctantly, since the sentence of capital punishment was to be carried out in just two hours' time, he listened to her request for a telecom link with Prisoner 2897436, Jacqueline Boothby. Only when Alma succeeded in convincing the warden that she was Akiko's long-lost sister did he finally relent.

After a five-minute pause, Akiko's face appeared on the monitor of Alma's cellphone. It was like looking into a mirror from the future—Akiko looked twenty years older than she really was, her face drawn and haggard, with deep worry lines at the corners of her eyes and mouth. Her hair had been shaved down to stubble, and she wore prison grays. She looked at Alma with open skepticism for a moment or two, as if not really believing that another Superkid had actually telecomed her, and then gave her a grim smile.

"Hoi, Al," she said. "I like the blond hair."

Akiko's voice was much harder than Alma remembered, and her body language was all wrong—different from the poised grace that Alma remembered. She supposed the two years Akiko had spent in prison were responsible.

Three days ago, when Ajax had broken the news that Akiko was on death row, it hadn't really sunk in. Akiko had been a distant memory that had paled in comparison to Alma's joy at finding Ajax again. But now that Alma was looking into the eyes of the condemned woman, it was hitting home. She was suddenly sorry that she was bothering Akiko with a frivolous question at a time like this.

She gave Akiko the heartiest smile she could manage. "Hello, Akiko," she said. "I just heard about your . . . about what's happening today."

Akiko was blunter: "My execution."

"Yes. Ahmed was the one who tracked you down and told me where you were. I'm sorry that—"

"I'm not. This place chews. I'll be glad to be out of here. Now quit the bulldrek and tell me what the frag it is you want."

Alma fought down the lump in her throat. She might as well get to the point; Akiko looked as though she'd like to cut the connection.

"I just learned something about Poppy's death," Alma told her. "I always thought he died of a heart attack, but that wasn't what happened. He—"

Akiko said something, and Alma had to stop and ask her to repeat it.

"I said, 'You ought to know,' " Akiko repeated impatiently.

"I'm sorry? What do you mean?"

Akiko stared out of the cellphone's tiny screen, shaking her head. "You were the one who found his body."

Alma frowned, confused. "I did?"

"You came running down the hall, screaming something about a head. I looked into Poppy's office and saw a body lying on the floor, minus its brainbox. They tried to tell me, later, that it was someone else—that it wasn't Poppy. But I never believed them."

"That . . . wasn't me," Alma said. "It was Abby."

"It was you, all right."

"It couldn't have been," Alma insisted. "I'd remember something like that. It wasn't until I was placed with a family that my foster mother told me Poppy was dead. You must have mistaken Abby for me. According to the police report, she was the one who found the body."

Akiko gave a harsh laugh. "What do the police know about anything? Half the time they get their data scrambled. If they were even the slightest bit competent, the fragger that raped me would have been put away for good. Did you know that he murdered three other women? If I hadn't been a Superkid, he would have killed me, too. I could have finished him off then and there, but oh, no, I was too honest. And later, I trusted that the cops would be smart enough to collect enough evidence to link the crimes. But they bungled it. So don't talk to me about police reports." Akiko emphasized the last two words with a twisted mouth, as if she was getting ready to spit.

"I see," Alma said, not knowing what to say next. "Uh, if there's anything I can do, Akiko . . ."

"There isn't. In one hour and forty-two minutes, I'm going to fry. But thanks for calling," she added in a sarcastic tone. "Talking about Poppy has brightened up what's left of my day immensely."

The cellphone's monitor went blank.

Slowly, both hands trembling slightly, Alma folded the cellphone shut.

Later that afternoon, after Alma had done a thorough recon of the restaurant and plotted her best surveillance position, she returned home to her apartment. Out of deference to Gray Squirrel, she'd been religiously following the test schedule that he'd laid down; she was in day sixteen of a twenty-one-day period of leaving the REM inducer in passive mode—the final portion of the beta test. But now it was time to break that pattern. She needed to be as fresh as possible tonight. As a Superkid, Abby would be Alma's equal in terms of strength, speed and intelligence. The last thing Alma needed was to give her an edge by being overtired.

Alma had no choice but to break with Gray Squirrel's orders. She'd have to use the REM inducer to catch a fifteen-minute catnap this afternoon, in order to stay fresh.

So lost in her thoughts was she that she touched the wrong icon when she got into the elevator. Alma only noticed her error when the doors opened on the underground parkade. She couldn't imagine why she'd hit that icon: it wasn't as though she ever came down here, since she always commuted by SkyTrain or cab. She could hardly use the "running on autopilot" excuse.

The elevator gave a soft *ping*, and then the doors began to slide shut. It wasn't until the last moment that the design on the motorcycle Alma was staring at registered in her brain. Painted on the gas tank was a winking owl, in front of a night sky speckled with stars and a crescent moon. Alma lunged at the doors' "open" icon as two words came together suddenly in her mind: Night . . . and Owl.

"No," she whispered. "It isn't possible. This is *my* building."

As the doors opened again, Alma slid into the underground parking lot, keeping a wall at her back. She increased her cyberear's amplification until the hiss of the air vents sounded like the roar of a hurricane, filtered out that and her breathing, as well as the pounding of her heart, and listened for sounds of an intruder. Her cybereyes swept the parkade, both at ground level, where she'd see the feet of anyone hiding behind a car, and higher up, where an intruder could cling like a spider to the pipes.

Nothing. The parkade was clear.

Every sense still on alert, Alma approached the motorcycle. It was a Harley Electroglide—a brand-new 2062 model, by the look of it. Alma did a slow circuit of the spot where it was parked, her eyes searching the concrete floor for clues. A crumpled Stuffer Shack paper cup lay up against the wall where someone had dropped it, and there were a few bootprints on the cement where someone had walked through oil. Otherwise, the area was clean.

Alma squatted and touched a finger to the bike's exhaust pipes. They were cold; the motorcycle had been here for some time. And that, perhaps, was the most worrying thing of all. Was Abby lying in wait for Alma, up in her apartment?

Alma smiled. If she was, that would certainly simplify things.

She told herself not to rush: to be thorough. She continued her inspection of the motorcycle, opening up the seat to look inside its built-in storage compartment, and flipping open the leather saddlebags that hung at the back. Both were empty. On a whim, she peered up the exhaust pipes and spotted something glinting in one of them. Sticking a finger inside, she fished it out.

It was a stylus-thick cylinder of silvered plastic with a magnetic strip down one side: a maglock key. And not just any key, but one Alma recognized at once. The key was identical in shape and size and color to the one in her own pocket, except for a faint X that had been scratched into one end. It was a key to another apartment in her building.

She stared at it a moment longer, wondering what it might mean. Had the tables suddenly turned—was Abby staking Alma out from a neighboring suite? But if she was, what was the key to that suite doing hidden inside the motorcycle's exhaust pipe? If Abby was in the building, wouldn't she be carrying the key with her?

Alma needed answers. Following up the clue in her hand seemed to be the best way to get them. She strode back to the elevator, got inside, and pressed the icon for the twelfth floor. When she got off, she opened the fire door carefully and quietly climbed the two flights up to her floor. After a careful check of the hallway, using the magnification system of her cybereyes to search the most likely spots where a surveillance camera might have been planted, she crept down the hall, trying the key she'd found in each door she passed. It didn't work in the doors of the suites to either side of hers or in the one across the hall. Three doors down from her apartment, however, the maglock flashed green when she slotted the key.

Alma opened the door a crack and listened for any noise coming from inside the apartment. Every muscle in her body was tensed for action; there was a good chance that Abby was just behind the door, poised to jump her the moment she entered. Alma slid a hand into her pocket and drew out the gamma scopolamine injector she'd carried to her meeting with Hothead as a holdout weapon. She flicked the lever that primed it and heard the soft hiss of air compressing. Then she crouched low and to the side and eased the door open.

The apartment was a mirror image of her own—as far as the layout was concerned, at least. The bathroom was on the left, instead of on the right, but the kitchen and living room were one big open space, with no one in sight.

One big mess, was more like it. Everywhere Alma looked, the floor and counters were strewn with clothing, pieces of electronic equipment, piles of newsfaxes, and empty fast-food containers nested together in tall stacks. An enormous handgun lay in its holster on the kitchen counter: an Ares Predator. The bathroom—which Alma glanced into to assure herself that it was also clear—had shelves that were filled with cosmetic containers of every description. Most were tubes of the brightly colored "Beijing Opera mask" makeup that was the latest trend, out on the fringes of fashion.

Alma shut the hallway door softly behind her and slipped the injector back into her pocket. She made a slow sweep of the apartment, picking her way through the stacks of junk. She'd expected to smell rotten food and mold, but the room smelled faintly of sandalwood instead. The fast-food containers had been scrubbed out and stacked—saved for some purpose that Alma couldn't fathom. As she glanced around at the months' worth of accumulated debris, she slowly came to the realization that Abby wasn't just using the apartment as a stakeout. She *lived* here.

Which was just too weird to be true.

Alma searched the room thoroughly but learned nothing from the clutter. On a desk near the window, she spotted a cyberterminal that looked as though it had been cobbled together from spare parts. Alma powered it up and briefly considered jacking in, but rejected that idea as too dangerous. Lost in the Matrix, she'd have no way of hearing or seeing Abby if she returned to the apartment. Instead she activated the flatscreen display and scrolled through the menu that appeared on it.

There wasn't much: just a few application programs and eleven download files. Alma clicked on the first one, which was labeled DOURSAVE, and a schematic of some kind appeared. Scrolling down through it, she found a building map of something called the Technology Institute and what looked like laboratory research notes. She clicked on the second file, NUKESPEW, and found a report on the disposal of nuclear waste by the Gaeatronics Corporation, with the logo of the Western Wilderness Committee on the top. The third, labeled FRYBABY, contained a lab report that dated back to 2039, on a piece of headware that was supposed to modify the behavior of delinquent children by making them less aggressive. Alma skipped ahead to the fourth, INPUT, and found it was an e-mail file. She scanned quickly through the dozens of messages it held, but none of them contained anything of interest. They seemed to be tips from other shadowrunners on everything from how to crack a maglock to how to construct a remote-sensing listening system.

One by one, she checked the other files. It was the last one, labeled GRIMREAPER, that made her breath catch in her throat. The first page was a full-screen digipic of Gray Squirrel, with target crosshairs superimposed over it. Wincing, Alma flipped forward in the file. The next image to fill the screen was a document. At the top was a logo Alma recognized instantly: the curling tsunami of Pacific Cybernetics Incorporated.

The document was a memo from Gray Squirrel to Mr. Lali, dated ten months ago. Heart racing, forcing

208   *Lisa Smedman*

herself to slow down so she wouldn't miss anything
important, Alma read through it. Someone—maybe
even Abby herself—had highlighted three sections of
it in yellow. The first one read:

*Results from the alpha-test unit are unsatisfactory.
Seventy-two percent of subjects exhibit progressive loss
of muscle tone, which was only halted by removal of
test units. In twenty percent of these cases, side effects
not only persisted but increased, despite removal. Side
effects included narcolepsy, with attacks progressing in
number and duration and eventually leading to cata-
tonic state. Mortality rate to date of catatonia victims is
ninety-six percent in troll subjects; ninety-five percent
in ork subjects. Suggest we relocate testing project away
from Yomi to location that offers alternative stock.*

It was clear that Gray Squirrel was talking about
the alpha-test model of the REM inducer, which had
been tested overseas. The reference to "Yomi" told
Alma where that testing had been carried out: Yomi
was the island in the Philippines that Japan had exiled
its ork and troll populations to. It was an odd place
for PCI to choose as the site of a testing program.
The memo seemed to be indicating that only orks and
trolls had been accepted as volunteers to test the device—and yet the REM inducer was intended to benefit all races.

According to what Alma had just read, a horrify-
ingly large number of those volunteers had died, despite Gray Squirrel's best efforts. No wonder Gray
Squirrel had been so happy to have a subject with
Alma's stamina volunteer for the beta-test unit. She
glanced at her left hand, wondering how much worse
the tremors caused by the REM inducer were going
to get. If only Gray Squirrel were still alive . . .

With grim determination, Alma read on through the
report, lingering over the next highlighted section of
text.

Suggest you continue to stall Salish-Shidhe Council members. Alpha-test version is clearly not ready for testing in soldiers. Battlefield applications at this point seem limited, unless you can persuade Council to up acceptable "friendly fire" casualty rate from ten percent to twenty.

Alma paused. What was Gray Squirrel talking about? The soldiers who would be receiving the REM inducer were already casualties. Their brains had been injured by magic wielded by the enemy, not by "friendly fire."

Suddenly, another interpretation occurred to Alma. What if the REM inducers were intended not for wounded soldiers but for healthy ones? The cyberware would turn them into the perfect fighting machines: men and women who needed only a fifteen-minute catnap between battles to be fresh and ready to fight again. Alma shouldn't have been surprised by this proposed application, and she understood now why Gray Squirrel had done the first round of testing so far afield: if PCI was going to sell it to the Salish-Shidhe military, they certainly didn't want the Tsimshians finding out about the project. She marveled at the fact that Gray Squirrel had found so many test subjects— fifty in all, according to the numbers cited in this report. What would have motivated people who probably couldn't even find Salish-Shidhe on a map to volunteer for such dangerous testing? Certainly not patriotism.

The answer was in the final section of highlighted text.

Problems with alpha-test model are in process of being rectified, but imperative that you authorize either transfer of credit or move to new test area as soon as possible. Director of detainment camp is unwilling to risk exposure of project, in light of high mortality rate, and is proving uncooperative. He is refusing to provide more test subjects until further credits are transferred.

There was a little bit more—the usual salutations—
but Alma didn't read it. She stared at the flatscreen,
unwilling to believe what she had just read. If it was
true, there was a darker motivation for testing the
REM inducer on Yomi Island. The people who'd had
the alpha-test units implanted in their brains weren't
volunteers. They were lab rats. And Gray Squirrel had
killed them.

It all made sense now. Gray Squirrel's unwillingness
to provide detailed destinations to PCI security when
he went on his business trips to the Philippines, the
low-level tension that Alma had thought was caused
by Gray Squirrel's quarrels with his wife, and his re-
luctance to talk about the alpha-test models. When he
refused to provide her with details of the alpha tests,
she thought that he'd been trying to avoid biasing
Alma's assessment of the beta-test version. In reality,
he hadn't told her about those tests because he knew
she'd find them abhorrent.

What did you do when you suddenly discovered that
one of your best friends—a man you looked up to
as a benefactor of humanity—was really a murderer?
Alma's lips set in a grim line as she answered the
question she'd posed. You either try to deny the evidence and forget you ever saw it, or you confront that
friend with what you know and demand an
explanation.

She scrolled back to the image of Gray Squirrel that
had the crosshairs superimposed over it. Thanks to
Abby, Alma would never have that chance. Even
though her sinking heart told her that Gray Squirrel
was guilty of the crime he'd inadvertently confessed
to in the memo, Alma would have liked the chance
to hear an explanation of why he'd done it from his
own lips.

Part of her already accepted the fact, however, that
it would have made little difference. Hu's words

echoed in her mind: There are no excuses, only reasons. Even so, Alma still groped for excuses—and rejected them, one by one.

Maybe Gray Squirrel had been forced into carrying
out the experimentation on unwilling subjects—but
the tone of the memo didn't suggest this. Even scanning between the lines, Alma couldn't find a hint of
regret or sympathy for his victims.

Maybe the memo was a forgery, designed to accuse
Gray Squirrel of something he hadn't done—but if it
was, why had Abby murdered him, instead of
exposing him?

Wanting to see where the file had been copied from,
and when, Alma called up the summary information
on GRIM REAPER. She wasn't surprised to see that
it had been pirated directly from a private grid access
host that was separate from the main PCI system.
What did shock her was the routing code on the file
itself. Abby hadn't just accessed a secret system that
Alma herself didn't even know about—she'd done it
from Alma's workstation. And the date and time at
which the file had been copied—11:03 p.m. on November 10—was disturbingly familiar . . .

Alma suddenly realized why. That was the evening
she'd worked late at PCI, drilling the security staff on
counterintrusion measures, and come home too ex-
hausted even to flick on the lights before crawling into
bed. When she'd awakened the next morning, she'd
realized at once that her apartment had been broken
into the day before. Nothing had been stolen, but
there were subtle clues everywhere that an intruder
had been through the place from top to bottom. A
leaf on her orchid was broken, the window had been
left depolarized, the holopic of the Superkids was
crooked on the table, and the clothes in her closet
weren't in the same order they had been. The intruder
had even taken a container of soymilk out of the re-

frigerator, drunk it, and put the empty container into
the trash.

Alma had promptly reported the break-in to Hu,
and PCI had done a full investigation—with zero results. Alma had changed the coding of her apartment
lock and tightened up security at work for the next
few weeks, but there were no further incidents. She'd
eventually classified the intrusion as a random event,
unrelated to her work—a common break-in. The thief
had found nothing of value in her home and had gone
on his way.

Now she knew the truth. Abby had broken into
her apartment, probably as a test of Alma's security
systems. Then she'd gone the break-in one better by
infiltrating PCI itself. She'd copied the file that Alma
had just read and used it to whet the appetites of the
executives at a rival corporation—Tan Tien Incorporated. Then she'd carried out the extraction of Gray
Squirrel, framing Alma in the process.

No . . . not framing. Spitting on the camera was a
clue, just as the taunting messages on Alma's cellphone had been. Abby had probably assumed that
Alma, as PCI's counterextractions expert, would be in
charge of investigating Gray Squirrel's kidnapping.
She hadn't realized that Alma would miss the clue
she'd so deliberately left behind—that it would be
Alma's superior, Hu, who would spot it.

Abby hadn't been framing Alma. She'd been testing
her. Just as the Superkids had once been tested.

With a shiver of fear, Alma shut down the cyberterminal. Abby wasn't just a shadowrunner. She was a
damn *good* shadowrunner.

This morning's I Ching reading had warned Alma
to keep an eye on her immediate surroundings. *Observe the ups and downs of your own life*, it had ad-
vised her. *Observe your own life if you want to find
peace of mind.*

She could only think of one place left to observe that qualified as part of her "own life": her apartment. That was where she would find Abby. She was certain of it.

Easing out of Abby's apartment, she made her way down the hall.

Alma paced back and forth in her apartment, trying to decide what to do next. She'd found no signs of Abby—the apartment was empty, and everything was exactly as she'd left it that morning. She'd searched the apartment building top to bottom, including the roof, the electrical and utility rooms, the laundry and the storage lockers, just to make sure Abby wasn't hiding elsewhere in the building. She wasn't. As a final measure, Alma had mounted a miniature surveillance camera in the building's front lobby and placed another in the parkade where it would give a view of the motorcycle. She'd mounted a third in the hallway outside her apartment and a fourth in Abby's apartment, and then slaved all of them to a cyberterminal in her apartment.

For the past six hours and fifteen minutes she'd been sitting in front of the cyberterminal, staring at its monitor, watching other residents come and go. Although several people passed through the lobby and parkade, none of them resembled a Superkid. And none of them went anywhere near the motorcycle or came to the fourteenth floor.

Alma activated the clock in her cybereye and checked the time. It was 10:06 p.m. She still had to squeeze in a fifteen-minute catnap before she decided whether it was worth relocating her surveillance to Wazubee's. She placed the program she was using into record mode and then stood and stretched. She'd use the REM inducer to sleep from 10:10 to 10:25 p.m.

and then do a quick-frame review of whatever the surveillance cameras picked up during that time.

Alma curled up on her bed in a fetal position with her back against the wall—her usual sleeping pose—and closed her eyes. To activate the REM inducer, she had to use a code; Gray Squirrel had designed the beta-test model to avoid the "glitches" he'd found in his first design—glitches that Alma now realized must have been bouts of narcolepsy triggered by accidental activation of the device. The trigger was to count backwards by prime numbers from nineteen—something that a person would be highly unlikely to do by accident. Alma began, subvocalizing to focus her concentration.

"Nineteen, seventeen, thirteen . . ."

She felt a hot tickle begin deep inside her brain, a centimeter or two above the spot where her move-by-wire system had been implanted.

"Eleven, seven, five . . ."

Dreamlike, hallucinatory images began to flicker against her closed eyelids as she began the slide into REM sleep: composites of her thoughts, her observations that day, her fears. She was straddling Abby's motorcycle with Akira Kageyama clinging behind her, riding the roaring metal monster through a night sky. Something monstrous followed in their wake, flapping wings that made a sound like grumbling surf. The bike's twin exhaust pipes puffed out clouds of thick black smoke that rained maglock keys, became storm crows and flew away. Up ahead, the moon was a gigantic silver coin with a winking square eye and a big grin on its face. Alma smiled back at it—the grin of a fool.

"Three, two, one . . ."

Consciousness fled, and sleep claimed her.

Return

Night Owl opened her eyes, looked around, and saw that she was in Alma's apartment. Good. She hated it when Alma slept in a hotel, forcing her to figure out where the frag she was, or dossed down at the PCI office, which meant that Night Owl had to be extremely careful not to give herself away.

She sat up on the bed and patted herself down. She was fully clothed, in slashed leather jeans and a baggy fleece shirt: styles that Alma would normally never wear. Curious, she got up, made her way to the bathroom, and stared into the mirror. A bleached-blond reflection blinked back at her, surprise written on her face.

"What have you been up to, Alma?" she asked it. Then she sighed. "I wish you were the type to keep an e-journal. It would make my life so much easier."

She checked the clock that was built into the kitchen stove—Alma didn't seem to believe in knowing what time it was, since this was the only clock in the place—and saw that it was just after 10:30. Evening, judging by the dark sky outside the apartment window.

The window reflected a square of flickering light that was coming from a table on the other side of the kitchen counter. Night Owl walked into the section of the apartment that served as the living room, taking care not to disturb anything, and looked at the cyber-

terminal that was sitting there. Its flatscreen was split
into four views of the apartment building: lobby, parkade, hallway and . . . her apartment?

Night Owl had shoved her hands into the pockets
of the jacket to prevent herself from inadvertently
touching anything. Inside one pocket, she felt the
three coins that Alma used to cast the I Ching and
two cylindrical objects. Pulling them out, she saw that
both were keys. One had to be the key to Alma's
apartment, but the other had an X scratched into
one end.

Night Owl *tsk-tsked*. "You've been snooping,
haven't you, Alma?"

The other pocket held an injector. Night Owl had
no idea what drug was inside, but she didn't want to
mess with it. She laid the injector beside the cyberterminal and touched a finger to the PAUSE RECORD
icon that was blinking on the monitor. The digital
numbers that were displaying the time of the re-
cording froze at 10:34:18.

Letting herself out of Alma's apartment, Night Owl
padded down the hall. She opened her own door cautiously, every sense on the alert, but there weren't any
surprises. Alma had been content, it seemed, to
merely observe. She hadn't laid any traps.

Night Owl stripped off the clothes she'd woken up
in and left them in a pile by the door. She changed
into jeans and a crinkle-foil shirt and strapped the
Ares Predator against the small of her back. She
picked up the SkyTrain token that had been lying on
the counter beside it and slipped it into a pocket of
her jeans, together with Alma's I Ching coins. Then
she headed into the bathroom to paint her face.

She flicked on the light and stared into the mirror.
Which color to use as the base for her mask? The red
of loyalty, or the white of the evildoer? The black of
righteousness, the blue of the temperamental trouble-

maker, or the yellow of a tortured soul? Perhaps the silver or gold of the supernatural being . . .

Night Owl closed her eyes and reached out for one of the tubes, letting fate decide for her. Gold it was. She applied the makeup slowly and carefully, streaking a diagonal of black down either side of her mouth and a band of black across her eyes, then filling the rest in with gold. She could count on just six to eight hours in which to roam before a bout of yawning signaled that it was time to return. As soon as she started feeling sleepy, she'd have about half an hour to get back to the apartment, scrub off her makeup, change clothes, and crawl back into Alma's bed.

As she stroked the makeup onto her skin, Night Owl reviewed what must have happened. Alma wouldn't have searched this apartment without going through the files on the cyberterminal, one by one, in her usual methodical fashion. She'd have read the FRYBABY file and realized that the serotonin booster that was implanted in Aaron's brain in 2039 had led to his suicide.

According to that report, the Superkids of Batch Alpha contained a genetic flaw: a mutation of the serotonin 2A receptor gene that enabled the brain to absorb more serotonin than usual. Under normal circumstances, when serotonin levels fell within the average range, there were no ill effects. But increase the level of that neurotransmitter, and the brain became supersaturated with serotonin. Terrible things started to happen, like the suicidal depression that had caused Aaron to jump—and the fragmenting of personalities that had occurred in Alma.

Night Owl knew what she was: an alter ego of Alma's. Her earliest memories were those that Alma had stuffed in the deep, dark hole of her subconscious—the ones that were too painful for her to remember herself. The time she'd been touched *there* by the technician—Alma had never understood why her favorite tech got fired. The time her cybereyes had shorted out, blinding Alma for three terrifying hours. And the time she saw Poppy's severed head. She got all of the drek—and none of the benefits. She couldn't even access Alma's cyberware.

Night Owl hadn't really come into her own, separate awareness, however, until the REM inducer was implanted in Alma's brain. She could still remember the night she was "born"—when she'd found herself jacked into a cyberterminal, staring at the memo that Gray Squirrel had sent to Mr. Lali. She had no idea what the file was about—the last thing she could remember was being an eight-year-old girl. But she knew that the memo was both terrifying and important. If it wasn't, she wouldn't have had tears pouring down her face. She'd copied it onto an optical chip, tucked the chip into a pocket, and jacked out. Somehow, she'd managed to stumble out of the PCI building and, after wandering across half the city, let instinct guide her home. She'd spent the night rummaging around Alma's apartment, trying to figure out who and what she was, and then had collapsed into a deep sleep.

She'd awakened from that sleep the next evening, and the search had begun anew.

Night Owl hadn't liked what she'd found. Alma was a corporate drone, blindly obedient to the company she worked for and incapable of seeing her "friends" and colleagues for the monsters that they were. She worked long hours of overtime without being properly compensated for it and then came home to a sterile apartment each night, alone. The one time she'd found true love, she'd let her overblown sense of propriety and duty cause her to throw it away. She was pathetic.

Night Owl, on the other hand, was carefree and bold. Drawn to Vancouver's shadows, she'd used her runs to do some good in this world. She might not have been able to contribute as much cred as she'd like to Cybercare for Kids, but she was certain some child, in some dirt-poor backwater somewhere, appreciated the little she'd been able to give.

Night Owl had to assume that Alma had read the GRIMREAPER report in its entirety. Alma was smart enough to realize that the REM inducer inside her brain was allowing an alter ego to awaken each night, every time she drifted into REM sleep. Getting the REM inducer removed wouldn't be so easy now— not with Gray Squirrel dead—but Night Owl was sure that Alma would find a way. Why else would a business card from the Executive Body Enhancements clinic have been inside Alma's pocket? When Night Owl had called the clinic, posing as "Jane Lee," they'd confirmed her appointment for February 28: tomorrow. After chatting with the receptionist, Night Owl had learned that the cyberware the chopdoc was going to deal with was a "serotonin booster" that had been acting up. She could guess what that meant: the REM inducer was coming out tomorrow.

Tonight could be her last run. She'd better make it worthwhile.

Night Owl glanced out over the city from the rooftop of one of the few large buildings still standing in the Richmond Ruins: the Relax Hotel. Outside the sky-cab shelter in which she stood it was raining— hard. Raindrops pelted the cracked plexiglass and collected in large puddles on the rooftop outside the shelter before draining down through the rockworm holes in the roof. Across the river, the lights of Vancouver wavered like an underwater mirage. Night Owl wondered if it would be the last time she'd see the city and then shook off the melancholy she felt.

Time to get down to biz.

The first buyer—the blond Seoulpa ganger—was the easiest to track down. When Tiger Cat had confronted the woman outside the coin store, he'd called her Alma's "Johnson." On a hunch, Night Owl scrolled through the autodial memory on Alma's cellphone and found an entry for MS JOHNSON. She highlighted the number and touched a thumb to the dial icon. After five rings, Blondie's face appeared on the monitor screen.

"Yeboseyo?"

Night Owl saw a restaurant in the background, rather than prison bars. Blondie had either recovered from Tiger Cat's magic in time to stagger away from the police, or she'd talked or bought her way out of being arrested. Good. That saved Night Owl the difficulty of dealing with someone she didn't know instead.

As soon as Blondie saw who was calling her, she grimaced. Her image filled more of the monitor as she moved the cellphone closer to her face and peered into it; she was probably trying to spot background detail and figure out where Night Owl was calling from. Night Owl had anticipated this, however—in fact, she'd counted on it. The angle at which she was holding the cell would allow its vidcam to pick up the ruined rooftop and part of the jumbled skyline behind it. She hoped that Blondie was smart enough to recognize the Ruins—and that she would start moving in this direction. Night Owl didn't have all night to wait for her.

She pulled one of Alma's I Ching coins out of her pocket. Her friend Miracle Worker had cast a nova-hot illusion spell on all three of them—a spell she'd promised would hold up to a camera's scrutiny. Night Owl was about to find out how hot her friend's mojo really was. She held the illusion-cloaked coin up so that the cell's minicam caught it full frame. "Is this what your master is looking for?"

Blondie's indrawn hiss of breath told her it was. "How did you—"

"Tonight I'm selling it to the highest bidder," Night Owl announced. "Either Mang, Chiao or Li—I don't care which. I'll call you in five for your opening bid."

Before the ganger could reply, Night Owl cut the connection. She waited about ten minutes—long enough to let Blondie sweat about whether she really was going to call back—and then redialed. This time, the ganger answered on the first ring. She was no longer in the restaurant but in a moving car; outside the rear window, Night Owl could see the rain-blurred red W that topped the Woodwards Arcology receding into the background. Good. Blondie was on the move south.

"Well?" Night Owl asked.

Blondie looked guarded. "My master will pay fifteen thousand nuyen if it's the genuine article. But he insists on proof—"

"You call that an opening bid?" Night Owl rolled her eyes. "That's pathetic. I guess your master's not serious. Forget it. I'll call—"

Blondie's eyes spat venom at her. "Thirty thousand."

"That's more like it," Night Owl said. "Give me another five while I find out if the competition wants to bid higher."

"*Muyi*! Wait while I—"

Once again, Night Owl cut the connection. This time, she let fifteen minutes slide by. While she waited, she walked to the edge of the shelter and double-checked the floor, nudging the cement in front of her with the toe of her Dayton. From somewhere below came a faint *crunch-grind-crunch* of rockworms munching away. The cement under her toe shifted slightly, and she took a step back.

Night Owl redialed and spoke as soon as Blondie's

face appeared on the monitor. "Your competition countered with offers of one hundred thousand nuyen, and between them they bid the price up to five hundred K," she said. "Your master is looking at six hundred K to stay in the game."

Blondie gave her a sour smile. "Six hundred thousand nuyen will be his final offer. Take it, and I will guarantee your life. Refuse . . ." She let the rest of the sentence hang in the air unspoken.

There was no need to fill in the blank.

Night Owl kept her face carefully neutral, although inside she was grinning from ear to ear. She'd gambled that Blondie's master wasn't on speaking terms with his scaly rivals—checking in with the other dragons to see if they really were bidding on one of the Coins of Luck would be the last thing that Mang would do.

Night Owl's bluff had worked. Blondie had bought it—pun intended.

"Offer accepted," Night Owl said.

"Good." Blondie smirked. "How soon can you deliver?"

"That depends on how soon you can transfer the cred. We'll do this like a run, with fifty percent down, and fifty percent upon delivery. There's an internationally registered charity I use for this type of biz, called Cybercare for Kids. You make an anonymous donation of three hundred K in the account whose number I'm going to give you, to show me that you're serious about this buy. Then you ask the bank to set up a double-blind trust account and put the other three hundred K in that. As soon as you're satisfied that the coin is the real item, they authorize transfer of payment. Your client's confidentiality is assured, and the buy winds up looking like an anonymous charitable donation."

Night Owl pretended to check a watch. "I'll give you five minutes to make the first payment. When I receive confirmation that it's been made, I'll call you back."

She gave Blondie the bank name and the charity's account number and then broke the connection. Two minutes later, a representative of the bank called to say that the deposit had been made to the charity's account and that a trust account had also been set up. As soon as Blondie discovered the coin was a fake, of course, the cred in this second account would revert back to her master. But Cybercare for Kids would still have made three hundred K.

When Night Owl called Blondie back, the monitor screen remained blanked. Blondie was trying to hide the fact that she was in a sky cab, but the faint *chuff-chuff-chuff* of the helicopter rotors gave her location away. Looking north toward the city lights of Vancouver, Night Owl saw the strobed running lights of a sky cab heading her way. Blondie would be over the Richmond Ruins in a few minutes, at most.

"I've transferred the cred," Blondie said.

"Good."

"Now I want the coin. Where are you?"

Night Owl frowned, as if she were having second thoughts. "I'll need some time to set up a transfer," she said. "We'll need a meeting place where we can both feel secure. Perhaps . . ." As she spoke, she "accidentally" allowed the cellphone's minicam to pick up the hotel's rooftop sign. Only the upper half of the words Relax Hotel showed above the lip of the building, but it would be enough. Blondie was intelligent enough to pick up on this clue—she'd assume that Night Owl had stupidly given her position away. She'd be cocky during the meet, and less cautious. Which was just what Night Owl wanted.

"No. We do it tonight. Now. I know where you are: the rooftop of the Relax Hotel. Stay there. I'll come to you." Her voice sounded as if she was smirking.

Night Owl widened her eyes, as if alarmed. "All right," she said. "But tell your cabbie to hover three meters above the helipad, and jump down to the roof. Don't let him land; I want to see that it's just you getting out. If anyone else shows, our deal is off. And don't try to trick me by cloaking someone with an invisibility spell; I'll see them wading through the puddles."

The monitor screen sprang to life, showing Blondie inside the sky cab. The ganger rotated the cell she was holding so the vidcam picked up the otherwise empty passenger compartment of the cab. "Don't worry," she snarled. "I'm the only one coming."

Night Owl thumbed the cell off and watched the cab approach over the Fraser River. The sky cab came in high over the darkened ruins—the cabbie was obviously wary of approaching too close to the tangle of wires and concrete that lay below—and then circled over the Relax Hotel.

The landing spotlight on the belly of the machine sprang into hot white light, illuminating the pitted H that marked the landing pad, and then the cab sank slowly toward the rooftop, engines roaring and downdrafts rippling the puddles that covered the pitted concrete. The helicopter paused, and then the hatch opened. Blondie jumped down into the pool of light, landing with a splash on the rooftop. The sky cab withdrew, leaving her standing in the rain. It hovered a few dozen meters above, waiting for Blondie to conclude her biz. The ganger obviously didn't expect this transaction to take much time.

Blondie wasn't taking any chances, however. She already had her right hand shaped into a wedge, ready to cast a magical attack. Her hair was slicked down against her scalp by the pouring rain, her jacket already soaked, but she ignored these discomforts. She walked toward Night Owl, menace clear in every step. Her eyes were fixed on the coin in Night Owl's hand.

"That's close enough," Night Owl called out.

Blondie stopped, not noticing the way the concrete sagged down beneath her right foot. "Let's see the coin," she gritted. "I need to make sure my master is getting what he's paid for."

"All right." Night Owl slowly drew the coin from her pocket. The moment of untruth was at hand—this was when she'd find out whether Miracle Worker's illusion spell would pass muster. Even if it did fool Blondie, Night Owl knew what would follow. As soon as Blondie had the coin, Night Owl would be dead meat.

Night Owl took a step forward—a short step. "Here!" She flipped the coin into the air. It glittered in a lazy arc, spinning head over tails toward the ganger—an arc that would end just in front of where Blondie stood. Realizing that it would fall short, the ganger leaped forward to snatch the coin out of the air. She lifted the coin for a better look, and a smile of triumph spread across her face. She'd instinctively used her right hand to make the catch, but now she transferred the coin to her left and re-formed her fingers into a wedge shape, ready to launch a magical attack. Night Owl tensed, ready to hurl herself to the side . . .

She didn't need to. Just as Blondie's hand came up, the weakened rooftop gave way beneath the ganger's feet. Eyes wide with surprise, she disappeared into the gaping hole. Night Owl heard a muffled shout, but the sound was all but lost in a thudding rumble as chunks of cement cascaded down into the hole. A moment later there was a second rumbling crash as the floor below also gave way.

Night Owl listened a moment more, wondering if the ganger had bought it, and then heard a muffled cursing. Finally relaxing, she allowed herself a smile. Her plan had worked beautifully. Blondie was alive. With luck, she'd dropped the coin in the rubble and would spend the rest of the night searching for it. Even if Blondie had managed to hang on to the coin when she fell, it would take her a while to find her way out of the ruined hotel. She'd have to pick her way across the rockworm-weakened floors as carefully as a soldier in a minefield. By that time, Night Owl would be long gone.

Night Owl smiled and pulled her lucky SkyTrain token out of her pocket. Before she faded into the night, she needed to decide who the next sucker would be. Heads, it would be the Red Lotus; tails, Strange Eyes.

She flipped the coin and smacked it against the back of her right hand. Heads it was.

The Triple Eight Club was an enormous block of concrete, glass and neon, located a few steps away from the Stadium SkyTrain station. Built before the turn of the millennium as a combination theater and shopping arcade, it had been transformed into a casino when simsense made motion-picture technology obsolete. Now it catered to those who hungered for the thrill of old-fashioned games of chance: blackjack played with cardboard playing cards instead of the virtual cards that appeared on flatscreen tables; roulette wheels spun by human hands; slot machines with mechanical gears that clanked and rattled; and craps played with actual plastic dice. The only nods to modern technology were the gigantic, two-story-tall monitor screens that broadcast thoroughbred and greyhound racing in real time from racetracks in Tokyo, Shanghai and the Hong Kong Free Enterprise Zone.

Night Owl jandered into the enormous building, trying to lose herself in the crowd. Fortunately, she wasn't the only one in the crowd who had painted her face with a Beijing Opera mask. Even some of the Red Lotus gangers who were lounging at tables, sipping drinks and clicking mahjong tiles, had painted their faces. None of them paid any more attention to Night Owl than they did to any of the other "sheep" who bleated their way into the casino, begging for a chance to be fleeced. Her hunch had been correct: the gangers weren't expecting her to show up on their home turf. They'd be looking for her everywhere else in the city—but not here.

Night Owl stepped onto the escalator leading up to the balcony that ringed the second floor and approached one of the long lines of slot machines. She'd already purchased a bulging pocketful of "lucky eight" tokens at the exchange window below, and now she began moving randomly between the slots, feeding one token into each machine. She didn't even bother to watch the wheels as they spun and stayed only as long as it took to collect whenever she heard the ringing clamor that announced a payoff. She didn't care if she won or lost, but she knew she'd look suspicious if she didn't pick up the tokens that tumbled into the tray. She scooped each win up as quickly as she could and moved on to the next machine.

An hour later, she had slotted coins into three-quarters of the machines in the casino. She'd observed which of the slots were most heavily used: those near the entrance and closest to the escalators—slots that the casino had rigged to make small, frequent payouts to help spur the hopes—and empty the pockets—of those just arriving.

Choosing one of these machines, Night Owl pulled one of the two remaining I Ching coins from her pocket. It was roughly the same size and weight as the tokens used in the Triple Eight—close enough to

fool the archaic, mechanical measuring devices that
were built into the slot machine. Careful to hide the
hole at the coin's center with her thumb and forefinger—every centimeter of the casino was constantly
monitored by security cameras—Night Owl popped it
into the slot and pulled the heavy handle of the machine. She watched the symbols spin, and when three
cherries came up, she had to cup her hands quickly
to catch the shower of tokens that spilled out over the
slot machine's tray. She shoved them into her pocket,
suddenly aware of the hot jealousy in the eyes of the
gamblers next to her. The win had attracted some attention. She'd lose herself in the crowd, play a few
more slots, and then get out of here.

She began walking to another machine but was
forced to deke around a couple who were arguing
about whether to leave the casino. Without warning,
the woman stepped back to slap the man, and Night
Owl was jostled to the side. She collided with a massive troll who was standing in front of a nearby slot.
Although his back was to her, she recognized him in
a heartbeat by his V-shaped, spiral horns: the shaman
Wu—the one Red Lotus member who would recognize her instantly. After his run-in with Strange Eyes,
the shaman was in bad shape: one of his arms was in
a sling, and blood was still seeping through a bandage
on his face. But he still looked perfectly capable of
slinging spells. If he glanced back to see who had just
jostled him, Night Owl was going to catch some serious mojo.

Night Owl was already flashing for her pistol when
she realized that the shaman hadn't even noticed her.
His attention remained riveted on the machine in
front of him. She could hear him muttering in Cantonese and saw him stroking the side of the machine
with his fingertips. She realized that he must have
been using a telekinetic spell to slow the spinning

gears inside the machine. Then three symbols clunked home: a seven, another seven, and yet another. Coins fountained into the tray in front of Wu, and a feral grin lit his face.

When at last he glanced around—probably checking to see if the casino's security mages had picked up on the spell he'd just used—Night Owl had already done a quick fade. Although she was keeping her back to the shaman, her eye still twitched with the strain of having come so close to being spotted.

Ten slot machines later, she slipped out of the casino. She dumped the Triple Eight tokens she still had in her pocket into the grimy paper cup a streeter was using to beg with and then jandered quickly down an alley toward the loading bay where she'd hidden her bike.

Sheltering from the rain under the loading bay's overhang, she dialed the Triple Eight Club and demanded to speak to Wu. As soon as his face appeared on the monitor screen, he began shouting.

"You!" he roared over the rattle of slots and the clatter of roulette wheels. "You cheated Eldest Brother a second time. The statue wasn't—"

"Never mind that," Night Owl said. "I found the coin your master is looking for. I just delivered it."

That shut the troll up. "What do you mean?"

"It's in the casino—I fed it into one of the slots. For five hundred thousand nuyen, I'll tell you which one. Otherwise . . . well, the coin's likely to wind up in someone else's pocket and disappear out the door any minute."

Wu's eyes narrowed. "You're bluffing."

"No, I'm not. I was inside the club just a few minutes ago. I saw you coax a slot with your magic into coughing up triple sevens. If you don't believe that I was inside, check the casino's security camera recordings. Look for a woman with a gold face mask."

She watched a gleam creep into Wu's eyes and guessed what he was thinking. "If you're thinking about scanning the recordings to see which machine I played, don't bother," she added. "I slotted tokens into sixty-plus machines. You'll never figure out which play was the Fu Coin in time. Unless you want to piss off Elder Brother by letting the thing he's seeking slip through your fingers, you'd better get him to pay up. You've got five minutes to convince him. If I don't hear from the bank by then, the deal's off."

She repeated the bank account number she'd given Blondie earlier and hung up. Now she just had to keep her fingers crossed that the Red Lotus didn't get heavy-handed. The gang was a constant, visible presence at the casino, bleeding "protection" credit from it on a daily basis, but they didn't own the place. To search the nearly one hundred slot machines in the building, they'd have to cordon off the entire second floor and smash them open one by one—something that would bring the tribal police, with sirens wailing, pretty fraggin' quick. Night Owl was gambling that the gangers wouldn't want to attract that much attention to themselves. It would be easier—and much more discreet—to simply get their master to transfer the cred she'd demanded and then feed coins into the slot she identified until it paid off its magical prize.

This time, it took just over four minutes for the bank to call, confirming the anonymous donation of five hundred K to the Cybercare for Kids account. Night Owl disconnected with a grin and called Wu back.

"Payment accepted," she said. "The coin is in slot machine thirty-two."

As she hung up, her grin grew larger. Even if Wu used his magic to nudge that slot into a series of large payouts, it would take some time for the Fu Coin to work its way through the machine. The coin would be near the top of the pile; he'd be at it most of the night.

Night Owl straddled her Harley and gunned the engine. She wheeled the bike out into the street and headed back to her apartment for a change of clothes.

Just one more fake coin sale to pull off—but it would be the most difficult of all.

Strange Eyes had been the toughest of the three buyers to track down. Night Owl had caught a glimpse of the license plate of the limo that he'd bundled her into, two nights ago, and had traced the limo to a Seattle-based rental company. Strange Eyes obviously liked to travel in comfort and style, complete with a hired chauffeur, despite the fact that this made him stick out like a chromed thumb. Night Owl had assumed he'd rent another limo, this time from a company in Vancouver, and had called the handful of limo companies to find out if anyone matching his description had jandered in to rent a car.

No one had—her guess had been wrong. But not by much. On a hunch, she'd made a second round of calls, this time to local automotive dealerships that specialized in luxury cars. A clerk at the third dealership she called remembered the man who had walked in off the street and paid one hundred and thirty thousand nuyen for a Jaguar Z Type—a man with strange, all-white eyes. The Jag had come fully equipped, with global positioning system, cyberterminal with satellite uplink, surround sound and telecom built into the dash. And yes, the clerk was happy to give Night Owl the vehicle's telecom number, especially after she identified herself as Alma Wei, second in command of PCI's security force.

Night Owl repeated the sequence of calls she'd used with Blondie, telling Strange Eyes that she'd boosted the coin from Kageyama and was ready to sell it. Just

as she had done earlier this evening, she faked a bidding war, this time driving the price to eight hundred
K. When the Malaysian Independent Bank called to
confirm a third anonymous donation to the Cybercare
for Kids account and to let her know that another
four hundred thousand nuyen had been deposited in
trust, Night Owl called Strange Eyes and IDed the
spot where she would meet him and turn over the
coin: the middle of the Lion's Gate Bridge.

She had to reassure him that yes, he'd heard that
right. She explained that she'd kleen-tacked the coin
to the bridge in a place where only somebody with
her amazing agility and strength could reach it. She'd
be waiting for him near the south tower of the Lion's
Gate, on the west sidewalk, in five minutes' time. If
he didn't show within fifteen minutes, the deal was
off. That should set his tires squealing.

Pulling away from the darkened street corner where
she'd made the call, Night Owl turned her Harley
toward the northbound Stanley Park causeway—one
of two long tunnels that pierced the park's biodome.
She wasn't wearing a watch, but according to the cellphone's built-in clock, it was nearly 4:30 a.m. This time
of night, and with a storm pounding the city and
flooding its low-level roads, there was barely a car
in sight.

The biodome's grow lights were dimmed; the glass-
enclosed tunnel was illuminated only by normal streetlights. They strobed past overhead as the Harley
roared its way along the causeway, the full-throated
growl of its engines echoing off the empty tunnel's
walls. As the night-dark end of the tunnel hove into
sight, a curtain of rain obscuring the bridge beyond it,
Night Owl smiled grimly at the metaphor. She was
moving along a tunnel of light, toward darkness and
death—hopefully not her own.

The rain and wind hit her the second she exited the

tunnel. Most of her body stayed warm and dry, thanks
to the waterproof suit that she wore under her street
clothes; it covered her from her neck down to her
ankles and wrists. Her night-vision goggles kept the
rain out of her eyes, but rain pounded against her bare
forehead, cheeks and chin like sprays of ice water. Her
fingers were cold despite her fleece-lined riding gloves.
The temperature seemed to have dropped dramati-
cally in the last couple of hours—or maybe it was just
the chill that came with riding headlong into the wind.

She passed the two massive concrete lions that
guarded the south end of the bridge and roared onto
the bridge proper, climbing its gentle slope. Above
her, the wind howled around the massive suspension
cables that stretched high overhead. When she drew
close to the first of the bridge's two towers, Night Owl
pulled the bike to a stop. She propped it up on its
kick stand, next to the sidewalk, and swung down from
the seat.

Now that she was off the bike, the force of the gale
blew her back against the railing at the outer edge of
the sidewalk. After lifting her goggles away from her
eyes, she gripped the railing and leaned out over it,
peering down at the wind-churned waters of Burrard
Inlet, sixty meters below.

She saw what she was looking for near the base of
the tower: the red and green running lights of a boat
that was being tossed by the waves. She hoped it was
Skimmer, with his garbage scow. He'd promised to
drop anchor and wait for her there; she hoped he'd
be willing to ride out the storm for just a little longer.
He was an essential part of her plan—the only one
who could get her safely to her bolt hole.

Lightning flashed overhead, throwing the twin
towers of the bridge into sharp relief. A second or
two later, thunder boomed. In the bright flash of light,
Night Owl thought she saw a series of small dark

shapes winging their way across the sky—and a larger, serpentine shape. Shivering, she told herself that it was just a twist of cloud. A moment later, in the flash of lightning that followed, the smaller shapes were revealed to be storm crows. They landed, one by one, hunkering down like a string of beads along the cables of the bridge. Night Owl had the distinct feeling that they were watching her with their jet-black, unblinking eyes.

A pair of headlights in the causeway tunnel caught her eye. As the vehicle drew closer, she recognized the long, lozenge-shaped car as a Jag Z-Type.

Tearing off her gloves, Night Owl flipped open her cell and hit the icon that would automatically call the two numbers she'd preset: Blondie's cellphone, and the telecom at the Triple Eight Club where she'd contacted Wu earlier. As soon as she saw that the connections had been made and that the text message she'd input earlier had begun to transmit, she kleen-tacked the cellphone to the tower. The aperture of its lens was already adjusted to wide angle; the vidcam built into the cell would capture both the ladders that connected the deck of the bridge with the suspension cable above and the spot where Strange Eyes was most likely to stand. Then she turned and braced her back against the railing, just in time to see the Jaguar glide to a stop beside her Harley.

A gull-wing door swung open, and Strange Eyes stepped out of the vehicle. He stared at her with his bulging white eyes and held out a hand. Despite the rain that was pounding down onto the bridge, soaking Night Owl's hair and trickling down the back of her neck in icy rivulets, not a drop of water collected in his cupped palm. Strange Eyes seemed encased in an invisible, protective bubble that shielded him from both wind and rain. While Night Owl's jacket and

pants flapped like banners in the heavy wind, his clothing hung perfectly still.

"The coin, please," he hissed in a voice that carried
clearly, despite the roar of the wind. She wondered if
his telepathy was at work.

Night Owl gave him a mock bow. "Just a moment."
She turned and sprang into the air, letting the howling
wind slam her into the steel-cable ladder that was just
overhead. Then she climbed.

As she spidered up the rain-slick ladder to the place
where she'd kleen-tacked the last of the I Ching coins
earlier, the wind whipped her hair into her eyes and
numbed her bare fingers. She didn't care. She felt a
warm glow as she mentally played back the text message that her cellphone would be transmitting to
Blondie and Wu. The same memo would also be appearing on Strange Eye's telecom monitor—the one
inside his car. By the time he saw the message, however, it would be too late. He would have already
completed the buy.

HELLO, SUCKERS, it taunted. TONIGHT I
SOLD A COIN OF LUCK TO EACH OF YOUR
MASTERS: MANG, LI AND CHIAO. YOU'LL
SEE THE FINAL TRANSACTION LIVE IN JUST
A MOMENT. OBVIOUSLY, SINCE THERE IS
ONLY ONE FU COIN TO SELL, TWO OF YOU
HAVE BOUGHT FAKES. HAVE FUN FIGURING
OUT WHICH ONE OF YOU BOUGHT THE
REAL ONE!

Night Owl reached the halfway point of the ladder
and felt around for the patch of kleen-tack she'd used
to secure the last of the I Ching coins. She took her
time, pretending that it was harder to locate than it
actually was, in order to ensure that the cellphone
below would have switched over from text-only to
voice-and-visual transmission before she climbed
down again. As she peeled the kleen-tack free from

the ladder rung, holding the coin tightly so the wind wouldn't snatch it from her grasp, she smiled grimly, proud of herself for stealing Ryomyo's idea of pitting the dragons against one another and going him one better.

Each of the dragons, when it found out the coin it had purchased was nothing more than an ordinary coin cloaked with an illusion, would have to assume that one of the other coins was the genuine item. It couldn't afford to do otherwise and wouldn't believe the other dragons if they said their coins were also fake. The Red Lotus had already fired the opening shots in the war for the Fu Coin, by taking out Strange Eyes' limo. Night Owl could only imagine the escalated chaos her message was going to cause.

She peeled the kleen-tack off, popped the coin into her mouth, where she held it clamped between her teeth, and climbed back down the ladder. Just before she reached the bottom—and just as she'd suspected—she felt a command from Strange Eyes whisper into her brain. She didn't even try to resist it.

Show me the coin.

Night Owl parted her lips in a grin, giving Strange Eyes a good look at the coin. The man seemed far away; although his eyes were still white and blank, Night Owl knew he wasn't seeing anything on this plane anymore—he was looking into the astral. His mouth twitched into a smile, and Night Owl knew her plan had worked. He issued another mental command—without pausing to think about the circumstances.

Give it to me.

Night Owl spat the coin out of her mouth. It landed at Strange Eyes' feet, began to roll, and then was caught by a gust of wind and sent spinning toward the edge of the bridge. Strange Eyes dived after it, sprawling with his hand outstretched over the edge. Night

Owl laughed, thinking he had missed it, but then he picked himself up. Between two of his long fingers was the coin.

Strange Eyes looked up at her, an expression of pure hatred on his face.

Frag. Time to get out of here.

Night Owl frantically began to climb again, the right side of her face twitching. Her bare hands were nearly numb from the rain and wind; she slipped and nearly lost her grip. Only a meter or two more, and she'd be lost in darkness and out of range of Strange Eyes' spells . . .

The command came before she made it.

Jump.

Night Owl hurled herself from the ladder and felt the wind catch her. She fell, arms and legs flailing, tumbling like a spinning coin toward the water below. She had a brief glimpse of Strange Eyes peering over the bridge, watching her plummet to her death with a satisfied smirk as lightning flared overhead, and then he was gone. The wind roared in her ears, and the bridge spun off into the distance. From somewhere high above, she heard a chorus of cawing crows.

At the last moment, as the starboard running light of Skimmer's garbage scow flashed past, Night Owl twisted violently and forced her arms above her head. She hit the water in a dive and felt it smack into her body like a wall of cold cement, slamming into the top of her head, shoulders and chest. Then she was down in its icy depths. Although she'd flattened out her dive as much as she could as she disappeared beneath the surface, she plunged onward, downward, for what seemed like an eternity, until her brain was buzzing. Only when her descent had at last slowed could she begin the long, slow struggle to the surface. Red static was crackling across her field of view and her cyberears were roaring by the time she saw a green light dancing above her. A moment later she broke the surface and gasped in night air filled with pelting rain. Incredibly, the raindrops actually felt warm against her ice-cold face.

The rest of her body, although bruised, was still dry, protected by the drysuit she'd put on underneath her clothing. She owed her life to that drysuit—and to her incredibly augmented muscles, which had diffused the crushing blow of her sixty-meter dive.

As the choppy waves bobbed her up and down, Night Owl saw Skimmer leaning over the low railing of the scow, extending a pole-handled salvage net in her direction. She gripped the net with numbed fingers and clung to it as Skimmer hauled her up into the boat.

As she lay on the deck of the scow, gasping like a landed fish amid the bags of trash, Night Owl silently congratulated herself. Her plan had worked beautifully, down to the last detail. She'd tricked all three dragons' representatives into buying a fake coin, and by revealing that trick had ensured that the dragons themselves would be at each other's throats for some time to come. Best of all, she had "died" in a live cellphone transmission. That ought to stop them from looking for her.

Now all she had to do was wait out the coming storm. She knew just the place to do it, too: the last place any of the dragons would expect her to bolt to.

Forcing herself to sit up, she gave Skimmer his sailing orders.

Change

Alma woke up suddenly as fingers touched her hand. Her move-by-wire system kicked in immediately, and in one smooth motion she whipped the blankets off her body, yanked the hand that had touched hers away and down, and drew her legs up. A split second before she lashed out in a lethal kick, her mind registered the fact that it was Akira Kageyama who was leaning over the bed, wincing with pain at the pressure-point hold she was using to force his hand back against his wrist. Letting him go, she sat up in the unfamiliar bed and looked around.

The last thing Alma remembered was lying down on her own bed and activating the REM inducer with a prime-number countdown. She was no longer in her apartment. Instead, she had awakened in a room with walls and ceiling made from frosted glass. The bed she was in had a massive mahogany headboard and footboard, carved with entwined dragons; a matching bedside table stood next to it. One of the pillows was smeared with what looked like gold and black paint; Alma also saw a smudge of gold on the back of her hand. She touched her cheek, and her fingers came away streaked with gold.

There was one door out of the room; beside it was a long, low table that held a collection of tiny bonsai trees. A chair near the opposite wall was draped with a pair of pants and a jacket that dripped water onto the floor and a rubbery black garment; after a moment, Alma recognized it as a diver's drysuit.

"Where am I?"

"In my home." Kageyama stood beside the bed, rubbing his wrist. He wore only black silk pajama bottoms. His feet were bare, and Alma could see that he had only four toes on each foot. "You came here, early this morning, asking for sanctuary. I have granted it."

This morning? Alma activated her cybereye's clock and stared at the glowing red numbers that superimposed themselves over Kageyama. It was 6:22 a.m. Where had the last eight hours and twelve minutes gone? The only thing she could remember was a fragmented dream about riding through the night sky on a motorcycle and then falling from it, tumbling endlessly down into a cold, wet, dark place . . .

Her cyberear picked up the faint sound of trickling water coming from another part of the building. She realized where she must be: in the underwater condoplex that Kageyama had inherited from the dragon Dunkelzahn: Vancouver's most famous "leaky condo."

She had no memory of coming here or of asking Kageyama for sanctuary. Looking at him now, noticing that his chest was bare aside from the *pi* stone that hung around his neck, she wondered what else was missing from her memory. His smile was just a little too knowing, a touch too sensual. She realized that she was naked and pulled the covers back over her body.

"How long have I been asleep?" she asked.

"About fifteen minutes. You fought to stay awake as long as you could, but toward the end you were doing more yawning than talking."

Alma seized upon the one thing she was able to

understand: the fifteen-minute sleep. It must have been REM induced, since she felt as refreshed as if she'd slept all night. She couldn't have been sleeping for the past eight hours, since clearly she'd spent at least part of the evening traveling to the condoplex and talking to Kageyama. The only conclusion she could draw was that something must have gone wrong with the REM inducer—some glitch that caused her to move around and talk in her sleep, without any memory of having done so. She wondered if this was the first time it had happened.

"Was I sleepwalking? What did I talk about?"

Kageyama sat down on the edge of the bed and reached for her hand. Alma's first instinct was to jerk away, but the feel of his long, slim fingers holding hers was somehow reassuring—and disturbingly familiar. She could see from the expression on his face that he was searching for the best way to tell her something he thought might upset her. She braced herself for bad news.

"You arrived at my door just after five o'clock this morning, pleading with me to let you in. You said you had important news for me, that you knew what the three dragons were after: a magical coin."

Alma shook her head in disbelief. What would have possessed her to do that? Her subconscious mind had obviously been dwelling on Night Owl's offer. "I must have been talking about the coin that Night Owl mentioned in her message to me on the cell," she said, thinking out loud.

Kageyama stared at her, his eyes filled with questions. "Night Owl?" He paused, then tried again: "You're talking about her as if . . . but she said you knew . . ."

He shook his head in wonder. "She was wrong. You *don't* know, do you?"

"Know what?" Alma asked, exasperated.

"That you and the shadowrunner Night Owl are the same person—that you share a single body. As she so eloquently put it, you're two sides of the same coin."

Alma felt suddenly lightheaded, as if the air had been sucked from the room. It was difficult to take a full breath, and her stomach felt cold and loose. With the detached awareness of a person who has just gone into shock, she noticed that her breathing was very shallow and that her left hand was trembling.

"No," she whispered. "Night Owl is Abby, one of the other Superkids from Batch Alpha."

Kageyama released her hand and stood. He walked over to the wet clothes, unzipped one of the jacket pockets, and pulled a flat square of plastic from it. He turned it upright as he walked back to the bed, and Alma saw the familiar human pyramid of a dozen Superkids materialize above it. He handed the holopic to her.

"Night Owl wanted you to have this," he said. "She said to remind you that she's been a part of you since you were eight years old and asked me to plead with you to reconsider your decision."

Decision? Alma had no idea what Kageyama was talking about. She stared at the holopic, feeling as disconnected from the here and now as she did from the eight-year-old girl who flipped off the top of the pyramid and landed in a handstand in front of the other children, over and over again. Like the girl in the holopic, Alma's mind kept looping through the same cycle—question and denial, question and denial—as her eyes darted back and forth between Abby and herself, trying to sort out which one really was Night Owl.

What if it was true? What if the REM inducer was malfunctioning, causing Alma to act out dreams in which she played her polar opposite: a shadowrunner, instead of a security guard? Like dreams that fade with wakefulness, all knowledge of what she'd done while she was "sleepwalking" would have disappeared from her conscious memory—just as the memory of last night had.

No, she told herself. According to Hothead, Night Owl had been running the Vancouver shadows for at least three months. If Alma had been active as Night Owl for all that time, surely there would have been some evidence of her nocturnal excursions. It wasn't possible for her to have left no trace of her comings and goings.

But she had left traces: the first had been the "break-in" to Alma's apartment last November. It had happened exactly three months ago, around the time that Night Owl had first shown up in Vancouver. Then there were a handful of occasions when Alma had had the sense that something in her apartment was just *slightly* out of place. That had to have been Night Owl, touching and moving things as she crept around Alma's apartment.

No, she told herself. It had to be Abby who had broken into the apartment.

But what if it wasn't? What if it was true that this alter ego had been part of Alma since long before the shadowrunner "Night Owl" had appeared? Age eight was when the Superkids program had been shut down, and Poppy had killed himself. What if Akiko had been right: that it was Alma, and not Abby, who had found Poppy after his suicide? Perhaps Alma had tried to block the pain of his death by telling the police that her name was Abby, and over the intervening years had convinced herself that it really *was* Abby who saw the severed head.

No, she told herself—it was Abby who found the

body. Alma would have remembered something like that.

Then she thought back to the vivid images that had filled her mind as Hothead was describing what "Abby" had seen. The hollow feeling in her stomach grew as she realized that maybe, on some deeper level, she *did* remember.

One final question remained. If the REM inducer really had caused Alma to act out her darkest urges in bouts of sleepwalking, why hadn't Gray Squirrel noticed that something was wrong? Surely a glitch of that magnitude would have rung an alarm somewhere.

Alma noticed that her left hand was still shaking. Staring at it, she realized the truth. A warning bell *had* sounded—eleven days ago. The doctor at Executive Body Enhancements had been right: the tremors that had plagued Alma for the past week and a half weren't the result of TLE. They were caused by the REM inducer. Alma had told Gray Squirrel that her left hand had started mysteriously shaking, and he had agreed to run some tests. He'd been on the verge of discovering the glitch when Night Owl had killed him.

No—when *Alma* had killed him.

She heard a cracking noise and realized that she was gripping the holopic so tightly that she had fractured it. A thin line of static crackled across the image, cutting the pyramid of children—and Alma—in half.

Alma looked up from the holopic. "What did she— did I—mean: 'reconsider my decision'?"

"You were referring to your appointment, later today, at the Executive Body Enhancements clinic. When the REM inducer is removed, Night Owl will disappear, perhaps forever. She asked me to let you know that she never meant to hurt you—she was protecting you, although you didn't realize it. Gray Squirrel was a monster, and the experiments PCI was conducting were morally wrong. You—she—said she's sorry that she hurt you—that she tried several times to tell you what was happening, but you wouldn't listen. You wouldn't let her wake up."

"But I never . . . I wasn't going to . . ." The trembling in Alma's left hand grew stronger. The hand fluttered against the bedsheets as if trying to signal her attention. Alma was suddenly very tired and had to fight to stifle a yawn. Then she realized what was happening: Night Owl was trying to wake up.

With a mental effort that made sweat bead on her temples, she forced her hand to lie still. The exhaustion and craving for sleep instantly disappeared.

So it was true—it was all true. She *was* Night Owl. She nearly laughed at the irony. She'd finally learned who the killer was, and as a result she could never go back to Pacific Cybernetics. Her career as a security expert was over; everything she had built in her life had come crashing down. The flip side of her personality—the darker, brooding side—was a killer and an outlaw. Even though it wasn't really "Alma" who had committed the crimes, it was Alma who would pay for them. She would be an outcast, untrusted and unwelcome in the corporate world. The only community that would ever consider embracing her was one filled with murderers and thieves: the shadowrunners.

Then she realized that none of that mattered—the scenarios she'd just run through in her mind assumed that she still had a future. Activating the countdown mechanism in her cybereye, she saw that there were only five hours, thirteen minutes and thirty-eight seconds remaining until the bomb in her head exploded. Now that she could never prove her innocence to PCI, there was no escape. She couldn't have the REM inducer removed—not by a PCI technician—and that meant one of two things: brain damage, or death.

Her hopes rose briefly as she considered one possible course of action. She would go to Mr. Lali and explain to him that, yes, she was the one who had extracted Gray Squirrel, but that it was the REM inducer that had hived off the Night Owl personality—that his death was really PCI's fault. But that hope ebbed when she realized that Night Owl wasn't a separate entity—she was part of Alma. An alter ego, a part of herself that she had deliberately suppressed, but still very much a part of herself. She was guilty.

Even if Mr. Lali was willing to overlook that, Alma wasn't certain that she could trust PCI, now that she knew what Gray Squirrel had been involved in. The corporation had given its blessing to the callous murders of the alpha-test subjects and was more than willing to sacrifice Alma herself—the cranial bomb was proof of that. She'd trusted PCI and looked up to Mr. Lali as a father. Now she realized that she was no daughter to him. She'd been an employee, and then a test subject, and then a security risk to be eliminated—no more than that.

Weeping tears of frustration, she hurled the Superkids holopic across the room. "You said I came here 'asking for sanctuary.' From what?"

"The three dragons who were chasing you," Kageyama answered. "You managed to anger Mang, Li and Chiao to the point where all three wanted to kill you."

Alma's laugh was bitter. What did that matter now?

"Don't worry," Kageyama quickly added. His eyes twinkled with mischievous delight. "You also faked your own death—apparently in a very convincing manner. All three dragons think you died in a plunge from the Lion's Gate Bridge."

Alma's mouth dropped open, and for the first time since she'd awakened, she was consciously aware of the ache in her face, hands and shoulders. It felt as though she had been slapped across every centimeter of her body by something as hard as cement. Her eye fell on the wet clothes and the drysuit that lay over them. Something like the ice-cold waters of Burrard Inlet, for example.

"Why would the dragons want to kill me?" she asked, curiosity sparking her out of her apathy. "The only one I could have angered was Mang, when I aborted your extraction."

"You're forgetting Night Owl," Kageyama gently reminded her. "She also made enemies."

"I see." That explained at least one of the cellphone messages—the one in which Night Owl had been trying to warn Alma about the Red Lotus and a man with strange white eyes.

Kageyama sighed. "I still don't understand why the dragons think I have one of the Coins of Luck. I've heard of them, of course—three of the coins were listed in Dunkelzahn's will. The dragons obviously think that Dunkelzahn left me the fourth Coin of Luck, together with this condoplex, but they are wrong. The Fu Coin wasn't in the statue that you stole, and it isn't in this building."

Kageyama was going too fast for Alma. He was obviously talking about things that Night Owl had done; she didn't remember stealing a statue. "What's the Fu Coin?" she asked.

"It conveys great happiness to the person who owns it—happiness brought about by good fortune. You insisted that I must have it—that it lies hidden inside a jade statue marked with the character *fu*, somewhere inside this condoplex. But it just isn't here. I have no such statue."

Alma stared at Kageyama, not really listening. The realization that she and Night Owl were one and the same—and the gaping hole that the bomb was about to tear in her future—was just too overwhelming for her to concentrate on anything else. She found herself irritated by Kageyama's bemused smile and jealous of the fact that nothing ever seemed to faze him. He sailed through life, serene and happy, oblivious to the fact that the life of the person he was talking to hung in bloody tatters. She supposed he ought to be happy—just look at the wealth that surrounded him. It was all around him, from the multimillion-nuyen condoplex he'd inherited to the expensive gold chain and blue stone that hung around his neck . . .

Alma's racing thoughts came to a sudden halt as she stared at the *pi*. That wasn't just any stone. A *pi* was always carved from the same stone, one that came in a rainbow of colors, from white to yellow to red to lavender to blue, the most expensive coloration of all. And, of course, green.

That stone was jade.

"Akira." Alma interrupted. Strange, that the first name felt familiar on her lips. Angrily, she pushed that thought aside. "Lean closer."

When he did, she took the *pi* in her hands and peered at it. She found what she'd expected to, carved into the surface of the jade: the Chinese character *fu*.

"What's wrong?" Akira asked.

"Who gave you this?" Alma asked.

"My mother," Kageyama answered. "It was in her possessions—I found it after she died. I wear it to honor her."

"Take it off—please. Just for a moment. I need a closer look."

Kageyama hesitated, and then reached behind his neck, undid the clasp on the gold chain, and handed the jade to Alma. She activated the magnification system in her cybereye and peered at the stone closely. Once again, she found what she suspected she would: a hair-thin line, invisible to the unaugmented eye. Before Kageyama could ask what she was doing, she removed the chain, pressed the jade between her two palms, and twisted. It turned like a jar lid. When she opened her hands, the jade had separated into two halves, revealing a glittering bronze coin with a square hole at its center.

As she held the coin up for Kageyama to see, her smile broadened into a grin. She felt a rush of pure joy so strong that it was disorienting, and her mind flashed back to one of the happiest moments of her life: the day she'd beaten all of the other Superkids on an extremely challenging test and had been rewarded with a trip to the virtual zoo. All of the anxiety that had been growing like an icy finger inside Alma over the past few days melted away, and her vision blurred with unshed tears of joy. Only with difficulty could she focus on the here and now.

"You do have the Fu Coin," she said, forcing the words out in a joyful sigh. "You've had it around your neck since your mother died. It must feel . . . wonderful."

Kageyama's lips drooped as he stared at the coin. For the first time since she'd met him, he looked pensive, even sad. "I wonder," he whispered to himself. "Did Dunkelzahn know all along?"

He held out a hand. Reluctantly—not wanting to let go of the wash of happiness that was filling her—Alma let him tug it out of her fingers. Instantly, the lump of apprehension that had been pressing against her stomach earlier returned.

Kageyama placed the coin back inside the hollow halves of jade. He screwed them back together and then threaded the gold chain through the hole at the center. By the time he fastened the *pi* in place around his neck again, his smile had returned.

"Thank you, Night . . . er, Alma," he said. "You've provided an answer to a question that has been puzzling me for some time. You've forewarned me—and knowledge is power. Now that I know what Mang, Li and Chiao are after, I can take steps to protect it."

He stared at her a moment, eyes glittering. "My offer still stands. How would you like to be employed as my bodyguard?"

"That's a foolish proposal," Alma snapped. The brief taste of the happiness the Fu Coin could bring had left her irritable and depressed, now that she was no longer holding it. "I can be trusted—but it's not just me . . . in here." Alma tapped a finger to her head. "Night Owl tried to steal the coin from you, once before. What's to stop her from trying again, once I go to sleep and she wakes up?"

"That would be . . . amusing," Kageyama said. "But think of this: even if Night Owl does steal the coin, who would she sell it to? She has gone to great lengths to convince the three dragons that you're dead. The last thing you—she—wants to do is tip them off to the fact that you're still alive. And besides, I enjoy Night Owl. She is one of the few shadowrunners I have engaged who acts out of altruism. I feel it is only correct to treat her with the same compassion that she takes so much care to hide—but that shines through despite her efforts to conceal it."

Alma nodded, not really listening. Night Owl was a wild card inside her head. Whenever she was turned face-up, anything could happen. Fortunately, she too would be gone in—she activated the countdown function of her cybereye—four hours, fifty-three minutes and thirteen seconds.

"I can offer you a very generous salary," Kageyama continued. "It will include cosmetic surgery to alter your appearance, if you wish." He glanced briefly down at his fingers. "Dr. Silverman is very . . . discreet. She could do the surgery today—in fact, you told me earlier that you already have an appointment booked with her this afternoon."

He reached out and tipped Alma's head up. "Think about my offer, won't you?"

Alma didn't even bother to answer. She found herself staring at her own hands. The trembling that had seized her left hand a few minutes ago had stopped, but now it felt empty. She realized suddenly that she had yet to cast the I Ching for today. She only had a few hours left—but she might as well find out what they had in store for her.

Kageyama was standing near the door. He gave a slight bow, like a host bidding his guest good morning. "Is there anything I can get for you?" he asked.

"Yes," she said decisively, looking up at last. "Three coins."

Kageyama looked surprised. "Why? Are you going to flip one of them to decide whether you'll work for me?"

Alma smiled. "In a manner of speaking, yes. I'm going to cast the I Ching."

"So ka!" Kageyama laughed. "You do delight me, you know. Both as Alma—and as Night Owl. I think I'm going to enjoy having you around. Very much. Wait here; I will find you three coins."

Bowing once more, he hurried from the room.

While she waited, Alma activated the countdown sequence and glumly watched the numbers blink down. She shook her head slowly at the irony. Just like Akiko, she knew the time of her death and could count the seconds until it arrived. All she could do was sit and wait . . .

No. There had to be a way to deactivate the bomb. Carefully, she thought back over everything that Hu had told her about it. He'd said it would activate if all brain function ceased—if she died. No solution there.

The bomb would also activate if anyone other than a PCI technician tried to surgically remove the REM inducer. Which meant that the tech had to enter a code of some sort.

No—not the technician. As Alma thought about it, she realized that there was just one way to enter that code: input via a mental command. It was the same mechanism that Gray Squirrel had used as an activator for the REM inducer and that Mr. Lali had used to activate the bomb's countdown.

All Alma had to do to save her life was think of the right code.

Gray Squirrel had used a descending sequence of prime numbers as the trigger for the REM inducer and a descending sequence of squared numbers to start the bomb ticking. A similar sequence of numbers had to be the key to "defusing" the bomb.

Alma ran through every combination she could think of. She counted down by cubed numbers, by ever-diminishing fractions, in binary code, by units of measurement, and by right-angle degrees, from 360 to 270 to 180 to 90 to zero. When none of them worked, she tried each of the sequences in ascending order. Still nothing. The countdown just kept ticking.

Consulting her retinal clock, Alma saw that it was 7:30 a.m. precisely. As of this moment, she had exactly four hours and thirty minutes left to live.

She switched back to countdown mode to confirm this—and her breath caught in her throat. According to the countdown that was slaved to the bomb, she had four hours and *thirty-one* minutes to live. Somehow, she'd gained an extra minute—and she had no idea how. One of the sequences of numbers had *almost* worked. Which made no sense. Why would the countdown pause and then start up again?

She ran through all of the number sequences she had just tried and even ran through the series of numbers that had triggered the bomb, visualizing a different date at the end of it—one far in the future—but the countdown continued, just as it had before. Alma suddenly realized that the one-minute reprieve might not have been the result of anything *she* had done. It might have been Night Owl who . . .

Just at that moment, Kageyama returned. He placed three coins on the table beside the bed. They were Taiwanese commemoratives from the year 2000—probably part of a specially minted collector's set.

Without speaking, Kageyama bowed and walked to the door. He paused with one hand on the doorknob to glance back at Alma, his face set in a pensive expression, but she hardly noticed. Yet another bout of trembling had seized her left hand: Night Owl, trying to wake up and take over her body. Fortunately, the tremor was a light one—Alma still had enough control to scoop up the coins, rattle them between cupped hands and let them fall.

A deep sense of tranquillity descended upon Alma as the familiar motions of the I Ching soothed and steadied her. A second or two later, the tremor stopped. She cast the coins six times, shaking them briefly and letting them fall onto the table when she felt the time was right. Then she contemplated the hexagram she had just cast.

The result was lake over fire—the hexagram for Change. Alma nearly laughed out loud when she saw it—change was the very thing she was reaching for so desperately—and could not grasp.

As always, the reading was precise and ambiguous in one. She could recite it by heart: *Change is represented by two women living together, but at cross purposes. One lights the fire, the other extinguishes it with water from her bucket. One draws water from the well, the other hangs the bucket over the fire until the water has boiled away. Only when the two women live together in a civilized manner will the change be com-*

plete. Only when the change has happened is it believed possible.

A thoughtful expression on her face, Alma picked up her cellphone and recorded a memo. Then she lay down on the bed, holding the cell against her chest, and began counting backwards by prime numbers from 19.

Disruption

Night Owl awoke in the same place where exhaustion had overtaken her: in Kageyama's bed. The last thing she remembered was talking to Kageyama, telling him about the illusion Miracle Worker had cast on the I Ching coins and how she'd been correct in her guess that Strange Eyes would use his magic to force her to jump from the bridge, once he'd gotten what he wanted. She'd been yawning with every second word and fighting to keep her eyes open when she got to the part about Alma's appointment to have the REM inducer removed, and the fear that this would put Night Owl to sleep—permanently.

She sat up, and something fell into her lap: Alma's cellphone. Night Owl glanced at its clock, expecting to see that at least sixteen hours of wakefulness had passed—Alma's usual cycle. She was amazed to see that it was twenty after seven in the *morning*. Which could mean only one thing: instead of keeping her appointment and having the REM inducer removed, Alma had stayed awake for little more than an hour and then deliberately triggered it. Why?

Night Owl's quick glance around the room took in her drysuit and clothes draped over a chair, and the three coins on the table next to the bed. For a heart-stopping moment, she thought the dragons had come to the condoplex to return their coins—in person.

Then she realized that these weren't the coins that Miracle Worker had enchanted.

Night Owl had dreamed about coins—about holding the Fu Coin in her hand. Alma must have been casting the I Ching.

Belatedly, Night Owl realized that a red light was flashing on the cellphone. Alma had left her a message. Thumbing the memo icon, she watched as it materialized on the tiny monitor screen.

TWO DAYS AGO YOU LEFT ME A WARNING ABOUT THE RED LOTUS AND DRAGON EYES. NOW IT'S MY TURN TO WARN YOU.

THERE'S A BOMB INSIDE OUR HEAD—ONE THAT'S SET TO GO OFF AT NOON TODAY. PCI PUT IT THERE, TO SAFEGUARD THE REM INDUCER. DON'T TRY TO HAVE IT SURGICALLY REMOVED: THAT WILL ONLY TRIGGER IT.

THE BOMB CAN ONLY BE DEACTIVATED BY MENTALLY INPUTTING A NUMERICAL SEQUENCE, ONE THAT YOU MUST HAVE STUMBLED ACROSS AT SOME POINT DURING YOUR LAST PERIOD OF WAKEFULNESS. IT'S PROBABLY A DESCENDING SEQUENCE OF NUMBERS THAT ARE GROUPED MATHEMATICALLY: SQUARE ROOTS, OR COMMON MEASUREMENTS, OR SOMETHING ALONG THOSE LINES.

YOU MUST HAVE SEEN OR HEARD OR THOUGHT ABOUT THIS NUMBER SEQUENCE—BUT NOT COMPLETED IT. BY ONLY GOING THROUGH PART OF THE SEQUENCE, YOU MERELY PUT THE BOMB'S COUNTDOWN MECHANISM ON PAUSE. TO COMPLETELY "DEFUSE" THE BOMB, YOU NEED TO RECITE THIS NUMBER SEQUENCE

AGAIN, COUNTING THE NUMBERS ALL THE
WAY DOWN TO EITHER ONE OR ZERO.

I CAN CHECK TO SEE IF THE COUNTDOWN
HAS STOPPED USING THE COUNTDOWN SE-
QUENCE IN MY CYBEREYE—THE BOMB'S
TIMER DISPLAY HAS BEEN SLAVED TO IT. I
KNOW THAT YOU CAN'T ACCESS MY CYBER-
EYE—NOT WITHOUT A PLACEBO LIKE THE
"NIGHT VISION GOGGLES" THAT HOTHEAD
TOLD ME ABOUT. YOU NEED ME TO CHECK
TO SEE IF THE NUMBER SEQUENCES YOU'RE
USING HAVE WORKED. THIS MEANS YOU'LL
HAVE TO ACTIVATE THE REM INDUCER
AND ALLOW ME TO WAKE UP. TO ACTIVATE
THE INDUCER, COUNT BACKWARDS BY
PRIME NUMBERS, STARTING FROM 19.

LIKE IT OR NOT, WE'RE STUCK WITH EACH
OTHER. WE'VE GOT TO WORK TOGETHER IF
WE'RE GOING TO SURVIVE.

Night Owl realized her mouth was hanging open
and shut it. For several moments, she sat and stared
at the cell in her hand. Both gut instinct and logic told
her that Alma wasn't lying about a bomb being inside
her head—it reeked of PCI's usual methods. The corp
would do whatever it took to prevent its tech from
being boosted.

Alma was probably right, too, about numbers being
the key to defusing the bomb. All Night Owl had to
do was think back over everything she'd seen and
heard during her last run . . .

After several minutes of skull sweat, she came up
with a big fat zero. Not exactly the number she was
looking for. But even if she did manage to defuse the
bomb, it probably wouldn't prolong her own existence
by much. As soon as she allowed Alma to wake up
and see that the bomb's countdown had stopped tick-

ing, Alma would have the REM inducer chopped out and would kiss Night Owl good night.

Night Owl picked up one of the three coins that lay on the table beside the bed. Heads, she'd keep trying to figure out the number sequence that would deactivate the bomb. She'd trust Alma and work with her. Tails, she'd enjoy what little time she had left. She could have a lot of fun in the next few hours. Especially with a man as handsome as Kageyama. . . .

Tails.

Night Owl tossed the cell and coin back onto the rumpled bedclothes and went to find Kageyama.

Later, she lay on the bed beside him, watching his chest rise and fall as he slept. She envied his peaceful slumber—he slept soundly and deeply, oblivious to the bomb in the head of the woman beside him. His body was that of a man, lean and muscular, but his face, despite the mustache, had the blissful expression of a child. No—not quite blissful, Night Owl saw when she snuggled closer. A faint frown creased his forehead, which was otherwise completely unlined.

Night Owl was lying with a hand across Kageyama's smooth chest. As she shifted on the bed, her fingers brushed against the round blue stone he wore around his neck. It was the only piece of jewelry he wore. Intrigued by the translucence of the pendant, she gently lifted it and took a closer look. It was smooth on one side and had a Chinese character on the other.

The character *fu.*

Night Owl swore softly, cursing her own stupidity. The pendant wasn't just a piece of blue stone. It was jade—the most expensive color of jade there was. What's more, the pendant was exactly the size of a coin, but much thicker.

The dragon Chiao had gotten it wrong when he'd sent her into the condoplex to steal the Coin of Luck.

It wasn't a statue that held the Fu Coin; it was this pendant.

Cautiously, she shifted position on the bed, lifting her other hand up and over Kageyama's chest. She pinched the chain in her fingers and slowly pulled it taut. One gentle pull would break it, and then the stone would be in her hands.

In her hands . . . She paused, trying to remember the image those words conjured up for her. Then she got it: she was holding something between her hands, palms together as if they were raised in prayer. She'd twisted . . .

As if of their own accord, her hands moved so that the pendant was between her palms, and she copied the twisting motion that was playing in her mind. The chain around Kageyama's neck lifted, but just at the point where it was about to tighten enough to awaken him, she felt something come apart inside her cupped hands. Carefully, barely daring to breathe for fear of awakening the man beside her, she opened her hands.

The two halves of jade had come apart, revealing a bronze coin with four characters on its uppermost surface. The Fu Coin.

What now? Night Owl listened for a moment, to assure herself that Kageyama's breathing was still deep and steady. Her eyes fell upon something on the sheets that glinted faintly in the bedroom's dim light: the coin she'd flipped earlier. She glanced between it and the one in her hands, measuring them with her eyes. They were about the same size—and were probably about the same weight.

Moving with the slow grace of a tai chi artist, Night Owl reached across Kageyama and lifted the coin from the bed, and then fit it inside the two halves of his jade. Slowly, she screwed the hollow pendant back together. Then she laid it back on his chest, as gently as a feather.

Fu Coin clutched in her hand, she eased herself out of bed. She scooped up the cellphone and her damp clothes and then slowly slid open the door, praying it wouldn't make too much noise.

Behind her, she heard a rustle of sheets. She glanced back over her shoulder, about to make up a quick excuse about needing the washroom, but saw that Kageyama's eyes were still closed. Or were they open, just a slit? Night Owl had the distinct impression that she was being watched.

Then she noticed a movement in the hallway outside the door. Peering out into the darkened corridor, she saw that one of the glass panels in the walls was flickering into life, glowing like a dimly lit monitor screen. Peering out from it was an elderly Asian man with a bald, age-spotted scalp: Kelvin, the mage who had purposely trapped his astral soul inside the glass, like a fly in amber. Kageyama had ordered him to remain outside the bedroom earlier. It looked as though he had taken the order literally.

"Mistress," he whispered in a voice as transparent as his glass. "Where are you going?"

There was no use in lying. Kelvin's astral presence permeated every centimeter of the condoplex; he would follow her wherever she went. "This place makes me claustrophobic," she told him. "I'm just going to step out for some air. If Kageyama asks where I've gone, tell him I'll be right back."

"As you wish," the mage said. He lowered his head in a bow, but just before he did, Night Owl saw a twinkle in his eye that reminded her of the knowing look Kageyama had given her, the night she'd come to the condoplex to steal the statue.

Frag it. She didn't have time to worry about it now. She had the Fu Coin, and she knew exactly who she was going to sell it to.

No, she corrected herself. Not sell—give. And in return she'd ask for information—for the data that would save her life as well as Alma's. She just hoped that Alma would appreciate it enough to let her continue to exist.

Fu Coin clenched firmly in her fist, she headed for the elevator that would take her up to the surface, the one place in this bolt hole where Kelvin couldn't watch and listen to her.

It was nearly noon, but Night Owl wouldn't have guessed that by the weather. The skies overhead were black with clouds, the air charged with electricity. Rain sheeted down in torrents with a deafening roar that blended with the constant thunder. It pounded against the shelter enclosing the wharf that served as vehicle causeway, helicopter landing pad and dock for the condoplex. Night Owl had to scream into the cellphone in order for Egon to understand her, and she barely heard the phone trill when the return call came in.

A few minutes later, she saw the lights of a sky cab approaching. They tilted suddenly left and then right, rising and falling as the cabbie fought to steer his helicopter through the high winds. Night Owl heard only fragments of engine noise, a dull *chuff-chuff-chuff* in the spaces between the constant, grumbling thunder.

A moment later the sky cab landed with a thud that rattled the platform under Night Owl's feet. The hatch opened, and Tiger Cat climbed down into the rain, holding on to the helicopter's hand grips to anchor himself against the push of the wind. By the time he fought his way into the shelter, he was as wet as if he'd swum out to the condoplex.

"You'd . . . better have . . . the coin," he said, shivering as he wiped rain from his face. "We nearly crashed getting here."

Behind him, the chopper engine revved. The pilot was holding the sky cab in place by brute force, using the rotors to force it down against the helipad.

Night Owl held up the Fu Coin. Tiger Cat stepped forward and took a good look at it, then waved a hand and spoke a few words in Cantonese. Tiger Cat's eyes settled into satisfied slits as he raised a hand, fingers extended to pluck it from her grasp.

Night Owl balled it in her fist. "You promised me information," she said.

Tiger Cat glanced nervously up at the skies as lightning flashed overhead, followed a second later by a boom of thunder that rattled the windows of the shelter. He cringed—and something in his eyes told Night Owl that he wasn't just worried about a lightning strike.

"Just information? You don't want to sell the coin for nuyen anymore? That's a very wise decision."

Night Owl nodded. "That's right—no cred. Just the data you offered earlier. Give it to me—and hurry. I haven't got much time."

Tiger Cat inclined his head; Night Owl could see that he was going to spill the data in his own time, despite the fact that she was in a rush. "It was very clever of you to include an erase program on the credstick you gave Bluebeard," he began, "but Bluebeard's a smart man. He managed to copy the data before the program engaged. Then he called me to ask more about you. I told him the little bit I know— that you worked for Pacific Cybernetic. He took it from there and learned that you were suspended. He didn't discover why, but he did learn that you're under a death sentence. Do you know that there's a bomb inside your head?"

"I knew," Night Owl growled. She had no idea who Bluebeard was or what had transpired between him and Alma, but she could guess where Tiger Cat was headed—in fact, she'd already bet her life on it. "It's set to explode in less than an hour, at noon. Get to the fraggin' point."

Tiger Cat's eyes widened. Now that he understood

her rush, he spoke more quickly. "That bomb can be deactivated by placing yourself in an alpha state. You have to maintain your brain waves between thirteen and eighteen hertz for precisely one minute, then return to normal brain activity for one minute. Then re-enter an alpha state for forty-five seconds, then wait forty-five seconds. Then for thirty seconds, then for fifteen seconds. That's all it takes."

Night Owl nodded, realizing that it all fit. The key to defusing the bomb was a numeric sequence, just as Alma had predicted.

Tiger Cat held out his hand. "The coin, if you please. I must leave quickly, while the dragons are busy fighting."

Night Owl handed him the Fu Coin. He gave a brief bow, turned and fought his way back through the wind to the helicopter.

As Night Owl watched the sky cab take off, she pondered her next move. To defuse the bomb—to live—all she had to do was induce an alpha state four times and get Kageyama to snap her out of it at exactly the right moment. The waking up part was simple enough, but entering an alpha state at precisely the right second was going to be fraggin' hard. Night Owl doubted if even a Zen master could do that. Maybe with biofeedback equipment—but that wasn't something she could get her hands on in the short minutes she had left.

Even though she had the code, Night Owl was just as fragged as she'd been before. If she wanted to live, she needed help.

Then a thought struck her: maybe Alma could help. At least she had a countdown timer in her cybereye; maybe that would give her an edge.

With a start, Night Owl realized that she didn't even know how many minutes she had left. Turning back toward the elevator, she stabbed the call icon.

Solution

As soon as consciousness returned, Alma felt eyes upon her. Her eyes snapped open and, during the second it took her to figure out who was staring at her and where she was, her body tensed into a ready posture. Then she saw it was just Kageyama—that she was in the same bedroom in his condoplex. She started to relax, but the intensity of his eyes communicated a sense of urgency.

She placed her cybereye in countdown mode and saw that she had only twenty-six minutes remaining before the bomb inside her head would explode. The countdown was still ticking. She sat up, adrenaline pumping through her. What had Night Owl been doing all this time?

As if answering her silent question, Kageyama spoke. "Night Owl says there's a bomb inside your head, but that she's discovered the sequence to disarm it," he said. "You need to enter an alpha state for precise periods of time: one minute, then forty-five seconds, then thirty seconds, then fifteen seconds. Each alpha state must be followed by a period of normal brain wave activity that lasts exactly the same period of time as the alpha state that preceded it."

Alma nodded. Of course! Now that she knew the answer, it seemed simple—in theory. "But I've never even meditated," Alma protested. "And I don't suppose you have a biofeedback machine handy."

Kageyama shook his head.

"Then how will I know if I've managed to produce an alpha wave pattern, let alone time it?" Alma asked.

"You have to make your mind empty and still, to slow your thoughts. As you do, your breathing and pulse will slow. When that happens, squeeze my hand. I'll begin timing you and will tap you on the shoulder at the appropriate moment." He lifted an antique mechanical stopwatch with an engraved silver case.

Alma shook her head at the archaic tech. "Thanks, but no. I'll rely on my retinal clock instead."

"But that could distract you—"

"I'm not going to argue." She activated the countdown and saw that just nineteen minutes remained. "Please—be quiet. I haven't got much time."

Alma closed her eyes and tried to concentrate, but all she could focus on was the counter, slowly ticking down toward zero, and Kageyama hovering anxiously near her shoulder. She tried to empty her mind, but stray thoughts kept jumping back into it like unruly children. As the countdown reached the ten-minute mark, she felt tears well in her eyes.

"It's not working. I can't—"

Kageyama was standing less than a meter away, his chest at Alma's eye level. As soon as she saw his pendant, she knew the answer to her problem.

When she'd held the Fu Coin earlier, she'd felt an overwhelming sense of bliss. For precisely as long as the coin had made direct contact with her bare skin—exactly one minute, by some strange twist of fate—her brain had been in an alpha state. That was what had put the countdown on hold before—what had bought her the extra minute of life. She could use the Fu Coin's magic to induce an alpha state. All she had to do was touch the coin for the prescribed periods of time. It was as simple as that.

"Kageyama," she said in a strained voice. "Your *pi*

stone—quickly!" Not waiting for him to unfasten the chain, she snatched it from his neck, breaking the chain, and unscrewed it as quickly as she could. Despite the compensating efforts of her move-by-wire system, her hands were trembling.

There—the pendant was open. Alma held up the coin . . .

Both her eyes and Kageyama's widened in surprise in the same instant. It wasn't the Fu Coin that Alma held in her fingers. It was one of the coins Kageyama had given her earlier, to cast the I Ching. Alma stared at it for a long moment, stupefied, and then realized there was only one way it could have gotten there.

"Night Owl," she and Kageyama both whispered. Then Kageyama chuckled, as if at some secret joke.

"I don't see anything to laugh about!" Alma exploded. "The Fu Coin could have induced an alpha state. Night Owl's greed has just condemned us to death!"

Kageyama laid a hand on hers. Alma tried to jerk her hand away, but Kageyama held on tightly. His grip was surprisingly strong. Wired reflexes taking over, Alma raised her free hand to strike him. Before she could, he scooped up one of the two I Ching coins that remained on the table and held it up in front of her.

"I was prepared for this eventuality," he said. "I suspected that there might be others after the Fu Coin and that Night Owl would know who they were. She didn't disappoint me. Thanks to her, one more would-be thief has been thrown off the scent."

"What the frag are you talking about?" Alma asked heatedly. She didn't even realize that she'd slipped into street slang until she saw Kageyama's bemused glance.

Kageyama nodded at the wall where the two-dimensional Kelvin shimmered, watching. "Night Owl's friend Miracle Worker isn't the only one who can cast illusion spells. It was also Kelvin's specialty. This is the real Fu Coin, cloaked behind an illusion. The coin that Night Owl just sold was a fake. I hope she received a good price for it."

Alma suddenly realized where Night Owl must have gotten the information about defusing the bomb. Someone, somehow, had retrieved it from PCI's computer system and sold it to her.

"I think Night Owl got exactly what we needed," she said with a smile. "Now pass me the coin; our time is running out."

Only six minutes remained on the countdown—even if she entered an alpha state this instant, Alma would have only seconds to spare.

Kageyama pressed the Fu Coin into her hand, clicking the knob of the antique stopwatch as he did so. As its magic flooded through her body, Alma sank into the most rapturous bliss she had ever known—for sixty seconds precisely.

Then again, for forty-five seconds . . .

Then for thirty seconds . . .

Then fifteen . . .

Happiness

Night Owl awakened slowly, feeling as if she had been drugged. Something was wrapped around her head and face, pinning her ears against her scalp. Her cheeks stung in several places, and the tips of her ears were burning. Her eyelids felt thick and puffy, and her mouth was dry. A strange metallic taste lingered on her tongue.

Reaching up, she touched the wrappings around her head and realized what they were: bandages. Frag! Alma must have had the REM inducer removed. But if she had, why wasn't Alma the one who had just woken up? Had removing the REM inducer backfired on Alma, shutting her down permanently and leaving Night Owl in control of their body?

Night Owl sat up and looked around. She lay on a narrow bed with hospital-style railings on either side, in a small room that looked like a clinic recovery room. A door in one wall opened onto a tiny bathroom; another door—one with a lock on it—looked as though it might lead out into a hallway. Soothing music drifted through the air, and sunlight slanted in through windows that had a slight gold tint.

The view out the window was magnificent: a wide expanse of harbor with blue water that sparkled in the sunlight, colorful buildings that climbed the slopes of the North Shore, snowcapped mountains cloaked in lush green forest, and above it all, a turquoise-blue sky tufted with white clouds. To the west, the clouds were stained a bright orange and red by the setting sun. It was obviously late afternoon—hours after the time when the cranial bomb was supposed to have gone off.

"Congratulations, Alma," Night Owl said with a chuckle. "You did it. Assuming this isn't heaven, we're still alive."

For the first time that Night Owl could remember, she had awakened during a day when it was not raining. She stretched out a hand until the sunlight caught it and savored the warmth on her skin. Closing her eyes for a moment, she let out a contented sigh.

Like a bubble working its way up through thick, cloying liquid, a whisper of worry found its way into Night Owl's mind. She suddenly realized that she had no reason to feel this way. Alma had undergone some sort of surgery and locked Night Owl in a room—and Night Owl had no idea why. She should feel worried, apprehensive—even fearful. Instead she felt . . . happy?

It must be the drugs from the surgery. That had to be the answer.

Lowering one of the railings on the bed, Night Owl swung her feet over the side. She found that she was wearing jeans and a T-shirt: whatever the chopdoc had done to her, it hadn't involved the rest of her body. She crossed to the bathroom and peered into the mirror above the sink. The heavy wrap around her face and head was a bandage, just like she'd figured. Reaching up for one end of the gauze, she slowly unwound it.

Her ears were the first things to appear from beneath the wrapping. Night Owl was surprised to see that they now had delicate points, like an elf's.

When the rest of her features were revealed, her eyes widened in wonder at the changes she saw. Her cheeks were wider, her chin more pointed, and her lips thicker. Even her eyes were different. They now had a full epicanthic fold, giving her a distinctly Asian appearance, and the irises were a glittering gold, instead of the familiar brown.

Night Owl was used to seeing a different face staring back at her each night. She never left her apartment except in full Beijing Opera makeup, and she varied the design each evening, to suit her mood. But this time, the mask that stared back at her out of the mirror couldn't be wiped off. Faint red lines—the marks of a laser scalpel—showed where a surgeon had inserted collagen, shaved away cartilage, or tucked and folded skin. This mask—one of Alma's choosing, not Night Owl's—was permanent.

Night Owl slowly shook her head, wondering what Alma was up to now. Perhaps the biggest surprise was that she still felt no fear.

A cellphone was lying on the counter beside the sink, next to Alma's I Ching coins. The memo-alert light was blinking red. Night Owl picked up the phone, thumbed the memo function icon, and read the words that scrolled across the monitor.

HELLO, NIGHT OWL. THANKS FOR FINDING THE CODE TO DEACTIVATE THE CRANIAL BOMB AND PASSING THE DATA TO ME THROUGH KAGEYAMA. THAT WAS WELL DONE. I'M GLAD YOU DECIDED TO TRUST ME—FOR BOTH OF OUR SAKES.

I REALIZED, AFTER DEACTIVATING THE BOMB, THAT KNOWING THE CODE GAVE ME THE ABILITY TO HAVE THE REM INDUCER REMOVED. I DECIDED NOT TO FOR ONE SIMPLE REASON: I OWE YOU MY LIFE. IT SEEMED DISHONORABLE, SOMEHOW, TO "UNPLUG" YOU, ESPECIALLY SINCE YOU'RE REALLY JUST A PART OF ME. BESIDES, I THINK WE

MAKE A PRETTY GOOD TEAM. THERE AREN'T MANY SECGUARDS OUT THERE WHO CAN PROVIDE ROUND-THE-CLOCK PROTECTION, WITH ONLY TWO FIFTEEN-MINUTE BREAKS PER 24 HOURS.

AS A RESULT OF WHAT YOU DID, I CAN NEVER GO BACK TO MY JOB AT PACIFIC CYBERNETICS. THE POETIC JUSTICE IS THAT YOUR "CAREER" AS A SHADOWRUNNER IS ALSO OVER, UNLESS YOU WANT THE DRAGONS TO FIND US AGAIN. BUT THAT DOESN'T MEAN WE'RE NO LONGER PRODUCTIVE. AKIRA HAS OFFERED US A JOB AS HIS BODYGUARD. HE'S EVEN OFFERED TO HELP US GET IN TOUCH WITH THE MISSING SUPERKIDS FROM BATCH ALPHA. MAYBE SOMEDAY WE CAN EVEN HOLD A "FAMILY REUNION." BUT ALL THAT LIES IN THE FUTURE.

I'VE ACCEPTED AKIRA'S OFFER OF EMPLOYMENT, AND I SUGGEST YOU DO THE SAME. AS FAR AS I'M CONCERNED, THE RETAINER HE'S GIVEN US IS A MORE THAN ADEQUATE SALARY—EVEN THOUGH IT'S ONLY A SINGLE COIN. I THINK IT'S GOING TO HELP US LIVE TOGETHER IN A MORE CIVILIZED MANNER. JUDGING BY THE WAY IT STILLED THE TREMORS IN MY HAND, I'M GUESSING THAT IT WILL GUARANTEE THAT ONE OF US STAYS ASLEEP WHILE THE OTHER ONE IS AWAKE. AND I THINK THE FEELING OF CONTENTMENT IT GIVES ITS OWNER—US—WILL HELP US LAY TO REST THE GHOSTS FROM OUR PAST.

CAN YOU GUESS WHICH COIN I'M TALKING ABOUT?

Strange—Alma's message sounded like one that

Night Owl herself would leave, especially with the teasing question at the end of it. It sounded as if Alma was talking about the Coin of Luck, but that wasn't possible. Night Owl had stolen it from Kageyama and traded it to Tiger Cat for the data on how to defuse the bomb . . .

Hadn't she?

Night Owl looked down. There were *three* I Ching coins on the counter in front of her, when there should have been only two. One of these coins should have been inside Kageyama's pendant. The fact that it was lying here on the counter meant that Kageyama had discovered the switch and given the Taiwanese coin he'd found inside his pendant back to Alma . . . but why?

Suddenly, Night Owl realized the answer: Kageyama had expected her to figure out that the Fu Coin was hidden inside his pendant and had guessed that she would steal it. He'd swapped the Fu Coin for an illusion-cloaked fake, and then hidden the genuine article in plain sight. It had been one of the "Taiwanese" coins that Alma had left on the bedside table.

Stretching out a single finger, Night Owl slowly lowered it toward the counter. She touched the coin on the left and felt only cool metal beneath her fingertips. The coin in the center was the same. But the third coin she touched sent an immediate rush of happiness through her. It felt like a combination of falling in love, receiving the one thing you'd wished for all of your life, having a dream come true . . .

And receiving a reprieve from a death sentence.

Night Owl jerked her finger away and looked back into the mirror. She realized now why Alma had opted for plastic surgery. Night Owl and Alma were about to start a new life together.

Maybe.

Night Owl picked up the Coin of Luck and cocked

a thumb under it, ready to flick it into the air. Heads, she'd accept Kageyama's offer of employment. Tails, she'd slide on out of here, disappear back into the shadows, and try to find a way to get rid of Alma.

She flipped the coin into the air and watched it spin. She caught it in her left hand, and slapped it down on her right. Trying to ignore the rush of happiness she felt as it contacted her bare skin, she got ready to peel her hand back and take a look. If it was tails . . .

No. This wasn't any way to make a decision. Striking out on her own and ditching Kageyama would be stupid—suicidal even. She decided that whatever the coin said, heads or tails, she'd take Kageyama up on his offer.

Even so, she couldn't resist just a peek . . .

Heads.

The grin on Night Owl's face was only partially the result of the magical effects of the coin. She'd made the right choice. The coin had just been for confirmation—she wouldn't be using a coin toss to make life-or-death decisions. Not anymore.

Still smiling, she scooped up the other two coins and stuffed them, together with the Fu Coin, into her pocket.

About the Author

Lisa Smedman is author of the Shadowrun® novels *The Lucifer Deck, Blood Sport, Psychotrope,* and *The Forever Drug* published by Roc Books. She is also the author of the Crimson Skies™ novel *Ghost Squadron*, the second book in the Wings of Justice trilogy published by FASA Corporation. Lisa has also had a number of short science fiction and fantasy stories published in various magazines and anthologies, and in 1993 was a finalist in the Writers of the Future contest.

Formerly a newspaper reporter and magazine editor, she now works as a freelance game designer and fiction writer. Lisa was one of the founders of *Adventures Unlimited* magazine. She has designed a number of adventures and written short fiction for Tar's Ravenloft and Dark Sun lines, and has designed gaming products for Stars Wars, Indiana Jones, Cyberpunk, Immortal, Shatterzone, and Millennium's End.

Lisa Smedman makes her home in Vancouver, B.C., with her partner. She spends her free time gaming, hiking, and camping with a women's outdoor club, collecting stamps about the space race, riding her moped, and catering to her six cats.